Rajani Chronicles I
Stone Soldiers

Brian S. Converse

ISBN: 978-0-9987964-0-6

Cover Art by
Lawrence Mann
www.lawrencemann.co/uk

For LAZDE
Always

Thank you to all who contributed in some way to the
publication of this book, including
Kris, AHab, Jeremy, Gabe, Jim (KEP!)
Katie and Melissa.

I'm eternally grateful.

Prologue

The day was gray as the rain fell softly in downtown Detroit. It was a spring rain, meant to wash away the snow, blackened from passing cars, which still clogged the gutters and sidewalks; yet it only succeeded in giving the day a feeling of melancholy for all those who bore witness to the tragic scene laid out before them.

Police cars swarmed the front of a large hotel, their lights flashing, reflecting off the slick sides of other vehicles and the occasional rain jacket. Yellow police tape cordoned off an area of pavement and waved gently in the slight southern breeze.

The buildings were bleak, their architecture practical but brooding in the rain as they loomed over the proceedings below. The weather had darkened the day around the city, and the passing cars had their lights on, though it was midday. Some in the somber crowd held umbrellas, but most stood, the rain plastering hair to their skulls, while they watched events unfurl within the shiny yellow tape. They were used to the warm spring rains in Michigan. They hardly paid it any mind now, as the spectacle captivated them, its realness incapable of being captured by TV news cameras or movies of the week. For them, this was reality TV.

Workers from the coroner's office were placing the body of a young woman into a shiny black body bag; her hands were covered in small plastic bags to protect any evidence that could still be trapped under her nails. A crowd of reporters and onlookers were gathered outside the yellow barrier. Inside, a small group of uniformed officers watched the proceedings with quiet solemnity. Both crowds milled around restlessly, aimlessly. There was nothing anyone could have done for the girl; she had fallen too far.

Police Lieutenant James Dempsey arrived on the scene with his partner, Detective Steve Montgomery. Montgomery was slight and Caucasian, a man who would have looked more at home teaching history to high school kids or selling shoes at the local mall. His most distinctive feature was a thin mustache that sat atop his narrow lips like a lazy caterpillar. Dempsey was his polar opposite, large and dark, with an imposing presence that was more than an act. Their peers liked to tease them about being the odd couple of the police force, but they got along well.

James and Steve had worked together for eight years, long enough to know each other's preferences and talents. It was a comfortable partnership and had lasted through the end of Steve's first marriage and seen his second begin. James had not, however, been best man at Steve's second wedding; theirs was a working relationship only. James was sociable enough when it was needed, but in his heart, he was still a man content to be alone. Or rather, a man who had been left alone, and had learned to appreciate it, if not embrace it.

Steve had been driving with a Styrofoam cup of coffee in his left hand, and he winced as he took a sip of the lukewarm liquid. They sat in their unmarked police car and watched the water beading on the windshield after the wipers ceased their futile struggle against the relentless rain. Each of them was the epitome of the large-town cop. They wore their badges in more than their wallets. It was in their cheap suits, their set, shaved jaws, and their hard, cynical eyes.

They'd seen worse than this fallen girl.

"Another one," Steve said softly, wincing again as he took another sip of the near-cold coffee. He was five years younger than James, though his brown hair had already started to recede in front, leaving a lonely patch of hair above his forehead.

"Uh-huh," James replied. If it turned out like they thought it would, this would make seven women. Girls, really, considering their ages. He wished the rain would stop, though it didn't look like it would any time soon.

"Lotta people," Steve said finally, shutting down the motor of the car.

"Find out if it was one of ours who leaked this," James told his partner. "If it was, I want to see them back at the office. We don't need this shit."

Steve called in on the car's radio. "Twelve Adam One, on scene." They heard dispatch acknowledge before they got out of the car. Steve placed his cup on the roof of the car as he adjusted the shoulder holster under his drab brown suit jacket, redistributing the weight of his Glock 22.

They slowly made their way to the crowd of uniforms, stepping under the yellow tape. Steve went to find the pathologist, Cramer. He knew James and the antagonistic doctor didn't get along well. James tried to avoid talking to the man as much as possible, which was a problem, since he was the head of the Homicide Division, and it was a significant aspect of his job.

James grabbed the elbow of one of the uniformed

policemen and pulled him aside. "Sergeant Kelly, are you the OIC here?"

"Yes, sir," the officer replied.

"What's the story?" James asked.

"Same MO, sir," the uniformed officer told him, pulling out a small notebook from his chest pocket. "Our guy picks a girl at random and throws her off a building. No witnesses. Just another dead body on the sidewalk," he said disgustedly.

"We won't know it's actually him until we get the pathology report," James told the man. "Don't go spreading around rumors until we know for sure." He knew this was probably falling on deaf ears, but he had to say it anyway. He motioned toward the body, and could see the coroner's people zipping her into the bag. "The victim?" He looked up toward the top of the hotel, not really wanting to know personal details about the girl. This was someone's daughter. And he would have to tell her parents she was never coming home.

"Miss Jennifer Durand," Kelly answered. "College student at Michigan."

James stopped the attendant who was rolling the gurney by so he could take a look at the girl. "Hold on," he said as he pulled on his latex gloves. He unzipped the bag enough to see her face. The girl was young, white, and pretty. There was blood on her cheek, the only visible sign that she had fallen from such a great height. Her eyes were open, and James slowly reached over and closed them gently. They would turn dark soon. With her eyes closed, she almost looked like she was sleeping peacefully.

"Here with some friends to see a Tiger's game," Kelly continued as another uniformed officer walked to where they stood. "Last anyone saw of her was an hour before it happened. She and her friends were staying at the hotel here.

They say she planned to go for a swim to cool off."

"Looks like she dove a little farther than expected," the other officer said, smirking.

James stood next to the gurney, still looking down at the girl. "Keep your comments to yourself, Higgins. I don't want to hear them."

"Sorry, sir," Higgins replied, remembering too late that he wasn't talking to one of his peers this time, but to someone who could make his life very difficult for doing or saying something stupid, especially if the press heard it.

James sighed before turning to look at Kelly. "Okay. I want forensics on every building in the vicinity, not only the hotel. I don't care if they have to get on their bellies and crawl. I want some evidence." James looked back at the girl. "This has gone on long enough."

The girl's face still looked peaceful, though her eyes had opened once again.

Dusk engulfed the city, and found James in his apartment making a hamburger and listening to the television while going over his notes from the crime scene. He would have to attend the autopsy in the morning, something he dreaded for a number of reasons, many of them dealing with his relationship with the coroner's office in general.

He also didn't want to see the young white girl sliced open so they could say for certain she had died from a coup or contrecoup contusion to her brain, or before her fall by strangulation or some other form of foul play. As he'd told the officer in charge at the scene, this investigation had gone on long enough, and he was tired of the parade of dead white girls who had recently rolled through the morgue.

James was dressed in jeans and a number nineteen Red Wings jersey over his white T-shirt. He had never been interested in other sports the way he was hockey, which was shocking to most people he told, even members of his family. He'd also never been one to fit into a particular stereotype. His dad, and later his brother, Darryl, had been All-Americans in college basketball, but James couldn't make a jump shot to save his life. Maybe it was because he was built more like an NFL linebacker than a basketball player. Yet football had never interested him, and he had no time for baseball games.

Once a year, James would attend a Tiger's game with his dad and brother. It was a tradition by now; a way to reconnect to memories from his youth. Watching Sparky step over the first base line on his way to the mound. Seeing Sweet Lou Whitaker to Alan Trammel for a double play to first. The joy on his father's face when the last out came in '84 and the players all rushed onto the field, swarming Willie Hernandez and jumping for the sheer joy of being the best.

He knew from now on, though, he'd also think of a pretty young white girl who never made it to her own game; would never watch baseball again; never sit in the sun on a weekend and drink a beer and eat a hotdog with her friends. He was too tired to feel anything, even though hatred for this killer of young women should have been boiling up inside of him. He was tired of it all.

His cramped one-bedroom apartment was the usual bachelor pad, though neater than most. It had the basics: a bed, a bathroom, and a kitchen. He also had a computer and a book collection in one corner of the bedroom. Most of the books on his cheap fiberboard bookcase were poetry that he read from time to time when he needed to get over an unusually brutal investigation, such as the one he was involved in at the moment; but some were from various classes he'd taken to help him with his job.

These books were about managing people, public speaking, and others of the same type, although it had been a while since he'd taken a class. They wouldn't help to advance his career at this point, anyway. He was not the type of political creature who would try to climb to the upper ranks of the department with guile and charisma. He'd never make captain, and that was fine with him.

There was a large weight bench in one corner of the small living room, along with a recliner and TV. He still kept himself in great shape, and prided himself on posting better numbers on the annual physical exam given by the department than many of the younger officers. But he could tell he was slowing down as he aged. It wouldn't be long before he fell behind for good.

On the end tables near his old, battered chair was a framed picture of him and his wife in better times. She had died two years after they'd been married. It had been almost twenty years now, and he had never remarried; had never even come close. James looked at the picture, at the face still seen in dreams and memories; the smile, the line that she had hated that formed between her eyes, the dimple in her left cheek that only showed when she was happy, as she was when she had posed for the picture; a new bride with her entire life ahead of her.

There was still a hard kernel of pain whenever he thought of her. He doubted it would ever go away. He didn't think he wanted it to. He could live with it, only probing it once or twice a year. The pain hadn't lessened. It was part of who he was now. He couldn't remember her without also remembering his loss.

James turned off the stovetop and placed his overdone burger on a bun, hoping it wasn't as burned as it looked. He had a lot on his mind, and distractions didn't help his minor cooking skills.

On the TV, a well-dressed and polished-looking anchor

with a fake look of concern on his face was speaking. "...
the seventh murder by the so-called 'Infinity Killer.' Police
still have no leads. Commissioner Johnson is said to be
considering pulling the chief investigator, Lieutenant James
Dempsey, off the case due to a lack of progress in bringing
the killer to justice—"

James clicked the TV off and stood there a moment with
the remote in his hand. It took most of his self-control not to
throw it through the now-dark screen. He took a drink from
his rapidly warming beer and thought again about retiring.
He'd just turned forty-three. Not old, but certainly not a great
age to begin a new career. Maybe he could find work in some
technical field. He had always been good with computers,
and he could type, unlike many of the older members of the
force.

Who am I kidding? he thought, setting his beer and the
TV remote down on the counter between the kitchen and
the small dining area and walking over to the open window
of his apartment. He knew he'd probably be a cop until
he either died or got too old to perform the job. After he
graduated from high school, he'd served in the Marines, and
after that had gone straight into the police force. He'd been
there ever since.

James stepped out onto the fire escape outside his
window. He enjoyed sitting out there at night. It helped to
clear his head and calm him down. He would read poetry or
listen to the sound of traffic and people passing by and watch
the sunset—at least when the weather cooperated. The rain
had stopped only recently. He could hear the quiet dripping
as water worked its way from the roof to the concrete below.
It was a peaceful sound, and one that he needed to hear at
the moment, as his emotions swirled. He smelled the damp,
fresh scent left over after a spring rain in Michigan, mixed

with the smells of oil and exhaust from the motorists below, and the various aromas of food from other apartments in his complex. They smelled a lot better than his overdone burger.

He stood on the fire escape, trying not to think about the word that had been circling in his mind for a few months, but knowing it would finally have to be addressed: burnout. He wasn't getting anywhere with his investigation of the serial killer who had begun, within the last year, to throw young women from the tops of buildings in Detroit. There were no prints, no witnesses, nothing he could go on, except that all of the girls (with one lone exception) were white, and all of them were in their early to mid-twenties. Since most serial killers went after their own race, James knew that the killer was more than likely a white male in his twenties to early thirties.

There was no connection between the victims, and none of them had been sexually assaulted or had been able to scrape any DNA from the killer with their fingernails. Either the man was incredibly strong, or he was charming enough to lure the women to the top floor and take them by surprise, sending them over the edge to their deaths before they had a chance to fight back. James sat down on the guardrail of the fire escape, hoping that maybe the girl from that morning would pan out and they would find something beneath her nails. But he doubted it—this killer was too clever for that. He was beginning to feel like it didn't matter; they would never catch this killer unless the man wanted to be caught.

Police work could be terribly boring at times. There were the same people committing different crimes, or the same crimes being committed by different people. He became as tired of seeing the same faces pass through the precinct doors as he was of seeing the same crimes on the arrest logs. Yes, there were the exceptions; cases that caught his attention because of the interesting angle to the crime or the brutality of a murder, but usually, it was the same motives and the same outcomes. Someone thought they would get away with killing someone else, and most of the time, they thought wrong. Occasionally, someone would get away without being caught, and sometimes they were caught but got off on some legal technicality; an improper search, a mishandling of evidence or the evidence chain, a mistake on a search warrant.

Then there were the cases that were simply maddening, such as the Infinity Killer murders. True serial killers were rare, much rarer than most people believed. Many cops dreamed of making a name for themselves with a case like that, yet what they didn't foresee was what could happen if the killer was never caught. James had read all of the famous case studies of unsolved serial killings: the Zodiac Killer, the Alphabet Murders, and even the Jack the Ripper case. He hadn't been prepared for the magnitude of pressure that had come along with the case he found himself embroiled in at the moment.

The FBI should have been called in already, but someone high up in Detroit politics—whether it was the mayor, police commissioner, or the governor himself, James didn't know—had decided that the Detroit Police Department could crack the case without the help or interference of the federal government. Seeing as no congressional statutes could be enforced, all the FBI could do was sit back and observe silently, waiting for an invitation to the publicity party. It was all politics, and James hated it. He wanted to be a cop, not a politician. As head of the Homicide Division, though, he knew he had to play the game or he'd be sitting on the bench. Lately, however, he was beginning to think it might not be a bad thing to sit out a few innings.

He'd promised himself he would try to sleep more than the four hours per night he'd been getting lately; that he wouldn't stay up late poring over the case files, looking for something he might have missed. But he knew he would go to bed late that evening once again, too tired to think about it anymore. It was the only way he could fall asleep with the events of the days causing him to lie awake, watching helplessly while the red numbers of his digital clock slowly changed.

James turned to go back inside and eat his beef briquette when he felt a sudden pricking sensation at his neck. He was suddenly surrounded by a bright, white light, though he was unsure whether the light was real or only in his mind. He thought at first he was having a stroke, though there was no pain. The light disappeared as he lost consciousness, and he never felt rough hands catch him as he fell.

Chapter 1

James Dempsey woke to a brightly lit room, circular, with no distinguishing features to it. Everything—walls, floor, and ceiling—was white. The intensity of the light was aided by the brightness of the walls, and it took a moment for his eyes to adjust properly. There were no windows, and only a faint outline of what could have been a doorway, though it was taller and wider than a normal door, and there was no doorknob that he could see.

The first thing he noticed was he wasn't dead. His first fear of having a stroke was more than likely incorrect. The second thing was a clear plastic mask with a thin tube leading from it covered his nose and mouth. He reached his hand up to take it off, but then reconsidered. The mask was there for a reason, best to keep it on until he knew what it was. His mind was clearing now, but he was still confused. Had he been injured somehow and wound up in the hospital? The last thing he could remember was coming home from a long day at work and turning on the television news while cooking dinner; his normal routine.

James slowly sat up on the bed. His head spun a moment as if he'd been lying there a while. He saw he shared the room with four other people, and all of them were dressed in black robes. The robes were somewhat large on the two other men, and totally engulfed the two women. James was wearing one of the large black robes, as well. This was not what he remembered having on the last time he was awake. He couldn't remember ever owning a robe, in fact. Not his style.

The others were still sleeping peacefully, from what he could tell. They had the same oxygen masks over their faces. The beds they were lying on were pointed toward the middle of the room, where a strange-looking machine sat like a brooding octopus with arms ending in various devices. He wasn't sure what they were for, but a few of them looked like medical instruments and syringes. The tubes from the masks they wore led to this machine.

The mattress he was sitting on felt like it was filled with some type of thick gel. It reminded him of a mouse pad he had at home with a gel-filled hand rest on it. The mattress moved under him as he sat up.

His mind raced with various disaster scenarios. Was it some type of plague? Was he infected? Maybe a terrorist attack of some sort he'd survived, along with these people? Possibilities floated through his mind, but none of them added up adequately with the present situation.

Puzzling was the fact there were no antiseptic smells in the room. There was no smell at all, actually, though the slight odor of the mask could have been covering it up. James felt like there should be some type of medicinal smell if he were in a hospital. It was damn peculiar, but his most pressing need was an incredible thirst. His throat felt dry and swollen, as if he had not taken a drink in days.

A voice spoke from above James's head. It was rough and mechanical sounding, and had a peculiar background noise accompanying it. To James, it almost sounded like two radio stations bleeding together, one in English and one in a language he didn't recognize.

"Officer Dempsey?" the voice said in stilted English. "Officer Dempsey, please do not be alarmed. You are in no danger. We are choosing to remain unseen as of now, until you are better oriented with your surroundings."

"Where the hell am I?" he asked, his voice harsh to his own ears. He coughed and swallowed before speaking again, trying to ease the dryness of his throat. "Who are these people?"

Nothing strange about this situation, he thought sardonically. The robe he wore was at least comfortable, though he could tell he was naked beneath it. "What happened to my damn clothes?"

"Do not worry, Officer Dempsey," the voice assured him. "At the moment, we need you to calm down and know you are in no danger."

James jumped a little when the only door to the room suddenly whooshed open. It had been almost indistinguishable from the wall. What he'd thought was the door upon first waking must have led to a closet or another room.

"Please, exit when you feel ready," the voice told him.

"Can I take this mask off?" he asked whoever it was on the other end of the intercom.

"Feel free, Officer Dempsey," the voice replied. "Your lungs should be acclimated to the environment by now."

James took off the mask and stepped down from the bed. His legs felt shaky, but he didn't feel any pain in his body, so he most likely wasn't hurt, as he'd first feared upon waking up. With the mask off, he could smell a slightly antiseptic odor in the room, after all. He wasn't sure if it was a good thing or not.

The door led to a corridor with the same low ceiling as the room he was in, and it went on for maybe a hundred feet to his left and ended about twenty feet to his right. He'd almost expected the sickly neutral green of a hospital hallway, but the walls were a soft gray, and the floor a darker carpet that felt comfortable on his bare feet. Small lights were spaced along the corridor, where the walls met the ceiling about every ten feet or so. There were doors on either side of the corridor, spaced at about twenty feet apart.

He muttered a quiet curse as the door at the end of the corridor to his right opened. This wasn't a building he recognized ever being in before. Again, scenarios swirled around in his mind, from being in a CDC building somewhere to some secret government installation in the middle of nowhere, yet he felt no sense of panic. He walked down the corridor slowly and stood in the doorway to the room at the end, his eyes wide when he saw what was waiting for him.

Inside the room were three ... beings.

In front of them, on a small table, was a device that looked like a vintage microphone with a thin pole leading down to a wide base. As one of the beings spoke in their alien language, the mechanical voice came from this device in English. That explained the background noise he thought he'd heard when the voice first spoke to him over the intercom.

The room was twenty-five feet wide and ten feet deep and slightly curved on the side opposite him. There were two large high-backed chairs set two or three feet apart, each with a control panel set in front of it, full of buttons and blinking lights. Along the curved wall was a larger control panel, with four smaller chairs set along it, spaced about two feet apart. One of the chairs was occupied by a small figure with its back turned to James. There was what looked like a steering yoke in front of this figure.

In front of the smaller chairs, a large portion of the wall was either a window or some type of computer monitor, James couldn't tell which, showing an area of outer space, with a reddish-brown planet taking up half of the screen.

"Please," one of the seated aliens—for that surely was what they were—told James. The alien was older-looking than the other of his species. His white hair was in an intricate ponytail resting over his shoulder and across his chest. His equally white beard was long and flowing. Like the other alien of his species who stood next to him, he had dark brown skin, which was a striking contrast with his white hair. Looking closer, James could see it wasn't their skin that was brown. Their faces and hands were covered with hair. For all he knew, their entire bodies were covered in hair underneath their black robes.

There was something almost canine in the shape of their faces, but not quite to the point that they looked like dogs, especially because their noses were more reminiscent of human than mongrel. Their ears came to a point, each topped with a tuft of white hair. They were bipedal, but much larger than most humans. The one standing must have been at least seven feet tall and as broad as a bodybuilder.

"Be welcome," the older alien said, motioning toward an open chair near the viewscreen. "Rest yourself."

"I take it I'm not on Earth anymore?" James asked rhetorically, sounding calmer than he actually felt.

◊

Rauphangelaa tuc Nebraani could see the Human male standing before him was taking things quite well, considering he'd woken up aboard a spacecraft from another part of the galaxy. Of course, their strength was one of the reasons he had brought the Humans aboard the ship in the first place. He pointed back toward the *Tukuli's* viewscreen, which still displayed the red planet outside of the ship. "That's an accurate assumption, Officer Dempsey," he told the Human, unaware the question was not meant to be answered.

"Lieutenant," James said, automatically.

"Sorry?" the alien responded.

"Never mind, it's not important," James answered.

"Do not be alarmed, please," the alien continued. "We are still within your solar system. Mars, I believe you call the planet we are currently orbiting." As he spoke, he wondered if the translating device was working properly. He knew the device was primitive when compared to some of the newer models available, but it was all they had on the ship at the moment. Unfortunately, the device would take a while to learn the Human's language completely. The more the Human spoke, the quicker it would learn—much quicker than inputting the words manually, as Janan had done before the five Humans were brought aboard. His own translation implant would translate the Human's speech, but he needed Officer Dempsey and the others to understand him completely if the plan was to work.

Officer Dempsey stood before them, his arms crossed in front of him. "Uh-huh. You said all of my questions would be answered. So start talking. Why am I here?"

Rauphangelaa's Pledge, Bhakat tuc Rathaan, leaned toward Dempsey from where he stood next to Rauphangelaa's chair. His teeth were bared menacingly. "You will show respect to Rauphangelaa, Human."

Rauph sighed. No matter how long his Pledge trained in the ways of the Kha, Rauph was afraid Bhakat would never master one of the most important tenets: composure. He had a difficult time controlling his emotions, and now was not the time to let them spin out of control. He motioned his Pledge back. "Please, Bhakat, he meant no disrespect to me, I'm sure. We cannot blame him for being ... tense in this situation. Calm yourself."

Rauph looked back over to the Human. "Both of you, please, calm yourselves. Let me first start with the reason we are here, Officer Dempsey. Bhakat and I are known as Rajani." He bowed his head in greeting as he spoke, though his eyes were nowhere near downcast. He was an Elder; any bows of subservience were made to him, not by him. That was the way of things.

"As Bhakat said, my name is Rauphangelaa, but you may call me Rauph, if it is too difficult for you to pronounce." He motioned toward his ship's pilot, who was seated at the large control panel. "Janan'kela here is a Sekani."

The small, bluish alien Rauph referred to turned from his control panel and smiled at Officer Dempsey, showing very sharp white teeth. The Sekani's eyes were blood-red with black vertically slit pupils. "You may call me Janan," the little alien said, still smiling.

The Sekani looked like a cross between a cat and a monkey, and he would stand maybe four feet tall at most. Unlike the Rajani, he was not wearing a black robe, but was dressed in a tan coverall that fit his small, surprisingly muscular body tightly.

Rauph sat with his hands in an almost prayerful pose. "Please sit and listen to our story." He waited until the Human finally sat in the proffered chair before speaking again. "I will come right to it. We are here seeking allies," he continued. "Alien invaders known as the Krahn Horde attacked our home world. We are a peaceful civilization and had no defenses to repel the Horde. As far as we know, only we three were lucky enough to escape in search of help.

"When the Krahn attacked," Rauph continued, "they attacked all of the known Elders, like me, first. I was not at my residence or I would have been captured or killed as well. We boarded this ship and hoped we could make it through the blockade of Krahn ships, and past their large colony ship."

"We escaped, but our ship was badly damaged," Bhakat added. "The damage was not enough to stop us completely, but we have had to stop here to allow the ship time to repair itself."

Rauph leaned back in his chair. "That is when our ship's central computer first detected the radio and communication signals coming from your solar system. It took only moments for it to home in on your planet once it pinpointed the signals it was receiving and detected the artificial light coming from the planet's surface. We studied your society as much as we could in the short time we had, praying you were the help we so desperately need."

Rauph took a sip of water from a glass sitting on a small table near his chair before continuing on. "We found your species had certain ... talents in the art of warfare, but also that contacting your leaders at this present time in your progress toward a civilized society would be detrimental to your overall development. It was decided we would contact only a few select individuals. The computer picked the five of you using the parameters we set."

The Human sat, one ankle crossed over the other knee as he leaned back in the chair. Rauph wasn't sure what the expression on his face meant; it was somewhere between a smile and a frown. "What parameters?" Officer Dempsey asked.

Rauph folded his hands on the control panel before him. "We wanted Humans that were in good physical condition, had no discernible diseases, and were within an age group young enough to withstand the rigors of space travel."

"That's it?" the Human asked him, incredulously. "That's all you did? Fed that into your computer and out popped five candidates?"

"Well, more than five, of course, but yes," Rauph said. "You would be surprised at the information available in certain databases kept by your government and various consumer and medical agencies. It was easy enough for our ship's central computer to discover. You five turned out to be the best candidates from the list produced."

"So who are those other people?" Officer Dempsey asked, gesturing with his thumb back the way he had come in.

"They are people from your city," Rauph told him. "They were the closest to you at the time we had you brought to our ship. They live in your building. We thought you would be more comfortable with Humans you already knew in some fashion; those whom you lived with, in a common setting."

Officer Dempsey sat with his eyes closed, his right index finger and thumb squeezing the bridge of his nose. "Shit. You have got to be kidding me."

"There is something wrong with our logic?" Rauph asked the Human. He could feel his own muscles tightening from the stress of the conversation. He'd known it would be difficult to speak with an entirely new species. He hadn't counted on Officer Dempsey being so defensive.

"Oh, I would say so, yes." The Human looked Rauph directly in the eye. "Now, tell me why you brought us way the hell out here. How long have we been here?"

Rauph held up his hand, one finger raised to emphasize his point. "Please understand, all of us have lost so much. Our wounds are still ... fresh. We wish to wake up the others before we explain any further. It is a long story, and I do not wish to repeat it."

The Human leaned forward in his chair. "Then why wake me first? I'm no one special."

"Oh, but you are," Rauph told him. "You see, we learned about you from the transmissions from your planet. You are a protector of your species. You help those who are in need. Because of this, I,"—he looked at the others before continuing—"*we* wish you to be the group's leader. Please consider this an honor, as you would be second-in-command on this ship."

Bhakat made a small noise in his throat, and Rauph gave him a baleful look before turning back to the Human.

Officer Dempsey sighed. "I think we should wake the others now," he said after a moment. "There's so much you obviously don't understand. I think it would be better if all of us tried to explain it to you, together."

Rauph motioned toward the door and pushed a button on his control panel. The door opened again. "As you wish. You may help them to become more ... comfortable in their new surroundings. Bhakat will prepare them for waking from the suspension sleep we have placed them in."

◊

"C'mon, wake up now," a deep voice said. "All of you need to wake up as quickly as possible."

Gianni Moretti placed an arm over his eyes to block out the bright light. "If I'm in Heaven, why do I have such a headache?" he asked hoarsely. He moved his arm out of the way and opened his eyes, finally. The first thing he saw was the face of a tough-looking black guy looking down at him. The man was not smiling. "Nope. Must be the other place," he said. He felt disoriented, but he guessed he must be all right if he could still make jokes at a time like this. *What the hell happened?* he thought.

He looked over again and saw the black guy was big;

he looked like he could play football for the Giants. He also looked to Gianni like a cop, or maybe even a Fed. Gianni knew enough of them to recognize one when he saw him. He looked down at himself and noticed he was dressed in a large black robe, which was confusing in itself. Nothing was making sense.

The man was standing beside the beds with his arms crossed. Gianni saw there were other people in the room as well, some sitting up, rubbing their eyes and necks, presumably feeling as crappy as he did. "Now that I've got your attention," the man began, "let me explain our situation here in the simplest terms possible."

Great, Gianni thought. *I've been arrested, and I don't even remember it.* He sat up and felt a wave of nausea pass through his body. *Jesus,* he thought. *Did I get tasered or something?*

"My name is James Dempsey," the black guy was telling them. "I'll give you people a few minutes to let the effects of your long naps wear off. But it's imperative you prepare yourselves for what I'm about to tell you."

Dempsey, Gianni thought. *Why did the name sound so familiar?* Then it hit him: the man was a cop. In fact, the man lived on the top floor of Gianni's apartment building. *I knew I should have moved.*

Interlude

A press conference was underway inside the police headquarters building in downtown Detroit. A man in a rumpled suit and ugly tie was addressing a large crowd of reporters, who were packed into the tiny room. Steve Montgomery was standing next to him. The man in the rumpled suit happened to be the Chief of Police, and no one would comment on how aesthetically God-awful his wife's choice in neckwear was—at least not to his face.

"We regret that, due to his disappearance," the chief droned on, "Lieutenant James Dempsey has been pulled off the so-called 'Infinity Killer' case." The chief smiled and motioned to the man standing next to him as he introduced him. "His replacement is Detective Steven Montgomery, a veteran officer with twelve years on the force, who was already working hand in hand with Lieutenant Dempsey before his disappearance."

The chief motioned to Steve to come over and stand right next to him, and he placed his hand on Steve's back, as if holding him in that position. Steve knew this was a sell job to the press, and the chief wanted to make sure it looked good for the viewers at home. Unlike his missing partner, James, Steve was willing to play the game. He'd even shaved off his prized mustache for the occasion.

"I have every confidence Detective Montgomery will bring this case to a close, both quickly and efficiently," the chief continued. "All of our considerable resources are his to command. We'll answer any questions you may have now."

All of the reporters' hands shot up at the last statement. The chief pointed to one. "Yes, Ted?"

The reporter stood up. He looked like he'd been around the block a time or two, hence the first-name basis with the chief. The chief also knew Ted well enough to know he wasn't one to throw out controversial questions at a press conference. He'd save those for later, hoping for an exclusive. "Does Lieutenant Dempsey's disappearance have anything to do with the Infinity Killer?" the reporter asked.

"There's no evidence of a link of any sort, but we're still investigating that angle," the chief answered. "If anything new turns up on that front, we'll let you know. Next question, please."

Another reporter, this one unknown to the chief, quickly raised a hand. "What will happen to Lieutenant Dempsey once he's found?"

The chief paused for a moment before answering. "All we can hope for at this point is Lieutenant Dempsey is safe. There's no use speculating on his future in this force until we know for sure what his status and whereabouts are. Now, if you don't have any actual questions about this particular case, I have better things to do."

He walked quickly from the stage, to the stunned reaction of the assembled reporters. The public relations guy quickly began speaking, assuring them the chief was late for another important meeting, but would be available again soon. *Like hell*, Steve thought, though he kept his face impassive. He knew how much the chief hated talking to reporters. Besides, it was his job now to speak to the expectant faces gathered before him. He'd always kind of envied James for his ability to speak coolly and calmly with the mass of microphone-toting imbeciles, some of them from the local news, but many from all the major alphabet networks. It was something he'd have to learn. He put on his best fake smile and began to answer questions.

Chapter 2

Rauph waited on the bridge of the ship while Officer Dempsey went to wake his fellow Humans. He'd sent Bhakat along to assist, as his Pledge had a good deal of medical training; he had been a doctor, in fact, before becoming Rauph's Pledge. Bhakat would turn off the sleeping gas still flowing from the medibot through the masks the Humans wore over their faces. It would allow the Humans to wake up fairly quickly. Bhakat had unhooked them all from the various medical paraphernalia before turning off Officer Dempsey's sleeping gas.

The discussion he'd had with the Human had brought up memories of the events of the past Standard month. Rauph once again saw the carnage in his mind as he remembered the last time he'd seen Rajan.

The city of Melaanse sprawled along the eastern coast of Rajan's largest ocean. The city itself was about fifty Standard miles long, and its western edge bordered the Desert of Ambraa, a large expanse of sand covering most of the continent. Outlying areas to the north and south of the city were owned by a select number of Elders, and consisted of mostly farmland and orchards, with some animal ranches as well.

Melaanse was not only the largest city, it was the only city, and where most of the population of Rajan was located. It was filled with ancient spires, bridges, and skyscrapers interspersed with open grass parks and glittering freshwater lakes. Most of the buildings had been constructed hundreds of years before. It wasn't unusual to see marine drans flying over the city and roosting in various nooks of the buildings; their distinctive calls rising above the noise of city life below.

Rauph had enjoyed taking walks along the streets of the city as well as the sandy beach. Sometimes these walks were alone, and sometimes with another Elder or Pledge who wished to speak about some facet of the Kha. His estate to the north of the city was expansive, and had housed many Sekani and Jirina workers. He would always take the time to speak with them as they worked in the fields, orchards, and various manufacturing facilities he owned. Most of it was destroyed now, he knew.

In his memory, he saw small Krahn ships attacking the city; firing missiles into buildings. He was never close enough to see the Krahn ground troops, but he imagined they must be hideously ugly creatures. There were explosions and fire and the bloodied bodies of Rajani, Sekani, and Jirina lying on the ground where they'd fallen. Spaceships had screamed from the sky, firing bolts of energy and more primitive projectiles at everything in their paths on the surface of Rajan. Males, females, young and old, all were gunned down by the ships as they attempted to flee. There was no shelter to be found.

It had been early evening, and Rauph and Bhakat were returning from a trip to the city's central computer, which was housed in downtown Melaanse. He'd been preparing to take the *Tukuli* on a supply run to a nearby trading station, and having the ship prepped probably saved them enough time to escape. As he and his Pledge reached the city limits, they heard the sounds of gunfire and explosions coming from behind them. They'd turned to see the smoke of hundreds of fires and noticed the strange ships flying above the buildings, firing at the ground below.

It was night now, as his memory feverishly jumped from one event to the next. Rauph, Bhakat, and Janan'kela were boarding the *Tukuli*. Bhakat was carrying Janan, who was unconscious, his head bandaged and bloody. They had found the Sekani pilot lying near the remains of his family's dwellings.

All of the Sekani dwellings were completely destroyed, as were most of the buildings on Rauph's estate, as it turned out. Janan must have been on the *Tukuli* when the Krahn attacked, or he would have died with the others.

The *Tukuli* was housed a few Standard miles north of the estate, and Rauph had prayed the entire time it took to make their way in the darkness toward the launch pad. He'd been afraid they would find it destroyed, as everything else was, but it was whole and still prepped for takeoff. Either the Krahn had missed its location or they had purposely left it intact, confident they could salvage it later.

The *Tukuli*, now in space, was being pursued and fired upon by two Krahn ships. It was a credit to Bhakat's skill in piloting the ship that they had evaded the main blockade. *If only Janan'kala had been conscious,* Rauph thought, *we may have escaped without sustaining as much damage.* He didn't blame Bhakat in the slightest for his inability to outmaneuver the other ships. Normally, the *Tukuli* had a crew of at least three Sekani pilots and several other crew members for various tasks required aboard his ship.

Rauph remembered Bhakat turning to him after a few days and solemnly breaking the news they could no longer use the nulldrive of the ship or it could be permanently damaged. They needed to switch to the *Tukuli's* powerful auxiliary engines and let the mechanibots repair what they could. He'd reluctantly agreed with Bhakat's assessment. He'd watched the viewscreen as it displayed the outside of the *Tukuli*, seeing the small robotic mechanisms crawl over the hull, repairing the damage caused by the Krahn weapons. He knew that without the nulldrive, it would take more than a lifetime to reach the galactic core.

He had abruptly stood and left the bridge before beginning to cry silently, not knowing what to do or where to go for help. It was the lowest point of his life, not counting the day his mate had died. His only choice was to go and plead to the Galactic Alliance for help. The Rajani were still technically members, so he would at least be heard. He'd composed himself and returned to the bridge, telling Bhakat where they needed to go.

As Bhakat programmed their course into the ship's central computer, he and Rauph had spoken at great length about how they could best help their species. Neither of them wanted the Rajani to return to their war-like ways, but they had to help free their planet from the Krahn Horde.

Now, in Rauph's memory, he was sitting on the bridge of the Tukuli, along with Bhakat and Janan'kela, watching the viewscreen once again. Janan had recovered sufficiently from his head injury to pilot the ship, though he had no memory of events of the Krahn attack. On the screen was a transmission from a planet called 'Earth' by its inhabitants. A picture of James Dempsey appeared on the screen as the news program featured a story on the Infinity Killer, a Human who had been terrorizing the city with the random killing of young females of the same species, a crime almost unimaginable to the Rajani.

They had been moving slowly away from the Rajani solar

system for a few weeks when they had discovered the planet called Earth. As they studied the various electronic signals from the planet, they saw the civilization was involved with a multitude of armed conflicts, much like what he imagined his own ancestors had fought before the coming of Ruvedalin, founder of the Kha. They were also astounded to find the sheer numbers of Humans living on the planet. The Rajani, Sekani, and Jirina only numbered in the hundreds of thousands, at most, due to the restricted amount of habitable land on Rajan.

Besides being an Elder of the Rajani, Rauph also held the distinguished post of Keeper of the Stones. In this role, he was tasked with safeguarding the Johar Stones, both from other species and his own. This role also provided him access to what little history was known of the Rajani species. He worked closely with the Keeper of the Past, so he knew of the violent history of the Rajani like few others on his planet. Thousands of years earlier, the Rajani had been conquerors; ruthless killing machines encased in almost impenetrable energy armor. It was not a past he wanted his species to revisit.

As Rauph watched the footage of wars in deserts, jungles, and cities from Earth, an idea had crept into his mind, and he knew what needed to be done.

Later, Bhakat had stood, hands palm down on a table in one of the ship's meeting rooms, facing Rauph. "No! You cannot mean this! You'd free the Rajani by bringing yet another warrior species to our planet? You've seen what these Humans are capable of—"

"Be quiet," Rauph had almost hissed at his Pledge. He'd had enough of Bhakat's insolence for the day.

"But—" Bhakat had begun, shocked at Rauph's fury, before Rauph cut him off once again.

"No," Rauph had told him. "Listen to me. We *need* these Humans. You know as well as I. I have prayed for days, trying to come up with a better solution to our situation, but there really is no other option. Do as I say."

That night, he had felt regret for losing his temper, but at the time, he'd been too tired to care. They were all under a great deal of stress, but he'd made sure he apologized to his Pledge for his angry words after waking the next day. Afterward, they had set events in motion that had culminated in bringing the Humans aboard the *Tukuli*. He thought the initial meeting with Officer Dempsey had gone as well as could be expected. He sat on the bridge, waiting for the remaining Humans to wake, and hoped he'd made the correct choice.

◊

James tried his best to keep things calm as he woke up the others. The large alien known as Bhakat had come back with him to the room where he'd woken up and had taken off their masks. Bhakat had pushed a few buttons on the large medical machine in the middle of the room before leaving once again. James knew the others were feeling disoriented and probably pretty scared, but not as scared as they would have been had they awoken to a seven-foot-tall alien standing over them. They were still in the circular white room, sitting up on the beds. James saw they were all similarly confused about the black Rajani robes they were wearing.

"Okay, now that you're awake, I think we should start off simple," he began. "Like I said, my name is James Dempsey. I was woken up not more than an hour before you, so I don't have a whole lot of information to give, but what I do know is we have all been brought aboard an extraterrestrial spaceship."

"What?" the white female asked. "Did you say spaceship?

Like from outer space?" She was pale, and James couldn't tell if her pallor was normal for her or if she was going into shock.

"I did," James answered. "Look, I think it would be better if we all introduced ourselves. I figure we'll all be more comfortable with this situation if we know each other's names, and maybe you can tell us a sentence or two about yourselves." He was pretty good with names, given his job, and knew he could learn about these people both by what they told him, and what they didn't.

"Okay," the white girl answered. "My name is Kieren Gray. I've only been living in Detroit about a year. Before that I lived in Colorado Springs, Colorado." She smiled at the people around her, but James could see she was still very nervous. He guessed she was in her early to mid-twenties, and her blonde hair was cut short, not quite touching her neck.

"Hi, Kieren," he said, smiling to make her feel more comfortable. He looked at the other woman, who was a little older. Her long black hair hung down past her shoulders, and her complexion was darker than Kieren's.

"Yvette Manidoo," the woman said, frowning. James thought the name probably meant something, but didn't think it was the time to ask. He waited a moment, but that was all she said.

"Gianni Moretti," one of the men said. He looked like he was in his early thirties, with straight black hair almost as long as the Gray woman's. "I find it a little hard to believe I've somehow been kidnapped by little green men. I mean, c'mon, man, stop messing with us. Is this some type of sting operation?"

"Mr. Moretti," James said. "I have better things to do than mess with you. You can choose to not believe me, but it doesn't change the situation in any way."

"And what is our situation?" Gianni asked.

"Like I said before," James answered, "we've been brought aboard a spaceship, and are currently orbiting Mars. There are three of them, and they are asking for our help. That's all I know."

"Our help?" Gianni asked. "What, did they get lost and need directions to the nearest gas station?"

James was getting tired of the antagonistic tone of the conversation. "I think it's best if we let them explain why they brought us here. It's not like we can leave, regardless."

"So you're saying we can't go back home?" Kieren asked. James thought she still looked almost as scared as he felt. "We're stuck here?"

"Honestly?" James told her. "I don't know. All I know is what they've told me, which wasn't much." He turned to the last person, a fairly young man with short brown hair. He looked awfully young to have been chosen to come along, but he could have been older than he appeared. *Maybe I'm just getting old,* James thought. The kid didn't look old enough to shave, but there must have been something that led the Rajani to pick him.

"Oh, uh, David Morris," the kid mumbled. "Hi," he said to everyone with a nervous smile. "I'm in B2B marketing. That's, uh, business to business. Anyways, I grew up in Detroit, and I can safely say this is the farthest I've ever been from home."

At least he doesn't look like a small-time punk like Johnny Moretti. James thought the older of the two men looked like every perp he'd ever chased down a dark alleyway. Moretti also had an almost continuous smirk on his face, like he thought this was all a big joke someone was playing on him. James remembered seeing the guy around the building once or twice, and his 'cop radar' had gone off every time. There was something about him, but this was not the time or place to start an investigation.

Yvette was smiling now, realizing he was telling the truth. She seemed more excited than scared. The fact that she was beautiful registered in the back of his mind somewhere. "When do we get to meet them?" she asked.

The mechanical voice of Rauph answered her from the overhead intercom, and the doorway to the room opened with a whoosh. "At anytime, Yvette Manidoo. If you are ready now, we can proceed."

They all walked the short distance from the room to the bridge of the ship. Within a few moments they stood in the room with Rauph, Bhakat, and Janan, who had all turned to look at them.

"Holy shit, he was telling the truth," Moretti said, looking at the three aliens. His smirk had disappeared, and his eyes were wide with surprise. It was James's turn to smirk at him, having been proven right.

Rauph stood and bowed slightly to them. "Please, be at ease. My name is Rauph." He pointed toward the others on the bridge. "This is Bhakat, and this Janan'kela. Officer Dempsey was kind enough to tell you a little of our story. I will now tell you the rest."

"Officer?" David asked, looking at James.

"Yes," James told him. "I'm a police lieutenant for the City of Detroit. Or at least, I was a cop before all of this happened."

"I don't think your jurisdiction extends to outer space, Cowboy," Gianni said, looking around. The others were also wide-eyed as they took in the sight of both the aliens and the viewscreen on the bridge.

"No," James said, eyeing the other man. "I guess it

doesn't. Lucky you."

"Well," Kieren said, standing closer to James, "I, for one, am glad James is here."

"Thank you, Ms. Gray," James said, turning toward her. He could see the sight of the large aliens had done nothing to ease her anxiety.

"Kieren," she said. "Everyone calls me Kieren."

"Please," Rauph said. "We would like to move to a room offering more comfortable seating. If everyone will follow me, we can get settled and have some food and drink, as well. I'm sure you all are thirsty from your recent rest. Janan, set the *Tukuli's* navigation system to autopilot and join us."

David and Yvette were left by themselves for a moment while the others followed Rauph out of the room.

"So," David said. "Um, we haven't really been introduced. I'm David."

He held out his hand. Yvette didn't take it.

"I'm not impressed," she said, not even looking at him.

She didn't notice his expression change quickly from surprise to anger, but it was gone as they both turned to leave.

◇

Rauph led the procession of Bhakat and the five Humans down the corridor on the main level of the ship. He was encouraged that none of the Humans had become too upset when they had awakened aboard a starship. But then, he had ordered Bhakat to administer a slight sedative to each of them before they were awakened, so he didn't expect any of them to become hysterical. It would have been counterproductive to his goals.

He'd told Bhakat to set up a room with chairs around a round table and have refreshments set out for their meeting. When the Humans were brought aboard the ship, he had also made sure to request some of their native foods so they would feel more comfortable. The *Tukuli's* own food stores were getting low; yet another reason they had to quickly return to Rajan. Unfortunately, the ship had sustained some damage to its power cells and would take more than the mechanibots to fix. They would have to locate a space port to have it completely repaired.

They finally came to the meeting room, and the Human female designated as Kieren Gray gasped when she saw the various fruits, vegetables, and breads lay out on the table in the middle of the room. There were also pitchers of water and cups at each setting.

Rauph set down the translating device in the middle of the table and hit the power switch before speaking again. "I must also apologize for the use of this translating device," Rauph told them. "It is crude, but it works, as a last resort. The three of us have had translation implants inserted into our skulls, but I'm afraid this ship was not stocked with them. Please," he said, motioning toward the table. "Quench your thirst and satiate your hunger. I hope our accommodations are adequate."

The Humans sat down at the table and began pouring water into their cups and piling food onto their plates. Before long, the frenzied eating and drinking had subsided, and Rauph felt it was time to begin. Janan'kela walked in through the door of the meeting room and smiled. He sat down next to the Human designated David Morris, who involuntarily inched away from the pilot, Rauph noted.

"I will begin our story now," Rauph told the Humans as he stood up. "Please feel free to continue eating."

"Before you tell us how you got here," Officer Dempsey said, "I think we'd be more comfortable if you answered some of our questions."

"Yeah," the Human Gianni Moretti added. "Like how

long have we been here?"

"A short time," Rauph told them. "I believe in your calculations, it would be roughly fourteen days."

"Two weeks!" Morris exclaimed.

"I apologize," Rauph said. "We needed to keep you sedated until we were sure we had provisions aboard the ship, such as the food you see before you. Bhakat performed a thorough health check to make sure you were not carrying any potentially harmful viruses or diseases, and ensured you were acclimated to the atmosphere and gravity settings aboard the ship, which are different than what you are used to on your planet."

Rauph noticed the two women frown as they looked at Bhakat, presumably understanding what the health check may have entailed.

"I'm so fired," Morris said quietly, looking down at the half-eaten slice of melon on the plate before him.

"Maybe they'll write you a note so you don't get detention," Moretti told him, smirking. "By the way, if my cat is dead when I get back, I'm going to be very disappointed."

"So, you're a single man who owns a cat?" Yvette asked. It was her turn to smirk.

"What?" Gianni asked defensively. Rauph ignored this side conversation. He had no idea what a cat was, but supposed it was some type of servant.

"How is it we're breathing the same air as you?" Gray asked him. "I mean, you are aliens, right? From another planet?"

"Ms. Gray," Rauph said, "if you take on this mission, you will find most life in the Universe lives on planets similar to your own. There are billions of stars out there, and only a few have planets around them sustaining any form of life. Most of those planets have the same conditions; a yellow sun and a planet with an atmosphere the correct distance from the sun. There have been few documented life-forms found on the larger gaseous planets. Very little that is sentient. There are exceptions, of course, but again, they are very few."

Rauph was trying to be as general in his statements as possible. He wasn't sure if these Humans were educated enough to know anything about planetary physics or complex biology.

"So you're not from our solar system, I take it?" Yvette asked him, still scowling.

"No," Rauph explained. "Though both of our solar systems are located in what your scientists call the OrionCygnus Arm of this galaxy. Our planet is located farther away from the center. We were heading toward the galactic core when our ship broke down. That's where the seat of the Galactic Alliance is located. In relativistic terms, we're neighbors, though our planet is thousands of light years away from your own."

The group of Humans sat still and thought about this for a moment, trying to grasp what Rauph was telling them. Rauph thought the Humans all looked like placid beasts of burden; almost as intellectually dense as the Jirina back on Rajan. *Maybe we gave them too much of the sedative,* he thought.

He'd been thinking of the best way to present their plea for assistance, and had decided that starting from the beginning would be best. "If there are no further questions," Rauph said, "we can begin." He waited and saw no one else was eager to speak.

"My species has not always been as peaceful as we are now," Rauph began, the translating device again interpreting his language to English for the gathered Humans. "Our history is as bloody as it is long. Yet, for two thousand years we have lived in the peace brought about by Ruvedalin. Ruvedalin taught us the way of the Kha. The Rajani have had lives of prayer, meditation, and peaceful coexistence ever since. We have also lived secluded from the Galactic Alliance during that span.

"Our peace was broken with the coming of the Krahn Horde," Rauph continued after taking a small sip of water from his glass. "The Krahn are a younger member of the Alliance, who only recently invented inter-system travel, a prerequisite for inclusion. We've performed enough research in the Alliance's databanks to find out the Horde is comprised of the banished followers of Ronak. He is the younger brother of the Krahn's High Vasin, Maliq. Ronak was banished after a failed coup attempt on the Krahn home world."

"Nice family," Moretti said.

"No, they're not," Rauph answered. "Now, Ronak and his followers pirate the space lanes in hopes of one day returning to Krahn to overthrow his brother. Ours is the first planet they have attacked toward that end."

The female named Yvette Manidoo was still relaxed-looking, leaning back in her chair, though her expression would still be considered a scowl. "And why is that?"

Rauph turned toward her. "The Krahn Horde didn't attack until they had sufficient numbers."

"You mean others have joined them?" Gray asked.

"In a manner of speaking," Rauph told her. "You see, each female of the species has the ability to produce ten or more eggs in each mating cycle. Their young mature in three to four years after hatching, much like many of the reptiles of your planet."

"So up until now, they had not had enough offspring to fill their ranks," Dempsey said.

"That's correct," Rauph answered.

Moretti was smiling broadly. "Busy little guys, aren't they?"

"Killers are what they are," Janan responded, looking at each of the Humans in turn.

"And you expect us to do what, fight them?" Gray asked. "My God, I'm an elementary school teacher. I've never even fired a gun before."

"We've come too far," Rauph said. "We've been away too long. We ask you to be our champions of freedom. Of *peace*. We cannot fight. It is against the Kha." Rauph sighed. "I should not even be asking you to fight for us. I may be stripped of my title of Elder for it in the future, but right now, I have no other choice. I'm afraid there is no other way to free my planet."

◊

Yvette looked around the room at the others and wondered if the aliens could have chosen a more disparate group. The girl, Kieren, looked like she was going to either cry, puke, or both at any time. The guy with the short brown hair, David, was sleepwalking his way through this as if wondering if he was truly awake. Every time the little alien named Janan came too close, he would shy away as if he were sitting next to a leper. There was the man named Gianni, who looked at times like he was enjoying all of this, and at other times like he wanted to shoot someone. She would have to keep an eye on him. It wouldn't do to underestimate what he was capable of while they were all trapped on the ship together.

And then there was James, who was older, maybe in his late forties if she had to guess. Not handsome, but not ugly, either. Tough, masculine, and well-built. He looked like someone you wouldn't want to mess with, but also sad at the same time. In a word: mysterious. Maybe intriguing was a better word, she decided as she listened to him talk about their situation, and as he spoke, she decided he might be worth getting to know better.

It dawned on her it would also mean going along with the aliens on whatever adventure they had planned. She was surprised to find she felt no fear at the prospect, only excitement. She felt almost like she had as a young girl, before her father had moved them to Washington D.C.; not really knowing what to expect, but not at all daunted by the change coming into her life when her father was elected senator.

◊

James had decided to sit back and observe the discussion. He wasn't the kind who needed to be the center of attention, and he was observing the other people around him as much as the aliens. Then Gianni spoke, and that plan went by the wayside.

Gianni had his arms crossed now. "So you want us to fight your battles for you. What the hell do we get out of it?"

James leaned toward him. "Mister, you need to calm down." He turned his attention back toward Rauph. "He meant no disrespect. We're all still a little ... agitated."

"The Kha is too complex to explain fully," Rauph continued. "We do not have the time. Only know we will not fight. We cannot."

Rauph turned his back on the group as he looked at the stars outside the ship, which were being displayed on a handheld tablet set in the corner of the room. There were many tablets like this one scattered about the ship. They were the only way they could interact with the *Tukuli's* central computer when not on the bridge. The ship's crew could literally control the ship from anywhere on board or a short distance away from the ship, as long as they had one of the tablets. "Our ship is almost repaired," he said. "We need to return, with or without your aid. I'm afraid we may have already been away too long."

"There will always be time for vengeance," Janan said, a snarl on his face emphasizing his sharp teeth. David nearly jumped out of his chair.

James was surprised by the vehemence shown by the little alien, but he guessed if his entire family had been wiped out, he'd feel the same. He also noticed while the two Rajani believed in this 'Cah,' the pilot didn't act like he spent his days praying. Maybe the two Rajani were members of a religious sect, while the little alien and his family were the hired help.

Rauph turned from the tablet to look at the Humans. "Will you help us?"

"And if we don't?" David asked. He looked like someone had 'pissed in his oatmeal,' as James's grandfather used to say. "I mean, come on! The five of us against an army of space monsters? Are you serious?"

"He does have a point," Yvette conceded. "We could do little harm to this 'horde' of yours."

"But you could," Rauph told her. "With our assistance."

James thought Kieren was starting to lose her panicked look now that she was becoming more familiar with her surroundings and had resolved herself to the fact she was aboard an alien spacecraft. "What do you mean?" she asked.

"First," Rauph began, "know this: what I'm about to tell you is a secret my species has guarded for a hundred generations. I now share it with you only because of the desperate situation we find ourselves in. To even speak of it with outsiders breaks our laws and could cause my life to be forfeited upon my return to Rajan." He waited a moment to let this sink in before continuing. "There is a stone that, when implanted directly into the brainstem, strengthens a being's natural abilities a thousand fold. This was our edge in warfare long ago. No one could stand before us. Yet we found peace; a better way: the Kha. This way forbids our use of the Johar Stones. These stones, of course, are what the Krahn are ultimately after, I'm sure."

Rauph sat down in his chair and took another sip of water. "If you agree to help us, you will each be given a stone. I do not know what the result may be, only that you are physically capable of interfacing with the stones. If you decline, you will be sent back to where you were ... taken. You won't remember any of this ever happened."

"You can do that?" Kieren asked, incredulous.

"I'm sure they're advanced enough to scramble our brains up good," Gianni said.

"The implanting process is safe, I assure you," Rauph told them, hoping he hadn't broached the subject too quickly.

"Yeah," Gianni continued. "That's what they said about Thalidomide."

"Excuse me?" Rauph said, looking confused.

"Don't worry about it," James said. "It's not important."

"What is important," David added, "is the fact you want to implant us all with some alien steroid. Is anyone else here a little apprehensive of the fact we've been kidnapped by space aliens who want to perform experimental operations on us? Are we all fine with this concept? Can you at least take these stones out when all of this is over?"

"I'm afraid not," Rauph answered. "Yet, if they work like they're supposed to, you'll want to keep them, I assure you."

"When this is all over, huh?" Gianni said, looking more serious. "The kid has a good point. What happens when this little adventure ends?"

"You're free to do as you will," Rauph replied. "If you

wish to return to your home planet, then we will bring you back. If you wish to stay on Rajan, you may do that as well."

"Just like that?" Gianni said, the smirk returning to his face.

"I give you my oath, we will return you to your planet," Rauph said. "That's all I can give you. Is it enough to ease your worries?"

Yvette was sitting back casually in her chair. "All right. I'll do it."

David's jaw dropped. "What? Are you crazy?"

"Maybe," Yvette said, not bothering to look at David. "Maybe it's none of your business."

James was sitting forward in his chair, leaning on the table before him. "May we talk about this amongst ourselves? In private?"

"Time is short," Rauph responded, standing once again. "I can give you a few Standard hours to discuss, but then you must decide. Bhakat, Janan, please return to your duties on the bridge."

James waited for the three aliens to leave the room before speaking. "Okay, we've all been briefed on our situation," he said. And had the shit scared out of us, he wanted to add, but didn't think it would help matters. "Where do we go from here?" He waited a moment, but was met with stunned silence.

Interlude

Dennis Gray called his sister's house again, feeling like he shouldn't be as worried as he felt. It wasn't like Kieren to not call him back after a couple of days, though. She was usually very conscientious about such things. She hadn't even updated her Facebook status in a couple of weeks, which wasn't only strange, it was disturbing.

He was mentally kicking himself for not paying more attention to her lately and being too wrapped up in his own life to notice she hadn't been around for a while. He'd recently ended a relationship with a man he'd thought he'd spend the rest of his life with, only to find out Stephen had been cheating on him for almost a year. He and his sister hadn't gone out to dinner in almost a month while the messy finale had played itself out. If she didn't answer her phone this time, he would head over to her place after work to check on her.

When the call went to voicemail, he frowned and waited for the beep. "Hey, Squirrel, it's your favorite brother again. Where are you?" he said, as cheerfully as he could. It was an old joke between them, as he was her only brother. "The firm's annual picnic is this weekend," he said. "Sorry for the short notice. Anyway, uh, I was hoping you could come. Um, even if you can't, give me a call to let me know you're all right. I haven't heard from you in a while."

He gently hung up the phone, mentally kicking himself for being such a selfish asshole. He looked at the clock and made up his mind to go to her place, even if traffic would be a bitch trying to get across town. He had a copy of her apartment key, so he knew he could let himself in. He hoped she was out jogging or late getting home from the school where she taught, but his gut told him he was wrong.

Chapter 3

The discussion had been going on for nearly three hours, and James thought most of the others still looked a little shell-shocked. It reminded him of a scene from out of a movie; a courtroom drama where a jury had been locked away in hopes of coming to a consensus, and yet would be hung, no matter how hard they tried to work things out. They'd gone round and round, each bringing up the pros and cons of their situation. Many of them had stood or even paced behind their chairs; their bodies still felt stiff from lying in whatever suspended animation the aliens had placed them in when they were brought aboard the ship.

James had to wonder, though, how they could have been unconscious for two weeks without getting bed sores. There were still some things that didn't quite add up in the aliens' story of how they had been transported to the ship; something he'd have to think about on the voyage. James was not a naive person. In fact, his wife had told him on many occasions he was too skeptical, bordering on downright cynical. Partly, it was due to an upbringing by a father who had spent his entire life working in an automobile factory and had taught him to question everything and take nothing for granted. Partly, it was his personal outlook on life in general.

He had a difficult time trusting other people, or in this case, trusting aliens who professed to need his help. There was also the fact he'd been kidnapped by real live freaking aliens, which made him want to laugh and scream simultaneously. He was a little on edge, to put things mildly. He was never one to show his emotions openly, either. He'd learned as a cop to present a stolid exterior, no matter what he was feeling inside, and found it helped to keep the situation calm. A crime scene or the interrogation of a suspect or informant could get out of control quickly if people sensed the officer in charge was anything other than well-disciplined and in control of his own emotions.

Reporters could smell blood in the water if they weren't presented with a calm, detached demeanor. It was all a game; a farce perpetrated to stay in control of a situation. James wasn't sure what the others were feeling at the moment, but he was both scared and excited by the possibility of leaving Earth's solar system aboard an extraterrestrial craft.

His job had become a burden hanging from his neck like an anvil of despair. The alien named Rauph had been mistaken in what he'd said earlier. James was not some type of protector of his people. He was, at best, a means of vengeance, and at worst, a glorified caretaker. His job didn't begin until someone was dead. Where was their protection? If he found out through his investigation that the death was the result of foul play, then he'd continue the investigation. The murderer would go to jail for the rest of his or her life in the state prison in Jackson, and the victim's family would have their revenge, or the murderer would get away with it. Either way, James would go on to the next case.

He had nothing holding him back, he realized. No family obligations and no one to take care of but himself. With the realization came a sense of relief, and he knew he was leaving Earth, no matter what the others decided. He wasn't about to say no and go home. This was a chance of a lifetime. He hadn't felt this excited since he'd been on the plane heading toward Parris Island, going to recruit training for the Marine Corps. He felt the same mix of fear, excitement, and wonder as he'd had back then. It had been his first time on an airplane, and his first time being away from home.

"Yvette and I are going," James stated. "That's a fact. It's time for a head count. I'm not sure how long a galactic hour is, but we probably don't have a lot of time left to discuss this. Who else wants in?"

"I don't know," Kieren said. By this point, she was standing, her arms folded protectively across her chest. "I mean ... this is all too much. It's like we've fallen into an episode of the *X-files* or something."

"Or a bad comic book," Gianni chimed in, leaning back in his chair casually. James thought he looked like he was beginning to enjoy himself, and he had a feeling the punk was planning to come along, as well.

Kieren was looking back at James and doing her best to ignore Moretti. "They need our help. I mean, the whole reason I became a teacher was to help people. Of course, at the time, I thought it would mean human beings, but, I say yes. I guess."

"Are you sure?" James asked her. He didn't see what this skinny little white girl could contribute to the situation, but he'd learned over the years that appearances could be deceiving. He'd had plenty of little white girls kick his ass in the Corps, though he would never admit it to anyone, not even all these years later.

"Yes," Kieren finally said, after a moment of silence. "I want to help them. If I can." She smiled timidly, but James could see she had made up her mind.

Gianni was looking at Kieren. "Then I'll go too. It'll give me a good laugh to see Sandra Dee here make like Joan of Arc trying to help out a group of interstellar Buddhists."

"This isn't a joke," James told the other man. "You give your all, or you go home."

"Listen," Gianni said, "you may have been picked to be the leader here, but it wasn't by us. Just because they think you should be, doesn't mean I have to do what you say."

"You do what he says," Yvette said, leaning forward in her chair, her face as serious as it had looked since they woke up, "because he's the only one here who isn't freaking out about all of this. Would you rather be in charge?"

"I didn't say that," Gianni said, crossing his arms and frowning. "I don't see why we have to take this guy's shit when we don't even know what makes him the best pick. Am I right?"

"Mr. Moretti," James began.

"Call me Gianni," Gianni said.

"Johnny," James began again.

"Not Johnny. Gianni," Gianni corrected him. "You've been mispronouncing my name since we woke up. Gee-ah-nee, not John-nee."

"My apologies," James said. "Gianni, my qualifications as a leader aside, the reason why I'm heading this discussion is because they woke me up first, plain and simple. If you would rather have someone else do it, then you're welcome to take a vote. I didn't campaign for the honor."

"Don't be ridiculous," Yvette said. "It's clear to me you're able to do the job."

James smiled at her. "Thank you."

James turned his attention on David. "That leaves you, Mr. Morris."

"David," the man said. In his too-large Rajani clothing,

he looked like a frat boy waiting for a delivery from his dealer. "Call me David. Mr. Morris is my father." He sat there a moment, thinking. "Which, I guess, decides for me. I'll go. I don't have anything to go home to."

James stood, unable to keep the smile from his face. "Then it's settled. We go."

◊

Rauph sat on the bridge of his ship and prayed, having ordered Janan to turn off the communication system to the room where they'd left the Humans. He'd given his word they could conduct their discussion in private, and his sense of honor could not allow him to do otherwise.

But oh, the agony he felt having to wait for their answer. He'd told them he would give them a few Galactic hours to decide, but the time had come and passed. The truth was, he knew, he would give them as long as they needed, within limits. They couldn't go anywhere for at least a day or two while the mechanibots finished repairing the nulldrive. Until then, the *Tukuli's* engines would take them perhaps past the orbit of the fifth planet in the Human's solar system, at best.

He'd brought the translating device back with him to the bridge after his first meeting with the Humans, so when there was a knock on the door of the bridge, he turned it on before pushing the button to open the door. He saw Officer Dempsey outside in the corridor. He had a sick feeling in his stomach as the Human slowly walked into the room, taking in his surroundings again.

"Officer Dempsey," he said, apprehensively. "Have you reached a decision?"

"We have," the Human answered. He looked over at Janan'kela and Bhakat, and Rauph followed his gaze, wondering what the Human was thinking. "Yes, we'll help you," James said, refocusing on Rauph.

Rauph felt a smile break out on his face—the first true smile since leaving Rajan—as he rose from his chair. "Wonderful!"

"There are a few conditions, though," the Human said.

"Oh?" Rauph answered, looking over at Bhakat, whose expression hadn't changed since the Human had entered the bridge. He still didn't look happy.

"Yes," Officer Dempsey continued. "The first is, you tell us more about the operation you have planned for us, and the second," he said, smiling this time, "is you give us back our clothes. We're all pretty tired of these robes of yours."

◊

James was alone in his new room that night—at least, it felt like it should be night. Several hours had passed since they had all woken and discovered their situation. A long, emotion-filled day followed, and James needed to get some sleep. Rauph had agreed to tell them more about the stones, as James thought he would. Rauph had shown them diagrams of what would happen in the operation, and had assured them of the safety of the procedure. The Johar Stones were surprisingly small, from what James saw. They wouldn't displace the brain tissue much when implanted. He still had his doubts, because the aliens would essentially be giving him a brain tumor. He and the others would then be unconscious for five or six days while their skulls healed fully.

Rauph told them about the machine performing the surgery; the mechanical octopus James had seen on first waking up in the medical bay. James had been impressed. Clearly, the technology was decades, if not centuries, ahead of anything currently on Earth. After that, Rauph had told the little alien named Janan to take each of them to one of the crew quarters on the ship, where they could sleep. James had picked one of the larger rooms, which was a guest room for visiting Rajani, judging by the size of the bed.

James half-expected someone to interrupt him as he got ready for bed, so he wasn't surprised when there was a chiming sound from the door to his room. He'd taken a quick shower in the small bathroom and had just finished toweling off. It took him a moment to get dressed, throwing the large robe over his naked body and then clumsily hitting at and missing the button to open the door, before swearing and finally hitting it again—probably a little too hard. He was surprised who it was standing outside in the corridor. She smiled, somewhat nervously, and then spoke.

"Sorry if I'm disturbing you," Yvette said. "I couldn't sleep."

James sighed inwardly and moved away from the doorway, inviting her into his room with a sweep of his arm. She entered, and he pushed the button to close the door behind her. Sleep would have to wait.

"Please," he told her. "Have a seat. I'd offer you a drink, but I'm afraid all I've found here is water. I don't know if they even have alcohol on their planet, being a bunch of holy men and all."

"That's okay," she said, sitting on the sofa-like chair that was the only other piece of furniture besides the bed. At least it was comfortable, built as it was for the larger frames of the Rajani. There was a small table on either side of the bed, but otherwise, the room was bare of any adornments. The ceiling, like he'd seen on most of the ship so far, held small lights in the corners providing illumination.

James sat down next to her, but a comfortable distance away. He didn't want her to get the wrong idea about his intentions. Actually, when he thought about it, he didn't have any intentions. He'd only met the woman that morning, if that's when it was, and he had no idea what to expect from her.

"I really hate being in an environment I can't control," she said, looking around his room. He guessed hers was fairly equivalent, though if she had been placed in a Sekani room, it would be a wonder if she fit comfortably in the bed.

James had to stop himself from automatically switching to detective mode. He wasn't a cop anymore, at least not on this trip. He wasn't sure what he was now. So instead of checking for inconsistencies in her story and watching her body language, he just listened.

"My father is a lawyer," she began, now looking into his eyes. "At least he was before going into politics. A lot of people tell me I'm like him, always taking control of the situation and bending it the way I want it to play out."

"Are you a lawyer too?" James asked. He'd dealt with many of them over the years, and she was the type; sure of herself and driven.

"Not yet," she said, rolling her eyes when she said it. "Haven't taken the Bar Exam."

Something clicked in his mind about what she'd said earlier. "Wait a minute, you said your father went into politics. You wouldn't happen to be Senator Manidoo's daughter?"

"Right again," she said, her smile a little self-conscious.

"Well," he said, trying to lighten the mood, "I am a detective, you know."

She laughed, and he decided he liked the sound of it. It was genuine and full.

"Don't worry," he said. "I don't get into politics much. It never really interested me. I imagine your disappearance has caused quite a stir back home, though."

"Knowing my father, that's an understatement."

"So wait," he said. "You're a US senator's daughter, and you live in those crappy apartments?"

"You live in them too," she said, smiling.

"Yeah, but I live on a cop's salary."

"Well," she said, "Daddy has this thing about making your own way. I'm just another struggling law student, as far as he's concerned."

"You must have just moved in," he told her. "I don't remember seeing you around."

"Yes," she answered. "About two months ago. I moved from a place over on Knollwood. It didn't feel … safe."

"And you wound up getting kidnapped by aliens," he said, chuckling.

"Who knew?" she said, smiling once more. He decided he liked her smile too.

"I guess that's the elephant in the room," he said. "It's certainly not something I ever expected would happen to me."

"Me either," she agreed. "It's not like I'm some backwoods hillbilly living on a remote farm out in Podunk or something. They're not what I expected aliens to be like at all. Guess I watched too many James Cameron movies or something."

"I should tell you," James said, "I wouldn't be surprised if they were monitoring everything we say."

"You don't trust them?" she asked.

"I didn't say either way," he told her. "But it's what I'd do. They don't know us very well, either. I'm sure they must have based their choice of us on something, but it couldn't have been on close surveillance for any extended period of time. They probably need to verify we're right for the job, so to speak."

"Do you think we're doing the right thing?" she asked suddenly, and in her earnestness, he could see she might be younger than he had first thought, which really made him feel like a dirty old man. He could see she wasn't as confident in her choice as she'd appeared earlier in the day. "I mean, *really* doing the right thing?"

"All I know," he told her, "is the choice I had, based on the information I was given at the time. If they're telling us the truth, then I think they need our help. Whether we're the right individuals is a moot point. We're all they have." He didn't want to sugarcoat anything and was relieved she didn't show any additional signs of panic at his answer. *Good,* he thought.

"I've never had to have an operation before," she said. "No appendix. No tonsils. Hell, I still have my wisdom teeth. And now I'm ready to give aliens permission to operate on my brain? It's crazy."

"If they meant to kill us," James told her, "they would've done it by now, I think. They wouldn't have put on this ruse; they would have operated on us before we woke up. We're in no position to say no, really. Hell, we really have no way of knowing whether they've already been tinkering with our bodies."

"We were out for two weeks," she said, frowning.

"Exactly," he replied.

"So, basically, we have no choice but to trust they've told us the truth and move on."

"Right again. The defense rests."

"Ha-ha." She flashed a genuine smile at him. "Speaking of rest, we should probably get some now. Who knows how late it is, and how early they'll wake us up to prep for the operation tomorrow."

"Feel any better?" he asked her as she rose from the chair. He stood as well and followed her to the door.

"Not really. But I think I can sleep now, at least. Thanks for listening."

"No problem," he told her as she opened the door and

stepped out into the corridor.

"Good night," she said, and smiled.

"See you in the morning," he replied, returning her smile. He got undressed again and turned down the room light before falling into bed, exhausted. He didn't dream.

◊

The next morning, James and the others were back in the round room where they had first awakened, which Bhakat referred to as the medical bay. They had eaten a light breakfast and made a minimal amount of small talk. None of them seemed to want to discuss what would be happening a short time later. They had talked themselves out the night before.

James followed the proceedings as Bhakat prepped them for surgery. Sensors were placed against his temples and chest, and the oxygen mask was put over his nose and mouth again. They had been assured the medical machine was light years ahead of any medical devices on Earth, but James was still apprehensive now that the time had come.

"You're sure there'll be a minimum amount of scarring?" James heard Yvette ask. He smiled, knowing he wasn't the only one feeling nervous.

"Very little, Yvette Manidoo," answered Rauph's voice over the intercom. He was now in the control room across the corridor from the medical bay, as Bhakat programmed the machine with instructions for the operations. "Please, all of you count to ten."

James got to three before everything went dark.

◊

Rauph watched on a portable tablet as the medical machine performed the surgery on the Humans. When the medical bay doors were shut, the room emitted a gas, killing any pathogens or other viruses, which sterilized the room, as well as the medibot. No one could enter the room until the operations were completed, ensuring it would remain a sterile environment.

He replayed the conversation he'd had with Bhakat before initially waking the Humans up over and over in his head. Bhakat objected to implanting these Humans with the stones. It was against Rajani law to be implanted or to implant another inhabitant of Rajan with them. He'd told Bhakat he doubted that it mattered. There may not be any Rajani left to enforce the laws. They really had no other choice.

The largest concern Rauph felt was the fact there was no way of knowing what the Johar Stones would do to the Humans. They may have implanted the stones in beings who would show no discernible effects from them. Although the Rajani physiology was similar, there were differences, especially between the brains of the Humans and the Rajani, from what Bhakat had told him.

Rauph, as an Elder, and most importantly, as Keeper of the Stones, was one of the few Rajani allowed access to historical records relating to the stones. He had read files on data disks from past Keepers of the Stones explaining that the effects of the stones would become apparent eventually, no matter where they were implanted, due to their nature, which the Rajani had discovered after years of study. The quickest method was implanting them directly into the cerebellum of the individual. They needed enough time to see what those results were, which meant they had no time to wait.

For the Rajani, the stones had produced consistent results in those implanted. Their strength was enhanced far beyond a normal Rajani, and each bearer of a stone was surrounded by a protective energy field. This energy field could be turned on and off according to the bearer's wishes.

It took on a solid appearance most times, appearing as though the bearer were encased in stone-like armor.

The stones also appeared to have an effect on the physiology of the body, though Rauph saw there were some disputes over what these were among the various accounts of Keepers of the Stones he'd read. Most agreed the stones appeared to make the bearer become, or at least appear, younger. It was as if the stone restored the body to its physical peak, no matter the bearer's age when implanted.

Although the evidence collected by Bhakat suggested the Humans' bodies would respond to the stone, this would all be for nothing if they didn't. They would have to turn the ship around and continue their journey toward the seat of the Galactic Alliance in search of assistance, as they had first planned. Rauph strongly doubted assistance would be forthcoming, as the Rajani were not popular in the halls of the Alliance. It had been years since any official diplomatic contact had been made between the Rajani and most of the members of the Alliance, but memories of the war-like Rajani lingered, even after almost two thousand years of peace.

No, Rauph thought, *this must be our answer.* He prayed the Humans would respond well to the operation.

◊

James awoke a few days later. At least, he found himself lying on the operating bed staring at the ceiling. He had needles of pain sticking in his corneas, and his pulse was pounding in his temples. When he finished his self-examination, he found that something felt ... different, though not necessarily in a physical manner.

It was almost like the night his wife had died. The whole way to the hospital, he thought something was different, as if something important was missing. He hadn't even known at the time that his wife was already dead, but he'd somehow felt it. Now it was like he'd gained something back. He once again felt complete, though it was different than he'd ever felt before. He looked around at the others, all of them still sleeping, and wondered if the operations had been successful.

He stood slowly and stretched, feeling the same familiar tightness in his body, as if he'd been asleep a while once again. He wondered when, or if, his powers would appear, and what they would be. Suddenly, he felt a charge run through his body and saw a translucent outline around his arms. He blinked, surprised, and it disappeared just as quickly.

He concentrated again, and the energy field appeared once more around him. He looked at his arms, and then at the rest of his body, which were encased in the field. *That's it?* he thought, feeling disappointment. He sat back down on the bed and waited for the others to wake.

In the medical bay, Gianni rolled onto his side, rubbing his neck and grimacing. "Well, I feel great," he muttered. *Alien bastards aren't putting me under again,* he thought.

Soon all of them were slowly sitting up and rubbing at their necks and eyes, except for James, whose bed was empty.

The mechanical voice of Rauph came from the overhead intercom once again. "You must quickly become used to your stones. It will take us only a few Standard months to reach Rajan."

David yawned. He felt like his head was filled with cotton. "Wait. Where's James, uh, Mr. Dempsey?"

Kieren sat next to James's bed, which appeared empty. "I don't know," she said, standing up slowly and stretching her arms out.

"Maybe he changed his mind," Gianni said, feeling like he would puke if he sat up too fast. "Figures."

"Be quiet," Yvette told him. "He wouldn't have done that."

James's voice came from above his bed. "No, I wouldn't do that."

Kieren was suddenly encased in a field of energy. She flew off the ground and away from his voice. "Oh my ...!" Her energy field appeared like a blue gem surrounding her body.

James appeared. He was also surrounded by an energy field, which looked like lava rock; dark but not quite opaque. Kieren hung in the air a moment before returning to the ground clumsily. Her energy field disappeared as she touched the floor.

"Guess I've discovered one of my new powers already," James said. "So have you, Kieren."

Gianni threw his hands up again. "Great, I always was a slow learner."

"Not surprising," Yvette said.

David looked down at the black robe he was wearing. "Um ... can we please have our clothes back now?"

◊

Yvette was pleasantly surprised to see the operations had left only a very small scar at the base of the neck on all of them. Judging from the one she saw on the back of Kieren's head, hers was probably only an inch long, at the most. They hadn't even had to shave any of her hair, which she'd been growing out for a few years. She would have been disappointed if she was forced to cut it off and start over.

She'd woken up curious to see if she would feel any different. The only thing she'd felt was a slight headache for a few hours. When James's and Kieren's powers had manifested, she'd thought for sure her own would as well at any time, but it had been a full day, and still nothing.

She was beginning to have doubts anything would happen, and decided the best thing to do would be to take her mind off it all. She began to work out in her room, practicing her martial arts training. It helped to both relax her body and focus her mind. If it turned out she never got powers, she wouldn't be helpless in a fight, at least, though she would be very disappointed.

◊

After waking from the operations, the five Humans had all gone back to the various crew and guest quarters to rest and recuperate. James had felt like he needed to sleep, but after sleeping for so long already, he kept finding himself awake, his mind unwilling or unable to shut down so soon after regaining consciousness. Now, on the second night since the operation, he was once again awake and restless.

James had never been an eloquent speaker, though he'd held his own at the press conferences back on Earth. He found most of the people under his command didn't want a leader who used flowery language or large technical terms when addressing them. It was more of a mindset than anything. Most of the men and women in the force had at least an associate's degree, if not a bachelor's. Yet old thinking died hard, and the culture around the department was still of a workmanlike, blue-collar approach to the job.

James did appreciate good writing, especially good poetry, though he never let anyone see that side of him when he was working. Not even his partner, Steve, knew of James's collection of poetry. It helped him deal with the stress of his job. Without poetry, he knew he probably would have turned to the alcohol, painkillers, or other drugs many of his peers used to cope with the horrors they dealt with on a day-to-day basis.

When James discovered the little alien known as Janan had downloaded a variety of books and music to the ship's central computer, he was happy to see some of those books included classic poetry from Eliot, Poe, Yeats, Dunn, Frost, and Whitman; a few of his favorites. He was able to access the poetry using the handheld tablet Janan had given him, which was linked to the ship's central computer.

The tablet was an amazing device, able to physically expand from a screen only a few inches square to one two square feet in diameter, depending on the user's needs. Yet it felt like it weighed only a few ounces, and was as thin as a credit card. It put any of the electronic tablets back on Earth to shame.

James was also surprised to find there was the option of having the ship's computer read the books; sort of like an audiobook on Earth. He'd never heard the aliens talk directly to their computer or the computer talk to them, so it was interesting to find the computer was capable of that type of interaction.

The important thing, though, was the availability of poetry. It helped him to wind down when he was feeling anxious, and to remember there was more to humanity than the horrific acts they could commit against each other.

There were deeper truths to humanity than murder and deceit. Yes, there was darkness, but there was also light. He had forgotten that lately, and it felt good to remember it.

Interlude

Senator Josiah Manidoo was walking out of the Capitol Building, surrounded by other senators and their aides. A few reporters with cameras and recording devices hurried up to him as he was heading toward a waiting car. He hated how they always looked like scuttling insects. It was starting to rain, and his aide was standing by the open door of the car. Josiah sighed, wishing the man had thought to bring an umbrella.

"Senator Manidoo," one of the reporters asked. "Is it true you've filed a missing persons report on your daughter, Yvette?"

"No comment," Josiah said, hurrying as fast as he could on his bad hip. He was closer to the car, but the reporters persisted in their attention.

"Is it true you've hired a private detective to find her?" another reporter asked.

"No comment," the senator replied, his hip starting to really burn now. He finally made it to the car and scowled at his aide. The man would be lucky to keep his job after this. The door was open and waiting for him to enter.

"Is it true your daughter's disappearance has derailed your plans to run for the office of President of the United States?" the first reporter asked, aggressively sticking his microphone in the senator's face before he could close the door.

"No goddamn comment," he muttered angrily. The car door slammed, leaving a gaggle of reporters wide-eyed at the language used by the prominent senator.

He knew it was unwise to show anger toward a reporter in the run-up to an election year, but he didn't care at the moment. His daughter was missing, and that's all that mattered. He'd worry about his public image later.

Chapter 4

"Rajan is smaller than your home planet," Rauph intoned. He was standing before the gathered Humans in the same briefing room they had been in before their operations. It had been three days since the Humans had awakened from the procedure to insert the Johar Stones into their skulls, and Rauph thought it time to begin teaching them a little about Rajan.

He'd had Janan round up three of the handheld tablets and then programmed the central computer to display a picture of Rajan on each of them. "The days, therefore, are shorter than on your planet, and the gravity lighter. I assure you, though, you won't feel much of a difference when we arrive. You've been living with the decreased gravity since coming aboard this ship."

"Instant weight loss," Moretti said, patting his plump midsection.

Rauph saw Officer Dempsey give Moretti a frown of disapproval. He continued with his lecture quickly, not wanting to sit and wait for the two Humans to start up their feuding once again. "It's also a little farther away from our sun, though close enough, still, to sustain liquid water, which is essential for life on most planets."

He reached down to the closest tablet and tapped the screen, and all of the screens zoomed in closer to the display of Rajan's surface. "Because of the distance from the sun, Rajan is also somewhat cooler than the Earth," he said. "The two poles are much like Earth's, though they extend farther north and south, respectively. The population of Rajani, Sekani, and Jirina live along the equatorial region on Rajan's only continent, mostly living in the capital city of Melaanse."

He tapped the tablet screen again, and it zoomed in to the coastline of the large continent. "Melaanse is also the largest city on Rajan, and is located on the eastern coast of the continent, almost exactly on the equator. West of the city is a large uninhabitable desert, which means the population lives mostly north and south along the coast."

"Wait," Dempsey said. "Jirina? Who are they? You haven't mentioned them before."

"They are another sentient species living on Rajan," Rauph replied. "They are a ... helper species. I don't know if my words are making any sense translated to you. The Jirina ... serve in the houses of the Elders, mostly, though they also work on the farms outside of the city."

"So we'll have to save them too?" Gray asked.

"Yes, I suppose so, now that you mention it," Rauph said. "Forgive me for not bringing them up before, but it didn't seem important to our story at the time."

"Okay," Dempsey said. "But we need to know that kind of information if we're going to be prepared when we arrive."

"You're right, of course," Rauph said, rubbing his hand over his beard. "If there are no other questions at this time, I believe we should take a break for our midday meal and reconvene here afterward. We shall then begin learning the fundamentals of the Talondarian Standard language, which is spoken throughout the Alliance."

◊

Kieren found she picked up the alien language quickly, which was not much of surprise. She was a teacher, after all, and was used to learning in this type of environment. The words almost translated themselves in her mind before Rauph told the group what they meant.

She noticed James and David did well in the classes too. Yvette, it seemed, didn't care about learning the language, and Gianni ... well, Gianni never seemed to care about being there. She thought about offering to help him study, but was afraid to offer. She felt like a high school girl again, afraid to show too much interest in a guy, so she decided it felt too much like asking for a study date and kept silent. It was what she'd always done, played it safe, to avoid the risk of being hurt. Speaking up brought attention, something that always made her feel uncomfortable.

She'd always been a shy and reserved person, even when she was a little girl. Her brother, Dennis, was the wild one; the one who always had to have all eyes on him. She was happy to let him make a fool of himself as he strove to garner everyone's attention. She was content to sit back and observe people. Any time she chose to be assertive, she felt like a jerk afterward, like she was being too pushy with her opinions. It wasn't in her to boss anyone else around or to forcefully tell people off—though she could control a classroom of six-year-olds fine. Yet she also got angry with herself at times for not speaking up when she needed to. Dennis wasn't around anymore to do it for her. She sighed, wondering if her brother even knew she was missing.

◊

Police lights flashed in front of a hotel in Detroit, Michigan, on a cold and rainy night. Police officers and ambulance attendants milled about a section of the pavement which had been cordoned off with yellow police tape. Within the tape, two cars sat, mangled from a high-speed impact and the use of Jaws of Life in the aftermath. A crowd of people, some with umbrellas, and some without, stood around outside of the police cordon. Their breath steamed in the cold night air.

James Dempsey and his partner, Steve Montgomery, arrived on the scene in an unmarked police vehicle. James was dressed in his old Marine dress blues uniform, complete with medals and sword. This was his dream, and his mind mixed together parts of his life unrelated to each other.

"Another one," Steve observed.

"Uh-huh," James answered.

They stepped out of the car and walked to where Officer Kelly stood, writing in a small notebook. Steve drank from a white Styrofoam cup the size of a small bucket.

"Kelly, what happened here?" James asked.

Kelly looked at Dempsey and showed no signs of recognition. "Excuse me, sir, you shouldn't be in here."

The dream changed. Kelly was now a male nurse in a bloody green smock, holding a medical chart. James's partner, Steve, had disappeared completely. "Sir? I said you're not supposed to be in here."

James stood in the doorway of a hospital room, where nurses and attendants worked around a bed containing the body of a young black woman; they turned off lights and shut down medical equipment in a slow ballet of resignation. The woman was James's wife, Jennifer.

"Oh God, no!" James yelled, looking at his wife, who was covered to her chin with a white sheet. Nurse Kelly restrained James from entering the room. "No! What happened to her? What happened!" The two men struggled together for a moment, with the attendants still working in the room and paying no attention to them.

"Are you her husband?" the nurse finally asked him.

"Yes," James answered, and stared at the unmoving form of his wife.

Kelly motioned for James to exit the room ahead of him. "Come with me, sir. Please, there's nothing you can do for her now."

They stood outside the hospital room in the hallway. Nurses and doctors rushed by on their way to other sick and dying patients. James cried and held his crumpled barracks cover in his hands. "What happened?"

"Sergeant Dempsey," the nurse began. "Your wife's car was hit head-on by another vehicle. The other driver was intoxicated. I'm sorry—there was nothing the doctor could do for her or the fetus."

James placed his hand over his eyes. "A baby? Oh ... oh God, no. Please ... no!"

◊

James woke up, covered in sweat and wide-eyed from his dream. He was in his own private quarters on the *Tukuli*. It was the second time in two days he'd had the dream. After so long, he thought he'd put it in the past. The stress of the current situation was dredging up unwanted memories. *Lucky me,* he thought, sighing. Dreaming of the night his wife died was nothing new to him. He'd had it many times before. Events and characters were always different, but the end was always the same: finding out his wife had been killed, as well as the baby in her womb—a baby he had not known about until the moment the doctor told him.

He'd talked to her mother afterward. She was the only person who had known his wife was pregnant. He'd learned Jenny was waiting to surprise him after her first ultrasound. The embryo was only eight weeks along, but as far as he was concerned, it was a child. His child. It would have been born; would have been loved. Instead, it had died when she did, and was buried with her. Her name appeared on the tombstone, and under her name was carved, simply, Baby Dempsey. He hadn't known what name they would have given the child, and he hadn't wanted to pick one on his own, especially without knowing the gender. Not without his wife being able to give her opinion.

He'd thought at the time his world was ending. He had applied for and was granted a hardship discharge from the Marines, and had returned to Michigan to lick his wounds and decide how to move on with his life—or whether he wanted to move on at all. There had been a few tough weeks right after her funeral when all he could think about was whether or not it would be better to give up and join her and their child.

He'd gone to grief counseling and had come to the realization that leaving the Marines had been a mistake. He needed a challenge, something to keep his mind occupied instead of giving it time to dwell on her death.

The best therapy he found was to become involved in something important. Something that would allow him to gradually come to terms with his loss over time. He hadn't known what it would be until he saw an ad for a job opening at the Sheriff's Department. It had started him seriously thinking about law enforcement as a career, and he'd begun researching what it would take to become a police officer. He eventually took the test and started at the academy. That had been over twenty years earlier.

James blinked wearily, more awake now and aware of his surroundings. He had no concept of time, only the fact that it was dark in his room as he sat up, and he knew he probably wasn't going to fall back to sleep. There was no reason to fight consciousness. He still hadn't grasped the Standard Galactic hour that the aliens used. It was longer than an Earth hour, but he had no idea what standard was used to measure it.

The translating device the Rajani used was fine for making general sense of what was said, but James had come to believe there was still quite a bit of information lost in translation. There was so much he didn't know, both about the aliens and about the galaxy as a whole. As he pulled on his jeans, white T-shirt, and Red Wings jersey, he thought about the recent training they had received from Rauph. He could tell Rauph was sometimes to the point of exasperation when trying to explain everything to the five of them, but there was so much information, they were having a hard time taking it all in. Having their body clocks disturbed didn't help the situation.

James picked up the handheld tablet from the small table next to his bed and touched the screen to activate it. He looked at the time and saw by the numerals that it was morning. Janan had programmed the computer to display the time in Earth numbers so they would at least know an approximation of the time.

James had been thinking about something in the days (he thought it had been only days) since the Rajani had proclaimed the ship was repaired and had set a course back toward their home world. His team, for that was what they were now, needed training with their powers. So far, only he and Kieren had exhibited any special effects from the stones. Rauph assured them his records indicated it could take several days for the implanted stones to work, and that it depended on the individual.

James decided he needed to have an area where the humans could train without harming the ship, or each other. James had found not only could he become invisible when he was 'powered up' as he referred to it, his strength also had increased exponentially—a fact he discovered when he'd accidentally destroyed a table while in his powered-up form by simply brushing against it. He didn't want any similar accidents in their training, which could put a hole in the ship's hull, or worse, disable the ship again.

He stepped out into the corridor and headed for the bridge. He was beginning to become familiar with the ship's layout as they went along. He knew there was one main level corridor running from the bridge, which was located in the nose of the ship, to the engine maintenance rooms at the rear. In case of a hull breach, sections of the ship could be closed off to prevent a total decompression. The main airlock door was at the end of a cross-corridor above the left wing, and there was also a larger one in the cargo hold. The rooms off the main corridor were mostly meeting rooms and prayer rooms. He found the Rajani prayed quite a lot—at least Rauph and Bhakat did—so it made sense they would have prayer rooms for any guests they took aboard the ship. Crew quarters were located off of the upper cross-corridor that led to the wings.

The oxygen generators were located in one of the maintenance control rooms near the engines at the rear of the ship. Rauph had explained the engines actually aided in the production and cleaning of the breathable air aboard the ship. He hadn't become too technical or specific at the time. James would've liked to find out more later on, but was still too busy taking in all of the information as a whole to focus on such minutiae.

The lower deck had another, shorter corridor leading to a room at the rear of the ship containing the 'gravity well' as Rauph referred to it. Rauph hadn't even bothered with an explanation of how this device worked. James couldn't decide if it was too technical a concept to explain easily, or if Rauph himself didn't understand it. Maybe it was so commonplace that it wasn't worth talking about. There was still much they had to learn.

The lower corridor also led to the cargo hold, where the 'lander' could be found. James hadn't seen this ship yet, but had been told it was able to seat up to ten Rajani comfortably. The small ship was used when they needed to go down to the surface of a planet and back without having to land the main ship—and more importantly, without having to launch again from a planet's surface.

The upper corridor was where the housing quarters were located. The ship usually had a full complement of Sekani crewmen to pilot and maintain it, but Janan had been the only survivor the Rajani could hastily find as they left Rajan. The quarters were simple rooms with a large bed, a chair, and a table or two as their only furnishings. There was a restroom with a toilet, sink, and shower in his room. James would have to talk to Rauph about the incredibly large toilet seat—he'd almost fallen in the night before when he sat down, still half-asleep.

He'd felt sorry for the women; he'd assumed they were forced to squat whenever they used the toilet. He'd found out later they had settled into Sekani quarters, where the seats were much smaller. The Sekani rooms didn't have showers in them, but there was a central shower room for them to use.

There was a rudimentary kitchen, though most of the stores were various horrible-tasting protein and mineral bars. These had to be eaten with plenty of water or you wouldn't have to worry about using the over-sized toilet for a week. Rauph told him most of their fresh food supplies were used up on their journey from Rajan. There was still some food left from Earth, but he and the others agreed to only eat it at dinner time, when the humans would usually all eat together.

There was a communication system in each room,

allowing the occupant to talk to another person anywhere on the ship. James thought it was a simple intercom system until Rauph had explained he could also call someone in another room without their conversation being played for all of the ship to hear. This system was controlled by the central computer.

The lower corridor was bisected by another, smaller hallway. This hallway led to the bottom of the wings on either side of the ship, where the emergency ejection pods were located. These pods were only large enough for one Rajani and were equipped with survival supplies. They looked about as comfortable as a giant tin can. James hoped he would never have to use one.

Rauph had given everyone permission to wander the ship as they pleased. He had asked they not go in any of the various engine maintenance rooms or near the gravity well area. They also needed permission to enter the main bridge. James had complimented Rauph on the beautiful ship, but Rauph had pointed out the Rajani did not design nor create the ships; they bought them from another species. Whenever a new ship was needed, an Elder would travel off-planet to buy it.

There were only a few species in the galaxy who had truly mastered the design and construction of a ship worthy of interstellar flight, though all members of the Galactic Alliance had to have reached a point in their civilization where their technology was deemed worthy of inclusion.

The Rajani were an older race, and they had had the technology required for spaceflight for thousands of years. But after a drastic change in ideology and a religious awakening, they had settled down on their home planet, along with the two other species Rauph had explained about in their briefings. James didn't want to pry into Rauph's explanation too much, but he suspected these two other species, the Sekani and the Jirina, had been conquered sometime in the past.

Only the Elders of the Rajani were allowed to own an interstellar craft, and they seldom used them, if at all. This self-imposed exile was partly due to their religious beliefs, but also because of the resentment many other worlds harbored toward the past actions of the Rajani, when they were not a peaceful race.

James was lost in thought as he made his way down the main corridor to the bridge. He was surprised at how soon he found himself at the door. He pushed the communication button.

"I need to speak to Rauph," he said, talking into the microphone pad at the side of the button. "Is he available?"

The door to the bridge quickly opened, and Rauph emerged, holding the translating device. "Good morning to you, Officer Dempsey," the Rajani said, closing the door behind him and leading James over to a meeting room. James had told the aliens to call him by his first name, but Rauph still insisted on using a title.

"Good morning," James replied. Then he added, "I pray your rest was peaceful," using the standard Rajani greeting they had been taught. Rauph and Bhakat had been teaching them all basic greetings and other key phrases they might need when they reached Rajan.

"You need to work on your enunciation," Rauph said, producing a smile, showing off his long canines. "You sounded as if you said 'I pray your death was peaceful.' No matter, the two words are very similar to begin with, I suppose."

They went through the door of a meeting room and sat at the table inside. James noticed the tables and other furniture were made out of some sort of plastic-like material, which felt as solid as rock. It was definitely not something he would find back on Earth. He still felt both excitement and trepidation, thinking of how far he was from home.

◊

Kieren was fascinated by the fact the Rajani had thought to download reading materials from Earth. Not only items like books and magazines, but content from news sites from the Internet and even some blogs. Janan was a very curious type, and he had also downloaded music, movies, and even television programs.

She had been given one of the handheld tablet devices, allowing her to view files saved on the ship's main computer. It helped at times to ease her homesickness. She missed her brother, Dennis. She missed her students, too, though if anyone had ever told her this would happen, she would have called them crazy.

No, not exactly true, she thought, feeling guilty. Some of her students were really great, but everything at her current school was different from what she was used to back in Colorado. She had worked at a charter school in a suburban area, worlds apart from the inner-city school she'd ended up at in Detroit. The realities of where her students were coming from and the things they had to deal with on a day-to-day basis were as alien to her as the ship she now found herself on.

All that aside, she was lonely. Maybe not as lonely as she had been back in Detroit, where the only people she knew were her brother and her fellow faculty members. The other teachers were either old and cynical or young and desperate to escape their situations. Either way, making friends was not on the top of their lists. At least on the ship she knew everyone. James and David were nice, and she and Yvette were starting to become friends. She had her doubts they would become close friends, though.

Yvette didn't seem to want or need any close friends.

Then there was Gianni. She didn't know anything about him, even after a week on the ship together, except that he owned a cat. She was unsure whether that was because he wasn't interested in getting to know anyone else or if he wasn't interested in getting to know her specifically.

She decided if she and her fellow humans were going to be living together aboard the ship, they should be hanging out more socially. She would have to talk to James about setting up a room where all of them could congregate and get to know each other better.

◊

Rauph had begun to enjoy his meetings with Officer Dempsey. The Human had turned out to be quite intelligent once the initial shock had worn off. At least the Humans didn't appear to be as slow and timid as the Jirina on his home world, which was the first impression Rauph had garnered after initially talking to them. Kidnapping the Humans—and Rauph knew this was exactly what they had done—had been a desperate move on his part. He hadn't been sure if the Humans would be able to help them, even if they agreed. He only knew they were running out of time to do his home world any good. They had to return. The repairs to the ship had taken far too long.

As he sat down to speak with Dempsey, he wondered if the Human was the answer to his prayers, or if he was already too late to save his species. He hoped the Krahn had simply taken the inhabitants of Rajan prisoner, but had no idea how many had died in the initial attack and the time that had passed since then.

One of the tenets of the Kha was the limit on procreation placed upon the Rajani. A limit to the population was thought to discourage a need for expansion and the violence that inevitably came with it. Female Rajani could only produce one offspring in their lifetime. Males were permitted to mate until they produced a male heir, taking on mates until this feat was accomplished. Sometimes Elders would have four or five mates before one finally bore them a son. The result of this was female Rajani outnumbered males by a ratio of four or five to one.

In special cases of under-population, prominent males with a male heir were permitted to mate again. As before, they would mate only until another male was produced. The Second Son, or Taman, was considered special, and they were free to search for knowledge, without the day-to-day duties associated with the running of the household given to the firstborn son. In rare instances, when twin sons were born, the second son was known as the Tamal-Gaal, and this son was given over to the Elders to be raised strictly in the ways of the Kha.

With the attack of the Krahn, Rauph was afraid the resultant deaths of Rajani had placed them in jeopardy of becoming a non-viable species. The self-imposed limit had resulted in a decrease in the total population on Rajan. The Rajani didn't have the technology to artificially clone or recreate their species; nor would they use it even if it were available. Such technology was strictly forbidden by the Kha.

Rauph's first and only mate had died young, without providing him an heir. She had been more than a mate, though. He had loved her more than anything else, and after her passing, he'd chosen not to take any other female into his house. He had instead devoted his life to learning, and then teaching, the tenets of the Kha.

"I need to speak to you about training," Dempsey said, bringing Rauph out of his reverie.

"Training?" Rauph asked, not sure what the Human was talking about.

"Yes," Dempsey said. "You've given us these extraordinary powers, but they won't do you or us any good if we don't know how to use them properly once we get to Rajan. I know your religion forbids you from any type of violent behavior, and that's why your ship isn't outfitted with any type of training facility, but my team needs a way to hone our skills and learn to work together or we're not going to be very effective."

"I've also been thinking about this, though I did not know the word for it," Rauph replied, pouring himself a glass of water. "You should also know I must weigh the need to return to Rajan with the need for you to help us once we arrive there." Rauph sighed. "I'm afraid there is not enough time for us to stop and let you train somewhere."

"Then let us train aboard the ship," Dempsey replied.

"What do you mean?" Rauph asked, hating the translating device more and more each day.

"I mean," Dempsey continued, "let me set up a room where my team can train on the way to Rajan. We wouldn't lose as much time, and I truly think the better we're prepared for our arrival on Rajan, the more successful we'll be when we get there. Half my team hasn't even discovered their powers yet."

Rauph sat silently for a moment, thinking. The Human did have a point, unfortunately. Neither he nor Bhakat, or even Janan, had the knowledge to install a suitable training room aboard the ship. That left hiring someone else to do it. The only place anywhere close to their route that could possibly install the equipment on the ship was the Mandakan Space Port. That still left a few problems, such as how they would pay for it, and how long it would take to be completed.

There was no type of monetary system on Rajan, so it was always difficult when the need for bartering for goods or services came up when they were off-world. On Rajan, if you needed something, you asked. Population was calculated to determine how much needed to be planted or manufactured, and any excess was either stockpiled for emergencies or traded off-world.

We don't have time for this, Rauph thought. He looked across the table at the Human. He knew he had taken a big gamble, not only in placing his hopes for a chance to free his world on the Humans, but also giving them such awesome powers to accomplish the goal. He was well aware not only did the Humans outnumber them; they were also now vastly more powerful. He had to do what he could to make them happy. He couldn't afford any type of mutiny.

"I agree to your request," he said. "We must stop at Mandaka, a space station close to our route back to Rajan, and have the necessary equipment installed."

Dempsey smiled. "That's great. How long until we get there?"

"I would have to verify our location with Bhakat and Janan," Rauph said, thinking over the details. "I think it would be ten days, with a layover of two to three for equipment installation and ship repair."

Dempsey nodded, still smiling. "Okay."

"Before we end this meeting," Rauph continued, "there is something else I have been meaning to speak with you about."

"What?" Dempsey asked, caught off-guard.

"Your initial evaluation of your team?" Rauph asked, absentmindedly playing with his braid, a habit he'd developed years before. "You've made it abundantly clear we erred when we chose those Humans in your general proximity due to time constraints, but I want your honest assessment of them. Do you think you and your team will be able to succeed?"

The Human sat for a moment, looking down at the desk between them. Rauph could not read his face, either because of his unfamiliarity with Humans, or because Dempsey had the ability to hide his emotions well. He suspected it was both.

"I honestly don't know," Dempsey finally said, looking up. "I'll know better after we've trained together for a while. Hell, we still don't know if three of them will have powers, nor what those powers will be if they do manifest. I think it's too early for speculation at this point. I'm not sure Gianni is much of a team player to begin with. He's the one I'm worried about at the moment."

"I agree," Rauph said. "That being said, I will trust in your further assessment. If at any time in your training you feel that Gianni Moretti—or any other member of your team—is more of a liability than an asset, we can place them back into suspended animation until the mission is over and you return to Earth."

He disliked lying to the Human. He'd come to admire him, but he would make sure any Human who could not be trusted to help would never wake up again. The stones were too powerful of a weapon in the wrong hands, and once they were implanted, they could not be removed—at least not from a living being.

"I'll take it under advisement," Dempsey said, "but to do so could cost me the trust of the entire team."

"A valid point, I'm sure," Rauph said, standing up. "Now I must return to my duties on the bridge. Unless you have anything else to discuss?"

"No," Dempsey replied, standing himself. "I'll let the

team know we'll begin training as soon as the equipment is installed."

◊

David was surprised to find the little alien known as Janan was pretty cool to talk to. They had begun speaking at dinner the night before, and Janan had brought the translating device with him to David's room to continue their conversation afterward. The Sekani had a sharp wit and wanted to know everything about life on Earth. After about an hour, he excused himself, and a few minutes later, returned with what looked like a bottle of wine.

"It is a custom on Rajan to drink with newfound friends," Janan said, pouring the dark liquid into glasses. He handed one of the glasses to David. "What was it we were talking about before I left?"

"About Rajan," David replied. "The attack of the Krahn Horde on your planet."

"Ah, of course," Janan said, sipping the liquid. "You must forgive me if I don't know much. I was knocked unconscious by falling debris in the first wave of the attack. My entire family's dwellings, I've been told, were destroyed."

"Your entire family?" David asked the diminutive alien.

"Yes," Janan replied, sadly. "They're all gone."

"I'm so sorry," David said.

Janan held up his glass. "We'll drink to them. A custom on your planet, is it not? A roast, yes?"

"Toast," David corrected. He was looking at the dark liquid in his glass. "By the way, what is this?"

Janan looked at his glass. "It is called 'fernta' in my language. It is one of the few things left over from my world. We lost so much when the Rajani came ..." He paused a moment, looking at his glass. "To freedom," he finally said, holding his drink high over his head. "No matter the cost."

"Freedom," David replied, taking a drink for the first time. He gasped as the liquid burned a path to his stomach. It soon turned to comfortable warmth. "Whoa," he said, smiling.

Janan smiled as well. "Good stuff, yes?"

David held out his glass for more as they both laughed.

Interlude

Jebediah Morris was pissed off. He was known to his friends as Jeb and to everyone else—mostly his employees at the marketing firm he owned—as Mr. Morris. Angry, as anyone who knew him could tell you, was his usual state of mind. He was on the phone talking to his son's girlfriend, Lisa, when he should have been shutting down his computer and heading home for the night. He was pissed he had to talk to this stupid cow, when he would rather be enjoying a beer or three.

"Where the hell is he?" he bellowed into his iPhone.

"I don't know," Lisa replied, used to this man yelling whenever she talked to him. It was the only volume he had. *No wonder David doesn't get along with him,* she thought. *He's such a dick.* "The last I saw him was last month, after my birthday party."

"And you weren't worried almost a month has passed without word from him?" Jeb asked.

Lisa was incredulous no one knew where David was. "What?"

"He hasn't shown up for work for a month," he continued.

"Oh my God," Lisa replied. "I thought he was just avoiding me."

"Why would he?" he asked her. "What did he do this time?"

"He proposed," she answered, feeling miserable she would be the one to tell this man.

"Let me guess," he said, not yelling now. "You turned him down. Figures. The boy can fuck up making ice."

"For your information, sir," she told him, now feeling defensive for both of them. "I did not turn him down. I just ... didn't say yes."

"Well," he said, a new level of disgust in his voice now. "That explains a few things, at least. When he crawls out of hiding, you can tell him he's fired."

"But—" she began to ask if he'd called in a missing person report to the police, when she heard the unmistakable click telling her the current conversation was now a past conversation.

Chapter 5

James felt better after talking to Rauph the day before. He had been having some doubts about the situation, but then he reasoned, why shouldn't he? It was still unreal to him that he was aboard a ship traveling through space. There was no feeling of weightlessness, no sound of engines firing or shifts in the level of the floor underneath him. He could set the handheld tablet in his room to the view the space outside the ship, but even then, it was more like watching a dark television screen. There were no stars to be seen; no sweeping panoramas moving past the ship as it flew—the *Tukuli* was traveling too quickly. This brought him back to his present concerns. If he were to accidentally put a hole in the hull of the ship while powered up, it could tear the ship apart.

James also knew he eventually needed to have a face-to-face chat with Gianni. He wasn't looking forward to it, but knew it had to be done. He needed everyone on the same page on this mission, and even one person not buying into what they were trying to accomplish could undermine everything.

It would have to wait, though. He was going to have dinner with Yvette. Just the two of them. He'd been surprised when she asked him. Yes, he had mentioned something about getting together to talk, but she was the one who turned it into an actual dinner together. She was aloof most of the time, and while he was attracted to her physically, he didn't really know much about her, other than she was a senator's daughter and had a good sense of humor.

This would also be the first time in a several years that he had a dinner date with a woman, and he was nervous, even if the dinner consisted of eating protein bars as he spent his time hoping he didn't have anything stuck in his teeth when he smiled. At least they would have a chance to be alone together. He knew he was being foolish; she probably wanted to talk about the team and what he expected from her once they arrived at Rajan.

Have I really been that lonely? He thought about it a little while longer as he was heading back to his quarters after the daily information session with Rauph and the others, and realized the answer was an overwhelming yes.

◊

Rauph, Bhakat, and Janan had decided they would take shifts working on the bridge on their trip back to Rajan. With only the three of them, they had to improvise.

Bhakat was preparing to take over for Janan. He preferred the night shift. Most of the time there was no one to bother him, and he was left alone with his thoughts. When he was relieved by Rauphangelaa in the morning, he would usually go back to his own quarters and read or pray, preferring to stay away from the Humans. This night, he was feeling depressed and discouraged about the entire situation. Besides the fact he was having doubts concerning the Kha and the teachings of Ruvedalin, he also didn't think their mission could succeed once they arrived back at Rajan.

The odds were against them repelling the Krahn with

only five Humans, even if they were implanted with the legendary Johar Stones. There were thousands of Krahn on Rajan, and they were equipped with projectile weapons and a large colony ship outfitted with an energy cannon. As for the smaller Krahn ships, some had projectile weapons and some energy—it depended on what was scavenged from the various ships they attacked over the years since Ronak's exile.

The Galactic Alliance maintained records of all of its members, including the Krahn, in its Administrative Authority department. Anyone could access information at any time, as long as they had the proper security level. Not all information was free for everyone to see.

After they escaped Rajan, Rauphangelaa had accessed the Alliance Central Computer via the *Tukuli's* main computer and learned as much as he could about the Krahn Horde. They had known some about the Krahn, a relatively new race to the Galactic Alliance, but being as secluded as they were on Rajan, knew nothing of the Horde and the fact it had steadily been moving toward Rajan over the course of five years, pirating the space travel corridors and expanding its numbers exponentially.

The concept of a single ruler was foreign to the Rajani, who were governed by the Elder Council. The files on the Krahn suggested the Krahn had a stable government once Ronak was banished.

Bhakat had made his way to the bridge. He pushed the intercom button and waited for Janan to let him in. After a minute or two, Janan opened the door.

"Were you sleeping?" Bhakat asked irritably as he entered the bridge.

"No," Janan replied, wiping his eyes hurriedly.

Bhakat could see his friend had been crying, and his

demeanor softened. Janan was the only one he considered a friend. They had known each other since Bhakat had pledged to Rauphangelaa's house, and they complemented each other in many ways.

"I too grieve for your loss," Bhakat said quietly, sitting down next to the diminutive Sekani.

"It still doesn't seem real sometimes," Janan said, looking at the giant screen wall. "It's like we'll get back home and none of this will have really happened. My family will be alive and waiting for me like all of the other times I've returned."

He stood and wiped his face again. "My father will tell me about the gardens around Rauphangelaa's estate, and my mother will complain about the quality of food at the marketplace, and my brothers will pester me for stories about my adventures aboard this ship until I make up something good because nothing exciting ever happens aboard a Rajani ship." He smiled and looked at Bhakat, then turned serious once more. "But none of it will ever happen again. They're all gone. Even if we win this war and repel or kill all of the Krahn, it won't change the fact my entire family is dead." Tears began to stream from his eyes again, and he bowed his head, covering his face with his hands.

Bhakat said nothing. His friend needed to cry. It was part of the grieving cycle. He needed to accept his loss. Bhakat's parents were both dead, had been dead for a few years, and Bhakat still missed them. After a moment, Janan was able to compose himself. *It can't help matters,* Bhakat thought, *that Rajan was betrayed by a Sekani.*

Before the initial Krahn attack, the *Tukuli* had intercepted a transmission from the planet's surface to the Krahn colony ship that had given detailed information on the location of the Elders and their houses, as well as maps of Melaanse. Each individual on Rajan was given a computer identification number. Whenever someone logged into a computer console on Rajan, their number was sent to a log on the central computer system. Bhakat had discovered the transmission was sent by someone logged in with a Sekani number. They thought at first the central computer on Rajan must have been destroyed, because they couldn't access it to see who the number belonged to.

Then they couldn't access the full extent of the information given or the name associated with the identification number because parts of the Tukuli's computer memory were damaged in the escape from Rajan. The computer had been experiencing glitches in its memory even prior to the attack, but now an entire data section was missing, including everything right before the attack. Bhakat had been meaning to run a diagnostic on the computer to see if the Krahn had downloaded a virus to all of Rajan's computers through the central computer located in Melaanse, but other matters had taken precedent. He would get to it eventually.

"I suppose I'm just tired," Janan said, breaking Bhakat out of his reverie. "I've been spending too many late nights talking with David."

"Drinking fernta," Bhakat added, frowning disapprovingly.

"Ah, yes, that too. We're getting low, by the way. We'll have to restock when we get back," he smiled at Bhakat, who kept a serious expression on his face for as long as he could before he too smiled. He didn't smile often, but when he did, he usually looked like he was going to bite someone.

Janan always had a way of making him smile. He supposed it was why they were friends. Even though Janan was his only friend, he didn't begrudge the fact the Sekani was spending a lot of his free time with the Human named David. There was something fascinating about the Humans;

each in their own way, though Bhakat preferred not to become too familiar with them personally.

"Tonight," Janan said, "I'm going to bed. I've been staying up too late recently. I'm not going to be any good to the mission if I'm still hung-over when we get home." He walked to the door before turning back toward Bhakat. "Thank you for listening, Bhakat."

"Any time, my friend," Bhakat replied. He watched as Janan turned and walked out of the bridge, wondering if it was better or worse he had survived, when all of his family was now dead.

◊

James and Yvette were talking, seated on the comfortable couch-like piece of furniture in James's room. The bed behind them was much larger than a king-size. There was a small table with a few simple-looking plates on it in front of them, which James had brought into his room for them to eat on.

"Those nutritional supplements leave something to be desired," James said. "Hopefully we'll have something better for dinner tomorrow night."

"Yes," Yvette replied, smiling. "But we're probably far healthier than we were before coming aboard this ship."

They were seated at a comfortable distance from one another as they talked, though both were more at ease than the first time they'd sat together in his room, weeks earlier.

"True," James said. "You were pretty willing to come on this mission. Why, if you don't mind my asking?"

"Why not?" Yvette replied, still smiling, though James thought the smile now looked more like a cat's.

James leaned toward her, surprise on his face. "Why not? We haven't talked about this as a team yet, but you and I both know we're probably not going to win this fight. The odds are against us."

"Yes, I know, but there's nothing like a challenge to get the blood flowing."

"A challenge?" James asked. "This is going to be a war."

Yvette was still smiling. "Are you going to repeat everything I say or are you going to kiss me?"

James waited a moment before returning the smile. He slowly leaned toward her, his heart racing and his mind blank. Her lips were soft, warm, and he lost himself in the sensation for a moment. Then she ran her hand over his chest and was in his suddenly in his arms. He picked her up and carried her to the bed.

◊

Gianni was watching a love scene on a handheld tablet he had expanded to its full size and set up like a TV in his room. The doorbell rang as the woman on the screen said, "You had me at hello ..."

"Yeah," Gianni said loudly. "Come in."

He reached over to the tablet and turned it off. When the door opened, Kieren stood in the archway.

"Hey, Sandy," Gianni said glibly. "What's happening?"

"Why do you do that?" she asked him, folding her arms in front of her and scowling.

"What?" he asked.

"Make fun of everybody."

He held his hands up in front of him like a dog begging. "It's my poor upbringing. I was raised by wolves in the wilderness of Kentucky. I've only just been potty trained."

Kieren was still in the doorway. "I don't know why I bothered." She turned to go.

"Wait," he said, standing up now. "Kieren."

She smiled, knowing he couldn't see her face, and then turned, her smile disappearing as she did. "Yes?"

"Um ... I'm sorry," he began. "Please. Sit down."

"Better," she said, sitting down next to him. "What were you watching?"

"Uh ... *Apocalypse Now*," he replied quickly. "I wasn't really paying attention."

"Can you believe they downloaded all this stuff?" Kieren asked. "It's a good thing, too, seeing that nullspace is faster than TV signals. I think I'd be bored out of my mind without it."

"Nullspace?" Gianni asked her. Now it was his turn to look perplexed.

"Yeah," Kieren explained. "I was talking to Rauph, and he said the engines on the ship send it into a place called nullspace. At least, that's the closest word the translator came to in English."

"Huh. And to answer your question, yes, I can believe it," he told her. "They planned on having human passengers. I hear the munchkin loves soaps."

"See," she said, becoming angry. "There you go again."

"Listen, Lady," he said defensively. "This is the way I am. You don't have to like me."

Kieren stood up. "Fine. I'll see you later." She walked to the door and turned her head back to him. "How could anyone like you? You don't even like yourself." She walked out, and the door closed behind her.

Gianni waited a second, looking at the closed door and thinking. Then he turned the handheld tablet back to the love story. He sat, scowling, watching the two people kiss on the screen and wishing they would both drop dead. "Fine."

◊

Inevitably, Janan again found himself talking and drinking with David in the Human's room, though he'd told Bhakat he was going straight to bed.

"I believe this female loves you," Janan said. "You would be a fool to not see this."

"Oh right, shuuure," David replied. He'd drunk a great deal of the alien brew known as fernta. "She ripped out my heart and ... and ... shtuffed it down the toilet."

Janan's eyes widened in alarm. "And you lived? I didn't know Humans were biologically capable of—"

David waved away his concern. "No! No, it's an expreshun. Y'know?" He raised a glass. "To women—(burp). To Leesha." He promptly passed out, falling over onto the sofa arm, his glass falling to the floor, breaking, and spilling the small amount of dark liquid.

Janan shrugged. "Hmmph," he said, pouring himself another drink. "Can't handle his fernta." He took a large gulp of liquid and then stood on unsteady legs.

David looked comfortable enough where he was, and was too big for him to move anyway, so he left the Human where he'd fallen and cleaned up the broken glass the best he could before turning out the light. He opened the door and looked back at the sleeping figure on the floor. "Good night, my friend," he said softly before leaving for his own quarters.

◊

James's and Yvette's clothes were piled in a heap on the floor next to the bed. They were lying in bed, her head rested on his chest, and his arms were around her. After their lovemaking, words seemed to rush from each of them, and they had talked for hours.

"So I started taking karate, self-defense classes, and even shooting as well," she was saying softly. "I wanted to stop people who could do that. So I followed in my dad's footsteps and became a lawyer."

James was smiling sadly. "What did your dad say?"

Yvette smiled, now holding herself up on an elbow and

looking at him. "He was thrilled, of course. He had dreams of me becoming the first American Indian female president. He thinks I'll do my time as a prosecuting attorney, and then join him in Washington to begin my 'rise to the top.' Being the daughter of a US senator does have its perks, you know."

"I can bet," James said, rising up on his own elbow, looking at her. "Listen, they put me in charge, but I'm going to need someone I can count on down there when we finally land."

Yvette expression looked somewhat wicked. "Why, James, are you asking me to be your second?"

James looked bewildered. "My ... second?"

"In command," she said, in a teasing voice.

James looked relieved. "Oh. Yeah. I thought that's what you meant."

She laughed softly and kissed him. He felt the heat within him rise and the kiss became deeper. He was lost in her again.

◊

Early the next morning, James once again found himself awake and thinking. It was a little strange that the Rajani would have chosen such loners as the five of them to come along on the trip back to Rajan. Each of them, in their own way, was more comfortable by themselves than in a large group. Even Kieren, who was the most social out of all of them, could be found most times alone in her room, reading.

Perhaps they relate to us better, he thought. The Rajani were, after all, a species of loners. Janan was gregarious, but James didn't know if this was a species trait or not. Either way, the Sekani pilot had accepted the nature of the humans. Most of the time, he could be found either on the bridge or, when off duty, hanging out with David, who had found a kindred spirit in the stout little alien. This worked out well, since David seemed to be the odd one out in the team's pairing up.

James had also noticed how Gianni and Kieren looked at each other when they thought no one was watching. If they weren't together now, they probably would be soon. James wasn't worried about it, as long as the team could work together proficiently and without any problems.

It was difficult pondering the team's loner nature when he woke up next to a beautiful woman. He presently was sitting, propped up by pillows, watching her as she slept in the 'predawn' light.

They had discovered only recently the ship's crew quarters were equipped with 'windows' in the walls. There were panels programmed by the ship's computer to simulate the sun rising in the morning. It helped the body adjust better to long space trips. James only wished they had discovered them sooner. Their first few days on the ship after waking from their operations had left them all tired and irritable from lack of sleep and unnatural body rhythms. Now he sat and watched the light grow brighter. If he didn't know better, he would have thought he was in a house back on Earth. He had tried to figure out if the computer could program birdsong as well, but it didn't have any samples in its data banks. The closest he could find was from something called a dran, and its horrible screech was far from soothing.

He rubbed his hand along his jaw and felt how long the stubble was becoming. It had been difficult to explain to the Rajani the men's preference to shave their faces, and the women's preference to shave their armpits and legs. Finally, they had produced a crude razor by honing a knife-like utensil the Rajani had aboard the ship. Gianni and David had chosen to shave, but James wasn't keen on the idea, and had decided to let his facial hair grow. Yvette had teased him about how much gray was sprinkled throughout the black, but he thought it was better to weather a little teasing from her than to slash at his face every morning.

At least the Rajani were used to brushing their teeth, although it wasn't exactly a brush they used. Each room had a small device that would brush, floss, and even clean a person's tongue when inserted into the mouth. It had been a strange feeling the first time he'd used it, but not uncomfortable, and he soon became used to it.

His mind was bouncing from one subject to another, and he was half-asleep again when Yvette took a deep breath and stretched. She turned toward him and languidly draped a leg over his before settling into sleep again. *It's a good morning to not be a loner,* he thought as he drifted back toward sleep.

Interlude

Tomas Giovanni was banged up and bandaged, and he winced when the two Feds entered his hospital room, forcing him to move his bed into a sitting position. He could tell they were Feds even before they opened their mouths and started asking him the same questions as the cops. The Feds introduced themselves and asked him some preliminary questions before delving into their notes.

"So you have no ideas as to the present whereabouts of Mr. Moretti?" the older agent asked. He'd introduced himself as Agent Cooper, but Tomas thought he looked like Tommy Lee Jones in the movie where he was the FBI agent.

"That's what I've been saying," Tomas answered. "For all I know, he's enjoying cocktails in Maui as we speak."

"Why don't we start with your relationship to the missing person," Tommy Lee said, unsmiling.

"First off," Tomas began, "stop talking to me like I'm a suspect here. I'm the one who called you guys. Remember that. You keep this up and I'll have my lawyer in here so fast—"

"Now, now," the other agent, who had introduced himself as Agent Matchett, said. "We're having a friendly conversation, right?" This agent looked like Ned Beatty and had a southern accent. Tomas thought the guy must have done something horrible to end up in a shithole like Detroit.

"Fine," Tomas said. "Gianni is my cousin. My mother's sister's son, to be specific. We're also business associates."

"What kind of business?" Tommy Lee asked.

"Import/export," Tomas replied. "Olive oil. You wouldn't believe what you can sell the stuff for at some of these high-end boutiques and restaurants."

"Really?" Ned asked. "I'd always wondered. My wife ..."

He faltered on seeing the look Tommy Lee was giving him. He cleared his throat. "Uh, never mind."

Tomas smiled. "Anyway, I met him at his apartment that night. We had some issues with one of our customers and needed to talk about collections."

"So he was home when you arrived?" Tommy Lee asked.

"Yes," Tomas replied. "We talked for a while, had a couple of drinks, and then I had to take a piss, so I went in and took care of business. When I came back out, he was gone. Just gone, *poof.* No sign he'd even been there. Even the damn cat was gone. I thought at first he was out on the fire escape because the window was wide open, but he wasn't. I wouldn't have thought much about it, but then those men come busting in and attacked me."

"And you have no idea who they were?" Ned asked.

"None," Tomas replied. He'd find out one way or another, but no need to bother the Feds with his problems.

"You said earlier Mr. Moretti is a cousin in your family," Tommy Lee said. "You are referring to the Giovanni Family out of New York, correct?"

"Can't get anything past you," Tomas said, smiling. Truth was, he was surprised this hadn't come up sooner. His father was, after all, head of the Family. Tomas had been dealing with cops his entire life. There was nothing they could do for or against him in this matter. The cops would never have heard about it if he hadn't been admitted to the hospital. Besides his broken nose and a broken rib, he had some internal bleeding from a lacerated spleen and a bruised kidney. Payback was going to be a bitch once he discovered who they'd been.

When you show up at the hospital with these types of injuries and you're not a boxer after a big fight, the cops tend to get called. When you're a member of a major organized crime family, the FBI tends to get called. He made a point of calling them himself on his way to the hospital.

Tomas was still curious about what had happened to Gianni, though. If the men had taken him, he'd have to be rescued or ransomed at some point in the future, if he wasn't already dead. If he was in on this, well, then he'd be taken care of when and if he finally showed up again. Tomas hoped this wasn't the case. Gianni was one of his oldest friends, as well as being his first cousin.

It's not like the cops were actually concerned about his missing cousin. One of their own had to have disappeared at about the same time. Before the Feds showed up, the cops had grilled him, trying to find any connection between Gianni and the cop named Dempsey. As far as Tomas knew, there wasn't one. But then, Gianni had always played things close to the vest, even when they were kids growing up together, and he and the cop had lived in the same shitty apartment complex, so who really knew?

A nurse entered the room and looked at his chart. She was an older woman who looked like she meant business. "Mr. Giovanni, time for your sponge bath. You gentlemen will have to come back later. I assume you know our visiting hours?"

"Yes, ma'am," Tommy Lee answered. "We'll be back, Giovanni. Try to remember as much as you can for our next session." The two men left the room, neither of them looking very happy about the interruption.

"Hey, thanks for the save, Mary," Tomas said to the nurse.

"That's all well and good, young man," she replied, scowling at him and pulling on a latex glove. "But I was telling the truth."

"Oh." Tomas winced. "Damn."

Chapter 6

A day later, Yvette lay in her bed, in what felt like late morning, and thought about home. She could remember a time when she was one of the most popular girls in school. As the daughter of a seated US senator, she had been invited to all of the cool parties, which was strange to a girl who had grown up in rural Michigan. Her father had been elected for the first time when she was in the ninth grade. The culture shock she experienced after relocating to Washington DC had been extreme. There were as many political games in school as there were on the Hill. She'd learned quickly how to be garrulous and charismatic when needed, although it wasn't in her nature, and she would often find herself exhausted by the act at the end of the day.

It had all changed at the age of fourteen, when her mother had been killed by a mugger on a street in D.C. Afterward, she withdrew from her friends, preferring to be by herself. Her father had hired private tutors to home school her and allow her to graduate. All of the tutors had been women; her mistrust of men made it impossible for her to deal with them.

People who have never experienced it themselves don't understand what happens when you lose a loved one to violent crime. Many looked at her differently, as if it were her mother's fault. What was she doing out by herself at night? There were rumors going around her school that the senator's wife had been out with a boyfriend or hired escort. Her political enemies could be thanked for that one, she knew. Or maybe they had been her dad's political enemies. All she knew then was there had been surprisingly little sympathy for her from her peers or their parents.

After a while, she had started to blame herself. Her guilt was irrational, she knew now, but at the time, she had almost been convinced she was culpable for the entire incident. Her self-loathing and survivor's guilt grew to the point where she wondered whether it wouldn't be better to end her life than face each new day. She had her share of therapy, as well as personal defense classes. *Only the best for a senator's daughter,* she thought contemptuously. She was under no illusions; if her father hadn't been able to afford the private tutors and therapy, she would probably have ended up a basket case or dead by her own hand.

If the death of her mother hadn't been bad enough, she'd begun to have bad stomach aches that she had initially thought were a result of stress. She'd started to run low-grade fevers almost every day. She thought she had caught some kind of bug and didn't tell her therapist or her father until she was in so much pain that she begged her father to take her to the hospital. Her doctor had finally diagnosed the cause, but by then, it had been too late. She'd developed a condition called pelvic inflammatory disease. The damage from PID had left her fallopian tubes scarred beyond repair. She was infertile.

She had cried for days after finding out, and it had taken her years to overcome her anxieties in public and her fear of men. By then, she had decided to become a lawyer. Her ultimate goal, no matter what her father wanted, was to become a district attorney or a judge—someone who could take the criminals off the streets. She'd been angry at her father when he'd informed her she wouldn't get any assistance in finding an internship from him after graduation. She'd been even angrier when the only one she could find was in Detroit with an old friend of her father's.

But look what I would have missed, she thought as she got dressed. She wasn't only thinking about the situation she found herself in; on board an alien spacecraft, on her way to God knew where. She thought about James, who was so gentle and so sad. He'd been worried about the possibility of her getting pregnant. When she'd told him about her infertility, she hadn't been sure at the time if what she saw in his eyes was relief or disappointment. Either way, he had kissed her and held her until she hadn't felt like crying anymore.

He, in turn, told her about being a widower, though he hadn't gone into much detail, and she didn't think it wise to pry. They had plenty of time to discover each other's stories.

◊

It occurred to James he and the other human beings should learn as much about the Krahn as they could. If they were going to be fighting the creatures on Rajan when they arrived, they'd need to know all they could about their enemy. The idea still sounded a little ridiculous when he thought about it; him being on the way to fight aliens on behalf of other aliens. He knew it wouldn't be so funny when they actually arrived.

James was walking down the main corridor on the way to another training session. It was early in the morning, and he'd rolled out of bed, too tired to do more than dress himself. He felt like he wasn't getting enough sleep lately. He'd have to talk to Yvette about it. When he got to the briefing room, he saw David, Kieren, and Rauph were already there. Not surprising that Yvette wasn't. She was almost always late, wherever she was going. Who knew if Gianni would even show up?

"Good morning," he said, taking a seat at the table. He grabbed a nutrition bar from the middle of the table and began to eat it as Gianni arrived, looking as grumpy as James felt. *Guess he's not getting any sleep, either,* he thought. He looked over at Kieren, wondering if it was for the same reason. By her chilly reception of Gianni, he assumed the answer was no.

Finally, Yvette arrived, looking freshly showered. She smiled at James and sat down next to him at the table after grabbing her own nutrition bar. He winked at her and returned her smile.

Rauph stood and clicked on the translating device. "If you're ready to begin," he said gruffly. James thought he looked grumpy, as well. Maybe they were all in need of a vacation.

"Before you get into any more about Rajan," James said, "I was wondering if you could tell us more about the Krahn, and specifically about the Krahn Horde."

"Like what the hell they look like, for one thing," Gianni said.

"I don't know what they look like," Rauph answered. He turned and pushed a few buttons on the screen of the portable tablet set up to its full size. Some files appeared on the screen of the tablet, and he tapped one.

The screen instantly filled with alien text, and Rauph read for a minute before speaking. "There are only brief descriptions of the Krahn available. They don't believe in having their pictures taken, a lesson learned the hard way by the first envoys to their planet. When they agreed to join the

Alliance, it was under the stipulation no visual representation would ever be used."

Rauph read some more of the text, scrolling down the screen with his finger. "Shortly after they officially joined the Alliance, their king, or High Vasin of the controlling clan, died unexpectedly. A civil war began between the rightful heir, Maliq, and his younger brother, Ronak. The war lasted two Standard years between the followers of each brother before Ronak was finally captured. Instead of executing him, as was their law, Maliq sent his brother and some minor relatives into exile."

"And the rest is history," Yvette said.

Rauph stood and thought about the curious expression, then continued. "I suppose you could say the rest is *our* history."

"There isn't even a description of them?" Kieren asked. "Something to give us an idea of what to expect?"

Rauph turned to the screen and read once again. "I don't see anything other than that they are a bipedal, warm-blooded, oviparous, that is, egg-laying species."

"So, basically, they're walking lizards?" David asked facetiously.

"Great, we're fighting space alligators," Gianni said. "Do you know how stupid that sounds?"

James spoke up. "If that's what they are, then that's who we'll fight," he said. "It's what we signed on for when we agreed to this trip. By the way, alligators are cold-blooded."

"Thank you, Mr. Wizard," Gianni said, rolling his eyes.

James turned his attention back to Rauph. "You said there was another species on your planet, the Jur ... something."

"Jirina," Rauph corrected him.

"Yes, Jirina," James said. "Could you show us a Jirina, so we know the difference when we get there? I don't want any cases of mistaken identity."

"Yes," Rauph said. "Although, as you'll see, the Jirina are much different in appearance than the description of the Krahn I read to you." He pushed a few buttons on the screen, and then a picture of a Jirina filled it.

The Jirina was large and muscular-looking, though James had no visual frame of reference. Rauph pushed a button on the screen and another picture replaced the first. It showed a Jirina standing next to a male Rajani. James saw his first assumption was correct. The Jirina was probably anywhere from five and a half to six feet tall, but the horns protruding from the top of its head made it look even taller.

The Jirina had large brown eyes and enormous nostrils on each side of its nose. It had wide, flat ears resting against the side of its head. All told, it looked slightly bovine in appearance, at least from the neck up. Its thickly muscled arms ended in hands equipped with three fingers, each tipped with a thick fingernail. It had a broad body and stout legs. Rauph was right; they were nothing like the description of the Krahn.

"Now, we'll proceed with my regularly scheduled lesson," Rauph said, pushing a button on the screen. "We left off yesterday on some common words you may need on Rajan. We'll follow up with some more today, and maybe some simple sentences as well."

As Rauph droned on at the front of the room, James felt his mind drifting as he thought about the appearance of the Krahn. *Space alligators?*

◊

Janan was on duty aboard the bridge, checking the computer to ensure their course heading was correct. Not that he thought it would be incorrect, but he was bored, and checking the computer was one of the tasks a pilot performed while on duty. It provided a fail-safe, in case the computer's diagnostics were out of alignment, which happened from time to time on long voyages.

When traveling in space, there was no magnetic north to provide a point of reference. The *Tukuli's* central computer used a four-dimensional coordinate system to navigate. The computer used extensive Alliance star maps to provide a point of reference as they passed various planets and suns; the second point of reference was a planetary motion calculation determining the location of a planet in relation to its sun, which told the computer where the ship was in relation to the planet and at what Talondarian Standard time.

In this way, the computer could also control its orientation and heading as it calculated the direction it needed to travel to meet the next planetary body or sun in the path it was following. Basically, the ship "hopped" from one point in space to another along its heading. The transition was smooth, even in nullspace, since the computer made the calculations quickly, and the distances between solar bodies were so vast.

The nulldrive mechanism on the ship was based on technology created by the Talondarians. The secret of how their engines worked was lost with the fall of the Talondarian Empire. The term nulldrive itself was a misnomer, because the ship was not actually going any faster or slower than it did in regular space.

The Talondarians discovered the known universe was part of a multitude of universes that were expanding in nullspace, a sixth dimension outside of the five known dimensions. When the ship traveled in nullspace, it traveled in the spaces between universes, which were typically known as nullvoids, or NV Space, or just NV. Even this relatively minute distance of NV space was immense, and it still took weeks, sometimes months, to travel long distances. The First Rule of Space Travel stated matter could not travel faster than one percent of the speed of light, so it was better than trying to reach other solar systems at that speed. It would take thousands of years to reach the system closest to Rajan at one percent the speed of light.

Beyond that, Janan didn't know how the nullspace device on the *Tukuli* operated. As long as it worked, he was content to let the ship's central computer control it. He didn't know enough about the dark energy or string particles involved in the process. It was scary enough sometimes thinking about what would happen if the device malfunctioned at the wrong moment.

The computer aboard the *Tukuli* was also an artificial intelligence, though the Rajani always disabled their computers' learning mechanisms. They didn't want a computer becoming smarter, learning as it interacted with the pilot, crew, and the outside galaxy. Rauph had also shut off the computer's voice capability so it couldn't speak independently via the ship's communication system.

What a pity, Janan had thought many times in the past few weeks. It would have given him someone to talk to while he was on duty. At least they were almost to the Mandakan Space Port, although he didn't think Rauph would allow him to leave the ship this time. He smiled, remembering the difficulty he'd gotten into the last time he'd been at the port. No, it was probably better if he stayed on the ship. He was not, by nature, a troublemaker, but he attracted problems on Mandakan for some reason. It was so easy to do there.

Mandaka was also where the extraction crew was based. Rauph had hired the crew to bring the Humans aboard the *Tukuli* from Earth, and they had done their jobs effectively. He didn't think he would mention this to David or the others.

He suspected it was still a sore subject for them.

◊

The next morning, James sat with the others around a table in one of the meeting rooms. Rauph wanted to brief them about the space station they were about to visit. Most of the others sat and fidgeted, waiting for the briefing to begin. There was very little conversation.

James was used to this type of thing from years of police briefings and knew it could get monotonous to sit and wait. *Put down jury duty as another thing I don't miss about Earth,* he thought. He wasn't sure what to think about their upcoming stop at the space port. It still astounded him they were about to visit a space station built by an alien race, even if he had been living on a ship built by another alien race for almost a month.

The fidgeting stopped when the door opened and Rauph entered, carrying the translating device. The Rajani was understandably preoccupied. James was well aware of the time loss caused by this little side trip, but he was also sure they had made the right choice for the team.

"Officer Dempsey has told you we are going to visit a space station, I assume," Rauph began, still standing before them. "Unfortunately, I can only tell you about it. I'm afraid you will not be able to go aboard the station itself once we've docked." There was a collective groan from the group. They had all been looking forward to seeing the station for themselves, and to getting away from the confines of the ship.

Rauph held up a hand. "I know," he said. "All I can say is, if any of you were to be noticed by security aboard the station, we'd have a hard time coming up with a story to keep you from being quarantined for a lengthy period of time. As a new species, they would hold you away from the main station to make sure you weren't carrying any exotic viruses. Its standard procedure, I'm afraid."

"Well, great," Gianni said. "We've been stuck aboard this ship for weeks, and now we're supposed to sit tight and wait for you to come back so we can leave? What bullshit." He was dressed in a white tank top—what James's dad used to refer to as a wife-beater—dark slacks, black socks, and shoes.

He must have been changing clothes when he was brought aboard the ship, James thought. The others had all been fully dressed, thankfully. James was glad to be in his own clothes as opposed to the large Rajani robe he'd been wearing. The robe was comfortable enough, he supposed, but he felt like a monk while wearing it.

"We should be on our way again shortly after all of the repairs have been made to the ship," Rauph continued, tactfully ignoring Gianni's remarks. "Should I proceed with telling you about the station?"

"Why bother?" Gianni asked. "It's not like we really care."

"Then I need to get back to the bridge. Again, I'm sorry, but we'll have to make this trip as quick as possible and be on our way again." As Rauph left the room, everyone turned to look at Gianni.

"What?" he asked, glaring at them, then looking down to the floor, avoiding their disappointed expressions.

"Always have to push, don't you?" Yvette asked, before the room was left in uncomfortable silence.

"Well, who wants to play tic-tac-toe?" Kieren asked finally.

James sighed, wondering if the trip would get any more exciting after they left the space port.

◊

Rauph had spent the night praying he was taking the

correct course of action. His story about wanting the Humans to stay aboard the *Tukuli* because of quarantine regulations was true for the most part, but he also had an ulterior motive. He didn't want any of the Humans interacting with the occupants of the space station.

For one thing, he couldn't have the Humans run into the mercenaries he had hired to kidnap them from Earth. That would prove too sticky of a situation. For another, he was well aware of the reputation the Rajani held after all of these years. They were the monsters, the invaders. The ones mothers scared their offspring with to make them behave; the ones those same offspring had nightmares about and woke screaming in the night.

He'd done his best to play down that aspect of his species' reputation when he'd first spoken to the Humans. He was afraid the Rajani would be doomed because of events that had transpired thousands of years before. He still considered it a kind of luck they had encountered beings who had never heard of the Rajani. Most members of the Galactic Alliance would have celebrated the extinction of his species rather than helped.

Rauph had explained his plan for the space port to Bhakat, with less than desirable results. He'd finally been forced to order his Pledge back to his room for meditation. Rauph was thinking of this as they approached the Mandakan system. They had already been challenged by the Mandakan Imperial warship, which patrolled the system and had requested an explanation of their visit. A quick, superficial scan of their ship had shown the Mandakans they were unarmed, and they were allowed to proceed on their way for repairs. Rauph knew if the warship had found the *Tukuli* to be armed, it would have escorted the ship to the space port and then boarded it to inspect every inch.

Rauph, Bhakat, and Janan were in their usual positions on the bridge when they made their final approach. Mandaka was a small planet, much like Earth, whose inhabitants had made the most of living along a major travel corridor. The space port was enormous, and it orbited Mandaka like a small moon, its enormous meteor shield always pointed away from the planet.

Most of the money made by the port came from gambling—there were several large casinos aboard the station—as well as providing repairs, supplies, and a place to rest for passing travelers. That was the official story, at least.

Rauph also knew it had a large black market system, and this was how he planned to get the ship outfitted with the required training equipment without raising any 'official' eyebrows.

"Incoming call on subspace frequency," Janan said.

"Put it on intercom," Rauph told him.

"Ship designate *Tukuli,*" a voice said in Talondarian Standard. "You have been approved for docking. What is your purpose?"

"Repairs to my ship and lodging for my crew," Rauph replied.

"Acknowledged," the voice said. "Proceed to dock 10-KM and slow approach to .40."

"Acknowledged," Rauph replied. He motioned for Janan to turn off the intercom.

"Bhakat, you have the ship," Rauph said, standing slowly. Bhakat nodded, not meeting his master's eyes.

His Pledge was still angry about Rauph's orders to stay on the ship. Bhakat would have to get past it. Rauph had faith his Pledge would, given enough time. Bhakat was also angry because Rauph planned to ask Officer Dempsey to accompany him as a bodyguard, in his invisible mode, and allow the

Human to observe his dealings on the port. Dempsey would have to stay invisible throughout the negotiations—Rauph didn't want them to know they had someone aboard who was implanted with a Johar Stone. It would cause a panic among the denizens of the port.

Rauph walked to the doorway before turning again. "Please inform Officer Dempsey to meet me at the main airlock once we've docked, Janan." He turned and walked out the door of the bridge, hoping their trip would be uneventful.

◊

James waited at the airlock and wondered what was happening. Initially, Rauph had told them all they needed to stay on the ship due to concerns for their safety. He was still wondering when Rauph walked down the corridor toward him, carrying the translating device.

"Officer Dempsey," Rauph said when he had reached the airlock door. "Thank you for meeting me here." He placed the translating device down on the corridor floor. "My, that is heavy after a while," he said. "I'll try to find a more mobile one while aboard the station, if I have the chance."

James thought about asking the Rajani about the devices he, Bhakat, and Janan had implanted in their skulls, but thought better of it—perhaps they were too expensive or difficult to find. He wasn't sure about anything when it came to the workings of everyday alien life or technology.

"I'm sure you're wondering why I asked you to meet me here," Rauph said, breaking James out of his reverie.

"Yes, I am," James answered truthfully.

"I'm going aboard this station to barter the purchase of the equipment we need," Rauph continued pointing vaguely toward the airlock. "The beings I will be dealing with are not the most trustworthy, and I'd like to leave the station in the same condition I enter it in, if you catch my meaning."

James nodded. He could see where this was headed. "You want me to play bodyguard for you while you seal the deal."

"Precisely," Rauph said, with a rare smile. "In your invisible mode, of course. We cannot have them seeing you. As I told you before, they might take you into custody, and then all we have worked for would be undone."

"So you want me to follow you around and not draw attention," James said.

"Correct.".

"Why not take Bhakat? Wouldn't it be a lot easier?"

"Yes," Rauph replied. "And no." He scratched at his cheek for a moment, thinking. "You've seen how ... protective of me Bhakat is. One slight or show of aggression toward me, and he's liable to do something rash. This would not be helpful. Plus, as his Master, I must also protect him from outside influences. Believe me, there are plenty of bad influences aboard the space port. I was ready to tell you all about it in the meeting earlier, but Gianni said you wouldn't be interested. Do you understand what your duties would be?"

"Yes," James said.

"Follow my lead. You won't understand what's being said, but we cannot take the translating device with us. Please stay nearby, and I'll let you know if your assistance is warranted."

"Fine," James said. "How long until we arrive?"

"Oh, we've been docked for a short time already." He pushed a button next to the airlock door, and the inside door opened to a square room measuring about ten feet on each side. On the far side of the room was the outside hatch, round, and tall enough for a Rajani to walk through without stooping. Inside the room, there was a cargo storage net connected to the wall next to the outside hatch and one emergency space suit for outside repairs, as well as a small bench to sit on when donning the suit.

James was surprised to learn they were already docked. He hadn't felt anything to suggest the ship was no longer moving on its own through space. He'd have to remember to compliment Janan when they returned. It couldn't be easy to maneuver a large ship in such close quarters.

"Now," Rauph said, "if you could turn invisible ..."

James did as he was asked, powering up and then cloaking himself with invisibility. It was almost natural now, and almost instantaneous. He'd been practicing, so it was second nature, though he was still amazed he could do it at all. He had also learned that he could make the covering over his head turn invisible on its own, while the rest of him was shielded by the almost opaque power suit. He'd thought it had something to do with his power of invisibility, but he had shown Kieren, and after a few tries, she had been able to do it as well. He wondered if the potential power of the stones was greater than even the Rajani knew.

"Splendid," Rauph said, bending over to turn off the translating device.

They walked to the opposite side of the airlock, and Rauph pushed a button next to the outer hatch. The inside door closed behind them, sealing them in the airlock. Then he pushed another button, and the outside hatch opened with the hiss of air pressure equalization. Rauph stepped through, and James quickly followed, feeling the heavier gravity of the space port weigh his body down as he did so. Rauph closed the outside hatch and walked slowly down the corridor to a security station, as his body was getting used to the increased weight.

The security station turned out to be a simple guard booth set up outside of a wide closed door leading from the docking area to the space port's main level. James could see moving sidewalks and escalators lead up to the level they were on from various lower and upper levels of the docking area. There was a short line of aliens waiting to enter the station, and Rauph walked up and stopped at the back of the line.

The security station had one lone occupant, and James could only stare as they came to the head of the line and Rauph began to speak to it in Talondarian Standard. The alien had a multi-faceted head—at least, James assumed it was a head—like the eye of a fly. It was about four feet tall and dressed in a shimmering gown that covered its body and six appendages.

There was a translator device set up at the station, though this one was much more advanced than the one on the *Tukuli*. The alien made a low buzzing sound, and Talondarian Standard was broadcast from the device. Although he had started learning the language, James found the alien talked too quickly, and he soon realized he couldn't understand any of the conversation between it and Rauph. The conversation ended and Rauph bowed slightly. The alien pushed a button opening the doorway to the station, and James quickly followed Rauph inside.

Again, he had to stop a moment. The place was cavernous. There were walkways and stairways and blinking signs everywhere. The signs had Talondarian Standard but also various other alien languages and pictures. And everywhere, everywhere, there were aliens. Crowds of them; all walking or flying or slithering or hopping about in a wild mishmash of shapes, colors, and textures that assaulted his eyes wherever he looked.

The place was packed with aliens, all of whom were going about their business as if this was a trip to the local supermarket, which it might have been, for all James knew.

As he looked at them, something occurred to him. For every one of them with eyes, James could see when he looked at them, they all had that appearance in their eyes of 'sentience.' These weren't animals, but self-aware, cognizant beings.

James had to sidestep a creature that looked like a cross between a hippopotamus and a turtle yet walked on its two rear legs, and quickly followed Rauph as he headed determinedly through the concourse and toward a large corridor, ignoring the multitude of life-forms around him.

After walking down the corridor a short distance, James saw what looked like an elevator. He followed Rauph as the Rajani stepped onto one of the cars of the device. As James stepped through the doorway of the car, he saw it was, in fact, an elevator, except when the door closed, the car traveled sideways. It was occupied by two other aliens besides him and Rauph. One looked like a walking squid with deep blue cat eyes standing out of the top of its head on short stalks, and one appeared to be a robot with a clear abdomen containing a small salamander-like creature swimming in it that was hooked up to wires. The two aliens were speaking to each other in a language seemingly made up of wet burps.

Rauph paid them no mind, and they quickly exited at the next stop, each looking at Rauph while their speech became increasingly animated. James thought they sounded almost panicked, but he couldn't be sure. The doors closed, and Rauph quietly said "Dempsey?" in English. He had learned to say all of the Humans' names with little of his usual accent in their time aboard the ship. James tapped him lightly on the shoulder twice. Rauph nodded, and this time the car did go up after the doors closed, and Rauph pushed a button on the console.

When the car stopped and the doors opened, James followed Rauph and found they had entered a different part of the station. There were no crowds here; no flashing lights or beckoning aromas. The light was dimmer, and the doorways along the corridor looked more like rooms than shops. *These must be for lodging,* James thought as he saw the doors were spaced evenly along the corridor like any other hotel he had ever seen.

Rauph walked down the corridor and stood for a moment, looking at a digital monitor set into one of the walls. Then he was off again, turning right when another corridor intersected the one they were walking down. Things progressed this way for a while, with Rauph checking directions on the monitors he found and then making a left or right turn until James had lost all sense of direction. He hoped he didn't lose track of Rauph, because he'd be utterly lost on his own.

Finally, Rauph found the door he was looking for. He pushed a button next to it, and a voice came over the intercom. Rauph replied, stating his name, and the door opened. James barely had enough time to avoid the door before it closed. Inside, he was once again stopped short, his mouth wide open in awe.

◊

Bhakat didn't know how to feel about the presence of the Humans aboard the Tukuli, even after they'd been on the ship for so long. His first priority, however, was to return to Rajan and make sure his Master stayed safe in the process. When Rauphangelaa told him he was taking the Human named Dempsey aboard the space port, he couldn't help but think of it as a question of his own honor. Rauphangelaa either didn't trust Bhakat to ensure his safety, or he did not trust him to uphold the tenets of the Kha. Either way, it was a blow to Bhakat's faith in his Master, as well as his own ego.

It was a great honor among the Rajani to be taken as

a Pledge by an Elder, and Bhakat was grateful he had been chosen by Rauphangelaa. He did his best to study the teachings of Ruvedalin and live his life in peaceful meditation, as Rauphangelaa had taught him. It was difficult, though. He did not have the temperament for it. Because of this episode with the Krahn, he wasn't sure if it was a loss of faith in the Kha or a realization he had never had faith to begin with.

Rauphangelaa had told him to go pray in his room while he and the Human were aboard the port, but Bhakat found once he got there, he had no desire to recite the words of Ruvedalin or to sit quietly. He was too anxious about his Master; he knew the creature Rauphangelaa was planning to visit.

Interlude

Steve Montgomery was stumped. The Infinity Killer had not harmed anyone for weeks. The investigation was falling apart as the political pressure began to take its toll on everyone involved.

After a month with no progress, the FBI had finally been called in to take over the investigation. The Detroit Police Department was still assisting, but had taken a back seat. The chief and mayor were both beside themselves at the turn of events.

Steve didn't take it personally. He'd never wanted to head the investigation. His only regret was the fact that James's reputation had taken a huge hit throughout the time he'd been missing. He didn't deserve it. If he was still alive, Steve doubted James would ever be able to return to the force again.

Chapter 7

Rauph had been to the Mandakan Space Port before and knew what to expect. He was not daunted by the sheer size of the port, nor the immense crowds of aliens found there at any given time. Most of his past visits had been to meet and work out a deal for the few items they didn't produce themselves on Rajan, but a few times had been to meet with distributors of various technologically advanced items; mainly ships for the Elders or devices such as the translation implants he, Bhakat, and Janan had been outfitted with.

As an Elder, Rauph was one of the few privileged enough to own his own ship and have the ability to travel off-planet. Because of this, he'd made contacts on the station, and it was with one of them he hoped to meet now, though he had become more and more nervous as he wound through the maze of corridors, nearing his destination.

The being he was going to see was a Cauterfan named Zazzil. He could be trusted, for the most part, to keep things confidential, and what Rauph needed at the moment was just that—someone who could be quiet for as long as it took to repair the ship. He had no worries about afterward; he doubted he would be returning to Mandaka any time soon, if ever.

He had moved slowly through the intersecting corridors to make sure the Human could keep up. He had checked once, on the hydrolift, to affirm Dempsey was still with him, and had been satisfied the Human wouldn't lag behind.

Showing up on the Cauterfan's doorstep, though, was going to be tricky. Zazzil was not fond of surprises, and his species was generally not known for adapting to changes easily. Rauph hoped the price he was willing to pay would be worth any inconvenience the Cauterfan experienced. Otherwise, he might have to find someone else, which would waste even more valuable time. Zazzil was the only one Rauph could think of who could provide the equipment he needed.

When the door opened, Rauph was stopped by one of Zazzil's bodyguards, a Makerfy. The creature walked on two muscular back legs and was covered in long black fur. If Rauph had ever seen a picture of an Earth gorilla, he may have thought the Makerfy was some type of distant relation, if not for the creature's almost equine head, which had sets of eyes both at the front and the side.

There was an intake of breath behind him from Dempsey. He should have warned the Human the Cauterfans were a species from a cold, gaseous planet, where they floated through the atmosphere on amorphous wings. He had told the Humans very few organisms could survive on a planet so much different than Earth or Rajan. The Cauterfans were one of the exceptions, and Zazzil had brought a little piece of home with him to the station. The room they had entered was forty feet high and twice as long. Most of it was filled with a large transparent enclosure. Inside the enclosure were billowing clouds of white gases.

As he was patted down for weapons, Rauph saw Zazzil pass by inside the tank and look at him before moving on, disappearing once again into the white gases. The Cauterfan's bulbous eyes held no expression, but Rauph had not been instantly expelled from the creature's room, which was a promising sign.

The Makerfy smiled, showing large, sharp teeth, and made a motion toward the meeting room, inviting Rauph to follow him. Rauph had been in the room before, but it still made him shiver to enter it, and not because the temperature was a full thirty Standard degrees colder. Cauterfa was a gas giant, and its temperatures were much lower than most inhabitable planets. The meeting room was basically a bubble in the side of the tank, surrounded by the sides of the enclosure. It subdued the light from the outer room and gave him the feeling he was sitting in a fog bank. Rauph sat on a chair, though it was slightly too small for his large frame, and waited. A tiny speaker near the chair crackled to life as Zazzil's voice filled the confined space.

"I don't recall us having a meeting scheduled for today," the flat, emotionless voice of the translating device intoned.

Rauph looked up but couldn't see the Cauterfan through the roiling gases. "I apologize," he said. "We did not, but I am here on a matter of some urgency." He waited a moment, but there was no reply, so he continued. "I'm in need of some repairs to my ship, as well as some ... alterations. I was hoping we could do business together concerning these matters." Another quiet beat and Rauph was thinking perhaps he should try somewhere else, when Zazzil spoke again.

"Our dealings in the past have been honorable," came the voice. Rauph looked up and saw Zazzil floating above him, the large gills below his wings opening and closing in a stately rhythm. The Cauterfan continued talking. "If you have brought trouble to my home, you will regret it, Rauphangelaa."

Rauph stood. "I assure you, the only trouble is my own. But my need is more about the lack of time. Would your employees be able to repair the ship and perform the necessary alterations in a day or two, at the most?"

"Depends on the condition of your ship," Zazzil replied. "And the nature of these ... alterations."

Rauph sat back down on the edge of the chair. "The ship's repair bots made emergency repairs, but we need to be sure the ship can make the journey to Rajan without breaking down again." He spent a moment thinking, choosing his words carefully on this part of his explanation. "As to the alterations," he continued, "I am willing to pay for those, as well as for your discretion. I need a training room set up, to my specifications, aboard the ship."

"A training room?" Zazzil asked. He was now floating nearer the floor, across from Rauph's face.

"Yes," Rauph answered, not volunteering anything else.

"And what do you propose to pay me for these services?" Zazzil asked. "This type of work does not come cheaply, as you well know."

"The ship's lander," Rauph said. "It's in pristine condition; hardly ever used, actually. It should be worth more than enough to pay for your services."

"We shall see," Zazzil said, now rising once again above Rauph's eye level and fading out of sight into the fog of gases. The Makerfy entered the room and motioned toward the door. The meeting was over. Rauph stood to leave, disappointed at the meeting's outcome, when the speaker crackled back to life.

"I have looked over my records," Zazzil said. "Your ship is Talondarian, correct? V series?"

"Yes," Rauph replied.

"Then the lander is a model XJ40, correct?" Zazzil asked.

"Yes," Rauph replied.

"Then we have a deal," Zazzil replied, though he had not reappeared from the fog. "My workers will arrive at your ship in one Standard hour to collect the lander and begin work on your alterations, if you have the specifications ready."

"Wonderful," Rauph said. "Thank you."

"We are always happy to help the Rajani," Zazzil said. "And the Talondarians."

Rauph stopped for a moment before making his way out of the meeting room and exiting the Cauterfan's living area. *Talondarians?* he thought. *What does this have to do with them?* He puzzled over this as he headed back to the ship, but other circumstances caused him to quickly forget about the conversation until much later.

◊

James and Rauph had only been gone for a few minutes when the argument started. It had been brewing for days; weeks, really. David, Yvette, Kieren, and Gianni were all in the common room, passing the time as they had been doing since coming aboard the ship; mostly trying not to be bored out of their skulls.

"Man, what I wouldn't give for some real music," David said, leaning back in his chair and closing his eyes while he stretched. Although Janan had loaded some music onto the ship's central computer, they all soon found most of it was either classical or country.

"What do you like?" Kieren asked. "I've always been a Beatles fan. Most of the stuff I listen to is classic rock from the fifties and sixties, with some early seventies thrown in."

"AC-DC, GNR, AIC," David said.

"Alphabet rock?" Yvette asked, smiling and looking up from her tablet. She was reading an old article in one of the trashy women's magazines Janan had downloaded about

Brad Pitt's beard, and hoping James's wouldn't turn out half as ugly if he continued to let his grow. She didn't know if she'd be able to kiss him if it did.

"Funny, David," Gianni said. "You always struck me as a Streisand fan. Maybe Liza Minnelli."

"Oh, piss off, Gianni," David said. "I suppose you only listen to Andrea Bocelli."

"Guy's a hack," Gianni said. "Can't hold a candle to Pavarotti or Domingo."

"Don't tell me you're into Opera?" Yvette asked, rolling her eyes.

"I didn't say that," Gianni answered, no longer smiling. "But if you're going to listen to it, why settle for the pop version?" He stood up and began walking around the room. "What the hell are we doing here, anyway?" he finally asked to no one in particular.

"Waiting for James and Rauph to come back," Kieren answered.

"We should have told Rauph to shove it," Gianni complained, turning toward the others. "Instead, we're stuck here going stir crazy while James goes to the space port. It's bullshit."

"No, what's bullshit is your attitude," David said. "Stop being such a selfish prick."

"What did you call me, you little asshole?" Gianni asked, turning toward David and clenching his fists.

"I called you a selfish prick," David said, standing up and facing the other man, and clenching his own hands into fists.

"Uh-oh," Yvette said. She looked at Kieren, who had a stunned look on her face at the prospect of violence between the two men. "The testosterone is getting pretty thick in here."

"What the hell is your problem?" David asked. "You're

such a jerk to all of us. You act like we're beneath you or something, and I'm sick of it."

"David," Kieren began.

"No," he said, still looking at Gianni. "I've taken enough abuse from this dick. I'm sick of his shitty attitude."

"Oh," Gianni said, smiling. There was no humor in it. "What are you going to do about it, tough guy?"

"Boys, that's enough," Yvette said.

"No, it's not," David said, still looking at Gianni. "You want to fight? Is that it? I'll fight you right now."

Yvette stood and quickly stepped between the two men. "Now you listen to me," she said, looking at David. She turned to look at Gianni. "Both of you. If we're going to get through this, we can't be acting like teenagers having a pissing contest." Kieren gasped silently, surprised at the other woman's language.

"Now," Yvette continued, looking at David, "I'm sure there was a good reason why Rauph asked James to go with him. Like maybe the fact that he can turn invisible?" She looked once more at Gianni. "I can see why he wouldn't want to take you with him. You'd probably get us all locked up or thrown off the space port."

"Hey," Gianni protested, frowning.

"We are going to wait," Yvette continued, ignoring Gianni, "and we will wait patiently. If you want to complain, do it somewhere else." She turned to David. "If you really want to fight, then bring it on. 'Cause I'll kick both your asses if you don't cut this shit out right now."

David looked at her, his eyes wide in surprise. "But he—"

"He nothing," she said. "We all need to learn to live with each other on this tin can. I'm sure James would tell you the same thing. We cannot be fighting each other when the real enemy is still out there." She pointed with her left arm vaguely in the direction of the door. "Do you understand me, gentlemen?"

"Fine," Gianni muttered, his arms crossed before him.

"Fine," David said, walking toward the doorway. "I'll be in my room."

"Good, I'm glad we have that settled," Yvette said, returning to her chair and picking up her tablet. She glanced at Kieren, who had a look of surprise mixed with awe on her face. "Oh, and personally, I've always preferred Elvis," she said, smiling.

◊

Rauph wasn't pleased after his meeting with Zazzil. The loss of the *Tukuli's* lander was especially difficult. He'd have to land the Tukuli on Rajan when they finally returned. It wasn't the landing so much as taking off again that worried him. The fuel it would take to leave the planet would cost a fortune on the off-market where the Rajani were forced to trade. He sighed as he made his way through the various corridors and the hydrolift on the space port. It couldn't be helped, of course. Nothing was as important as returning to Rajan. How things played out from there could be worked out later.

Rauph came to a sudden stop when he reached the main concourse. A group of uniformed aliens were sitting at a table at one of the shops, eating and drinking. There was a palpable tension in the area around them, and everyone was keeping a safe distance.

ASPs, Rauph thought. *Wonderful.* He stood and watched the Alliance Society for Peace officers a moment. He didn't think he'd been spotted, but he wasn't going to take any chances. He quickly turned and headed back the way he'd come. It would take a little longer to get back to the ship, but would be worth it if he didn't wind up being interrogated by the official regulating force of the Galactic Alliance. Seeing a Rajani this far from his home planet would be enough for them to start asking questions.

There was no refuting the fact they were in their own jurisdiction—all of Alliance space was their domain. It was their job to keep the peace between members of the Alliance. It didn't mean they didn't have their own ideas of the meaning of the word 'peace,' or there weren't political agendas and motivations behind everything they did.

He'd walked for a short time and had almost reached the elevators once again when it occurred to him he had not made sure Officer Dempsey was still following him after his about-face at the concourse. He stopped walking.

"Dempsey?" he whispered, making sure no one was around in the corridor close enough to eavesdrop.

There was no answer.

"Dempsey?" he said, a little louder, feeling panic well up inside. Still no answer.

Rauph wasn't sure if he should return to the ship and hope the Human would find his way back, or head back to the concourse so Dempsey could find him. Of course, this would also increase the chances of him being confronted by the ASPs. He stood there a moment, feeling his heart rate increase at the thought of being questioned by the ASPs. He would have to make a choice.

◊

James was surprised at the various smells permeating the air of the Mandakan Space Port. Most were strange to him, but some were almost familiar. Above the noise of alien languages, he could hear a low thrumming sound and feel a stir in the atmosphere; a consistent gust of cool air every few minutes. He guessed the station must employ some type of air filtration system to cut down on airborne viruses and bacteria brought aboard by the hundreds of ships docked there.

James visited Las Vegas once, soon after he'd been married. He'd gone with a couple of fellow Marines for a three-day weekend, and was surprised to find he didn't like it at all. From the moment he'd arrived, he could sense an air of desperation from his fellow gamblers. The casinos were more like traps for the weak-willed than providers of simple games of chance. Now he felt the same desperation aboard this alien version of Vegas. Maybe they weren't as different as he'd first thought.

He had not meant to become separated from Rauph. It sort of happened by accident. He'd observed as Rauph had stopped upon seeing the uniformed aliens eating and drinking together. He'd been fascinated, guessing almost immediately what they must be, but also knowing why Rauph wanted to avoid them. If the justice process was anywhere near as slow as it was in his precinct, they could be there a long time if the police took a sudden interest in them.

Most of the aliens were bipedal in nature, although one looked like he (she?) had paws instead of hands. One looked like an octopus, but with more appendages, each ending in tiny three-fingered hands. James smiled, wondering how the creature got dressed and if shirts with twelve armholes were difficult to find.

He looked back at Rauph, only to find the Rajani had already moved on. James walked down the concourse a few steps, attempting to see the tall Rajani amongst the rest of the alien life. He looked back the other way, and still no Rauph.

"Damn," he said quietly—yet loud enough for a small, furry alien walking near him to jump and look around, confused. James moved on hurriedly, trying to remember which direction led to the *Tukuli*. Finally, he made up his mind and walked in the direction he thought they had come from first. He couldn't very well make himself visible and ask the nearest alien for directions. Alien languages pervaded the concourse, and none of them sounded even remotely like English. He walked along, trying his best not to run into anything, and was successful more often than not.

Either by chance or by the fact he truly did remember the direction to go, he soon found himself at the security checkpoint. He noticed everyone leaving the space port was subject to the same strict security check as those entering. A long line of aliens waited to gain entry to the docking section of the station, but still no Rauph.

It wasn't right. He hadn't been far behind the Rajani. If Rauph had returned to the docking section, he should have still been waiting in line. James turned and retraced his steps to the concourse. When he finally reached it, he saw that all hell had broken loose.

◊

David had never been one to go against authority; at least, not until the last few months back on Earth. He had been so scared of his father while growing up, he hadn't dared step out of line, not even as a teenager. He'd done it a few times as a young boy, and the punishments had been severe. He thought he had escaped when he'd been accepted to Michigan State and received a scholarship to play football, but had quickly learned he'd traded one petty dictator for another.

In the short time before he injured his knee, he learned to hate his head coach, a big fish in a small pond who thought his every word was holy law. He'd almost been relieved when his knee buckled beneath the weight of two linebackers after he'd made an acrobatic catch in a game. Then back to his father, and all that entailed.

As he walked down the corridor of the *Tukuli* toward his room, still fuming from his fight and fingering the tattoo on his lower abdomen, he thought of Gianni and decided he was tired of always playing along and doing the right thing, even if it wasn't exactly right for him. It wasn't difficult to sneak off the ship. The others were still together in the common room, and Janan and Bhakat were still on the bridge for all he knew. Even if he set off an alarm when he opened the ship's hatch, he knew they wouldn't pursue him. They were following orders.

◊

Rauph had returned to the end of the long corridor aboard the space port and looked hopefully at the tables outside the bar. Unfortunately, the ASPs were still there. He knew he should head back to the ship and hope that Dempsey would do the same, but he couldn't take the chance the Human had either become lost, or worse, somehow been captured. Dempsey was critical to their mission to save Rajan. If it had been one of the other Humans, he might have left them, but not their leader. Officer Dempsey was the only one he had even a modicum of trust in.

He felt something walk up behind him and stop. Before he could turn, he felt a hand placed gently on his back.

"Rauphangelaa," a voice whispered. "We've been monitoring your situation. Do you require our assistance?"

Rauph could tell that it was the Makerfy, Zazzil's security chief. He breathed a sigh of relief and said, "I cannot afford to be seen by the ASPs, but I don't think I can return to my ship any other way." A small lie, but better to appear ignorant than tell them he had lost his Human companion.

"Then I suggest a diversion," the Makerfy said. Rauph could almost see the smile on the Makerfy's face at the word 'diversion.'

"That would be beneficial," he agreed, still not turning to look at the creature.

"Wait for the signal before you move," the Makerfy told him. "You will know what it is when it happens."

"Are you sure?" Rauph asked, still uncertain.

"Oh, yes, I am sure," the Makerfy replied.

"Then you have my thanks," Rauph said.

"It does Zazzil little good if his clients are obstructed by the ASPs," the Makerfy said. "At least until they pay. Of course, this may delay our work on your ship."

"That is acceptable," Rauph said softly, hoping it wouldn't be too long of a delay and wondering what the signal was going to be.

The Makerfy moved away silently. It was only a few minutes before Rauph found out the Makerfy's plans. He watched as a large creature, taller than him, and heavier, with a large beak for a face under small eyes, and hard plates covering its body, walked up to the table of ASPs and punched the nearest officer with one of its thickly muscled arms.

The reaction was like a bomb exploding. Suddenly, all of the ASPs were on their feet (or other various appendages), except for the one who had been on the receiving end of the punch, who was now out cold and lying on the floor of the eatery. In their haste to get to the large, plated alien, the ASPs began tossing chairs and patrons indiscriminately. In short order, there was a full-scale riot as ASPs and various customers at the establishment began fighting.

Rauph was amazed at the chaos that had erupted in such a short period of time. He said a prayer of thanks and quickly walked down the concourse toward the docking area. He felt like he was swimming against the tide as most of the inhabitants of the station seemed to be heading toward the fight, either out of curiosity, or a desire to join in.

Cheap entertainment, he thought as he was being jostled and assaulted by the various aliens in his path.

Suddenly, the jostling stopped. A space opened ahead of him, and the push of aliens parted a short distance directly in front of him. Could it be Dempsey? His chest felt like a large weight had been removed from it at the possibility. He quickly followed and found himself waiting in line at the security checkpoint.

It was only a matter of moments before he was through the checkpoint. Many who had been waiting in line had heard of the commotion and headed toward it, leaving the line considerably shorter. Rauph walked quickly to the *Tukuli.* He entered the security code and stepped through the hatch when it opened. After it closed, he waited anxiously for Officer Dempsey to appear, and finally, he did. Rauph breathed a large sigh of relief and sat down on the nearby bench.

"Well," Dempsey said, "that was interesting."

Rauph could only shake his head and wait for his heart to stop racing. It felt like it would explode if it didn't slow down; a sensation bordering on painful.

Interlude

Lisa turned the key in the lock and opened the apartment door before she had second thoughts. She had never been in David's apartment without him being there. He'd never given her a key to it, either. She'd had to plead with the super to borrow his copy, explaining that David was missing, and she was looking for any clues that might help the police discover his whereabouts. The super had finally relented, and she'd made her way up to his second-floor apartment.

It had irked her when she had presented a key to her apartment to him after they had been going out for six months, and he hadn't reciprocated. At the time, she had chalked it up to his need for privacy; she had come to realize that he was a very private person. But it had stayed in the back of her mind—his unwillingness to completely trust her. She knew it was partly the reason she had turned down his marriage proposal. She wasn't sure she was ready to marry a man with such trust issues.

She blamed Jeb mostly, knowing what an overbearing ass the man was, but it didn't change the fact that David had some things he needed to work out before she said yes. Perhaps it was where he was now, holed up somewhere or in some private clinic getting professional counseling. She hoped so. The alternatives were too depressing to think about.

His apartment looked exactly the way she remembered it from the last time she was there, and it didn't look like anyone had been in it recently. There were things growing in the refrigerator that looked like they would soon bear fruit. She quickly closed the fridge door, unwilling to think about cleaning up such a mess. She made her way to his bedroom and saw the various mounds of clothes, some clean and some dirty, she guessed. Again, although the bed wasn't made, it didn't look like it had been slept in recently.

She had made up her mind to leave when she noticed his cell phone sitting on his bedside table. That couldn't be a good sign. The red light was blinking, meaning he probably had messages on his voicemail. She hesitated a moment, deciding whether she should check it in case it held any clues to his whereabouts. Finally, she decided she should and called his voicemail.

"You have three new messages," the female voice said.

She pressed 1, and heard Jeb screaming. She quickly pushed 9 to erase the message. Then it was a recording reminding David to pay his electric bill. She was beginning to zone out when the message ended and a female voice began to speak.

"Hey, babe," the voice said, giggling. "Give me a call back. I miss you." The message ended with more giggling. She reached for the delete button, thinking it was a wrong number, but then hesitated. Was it really? Could she be entirely sure?

She felt tears come to her eyes when she realized that she couldn't. She dropped the phone and hurriedly left his apartment, wondering if she'd made a mistake—not only looking in on him, but about their entire relationship.

Chapter 8

James's heartbeat had finally returned to a semblance of normalcy when Bhakat's voice came over the ship's communication system. "Rauphangelaa, please report to the bridge immediately. We have a situation that requires your attention. Bring James with you."

James saw Rauph close his eyes and mutter a silent prayer. "What now?" he asked.

Rauph didn't respond, he only stood and motioned for James to follow him. When they finally made it to the bridge, not only were Bhakat and Janan there, but also Yvette, Kieren, and Gianni, all of them looking unhappy.

"We have a situation," Bhakat said, his words automatically translated by the device set up in the corner.

Someone must have come to the airlock to get it after Rauph and I left, James thought.

"Bhakat, what's wrong?" Rauph asked, sounding out of breath after the rush to get to the bridge.

"We're missing someone," Bhakat answered, looking at a readout on his control panel.

"Please don't tell me that David has left the ship," Rauph said, still out of breath and sounding exasperated, even through the stilted language from the translator.

"Yvette?" James asked, hoping David was in his room aboard the ship, but knowing from her expression it wasn't true.

"He can't have been gone long," she said.

"Shit," James said. "What happened?"

"He got into a fight with Captain Considerate here," she answered, pointing at Gianni, "and stormed out. We thought he had gone to his room to cool down, but when Kieren went to check on him, he wasn't there. We searched the ship and couldn't find him."

"I should have known," James said, looking at Gianni, who was standing with his arms folded across his chest.

"What?" Gianni asked, unfolding his arms. "It's my fault the kid can't take a joke?"

"We'll talk about this later," James said. "Right now, I have to go find David before he gets himself into any serious trouble."

"We're coming too," Yvette said.

"No, you're not," James said. "I can rely on invisibility; you can't. Besides, if we all go, we're all liable to get lost. You guys can't imagine how big this place is."

"So, we're supposed to sit here and wait for you to come back?" Kieren asked.

"I don't see any other choice," James said. "Thanks to Gianni."

"Hey," Gianni said. "I might be a jerk, but at least I didn't leave the ship like that asshole."

"You know, I've had about enough of you and your attitude," Yvette said, walking toward him.

"Yeah?" Gianni said. "What are you going to do, sic your boyfriend on me?"

"No," Yvette said. "James could probably kill you with one finger. I'm going to hurt you a little."

"Yvette, please don't," Kieren said. Yvette stopped and looked at her. "It won't solve anything."

"It'll make me feel better," Yvette said.

James couldn't tell if she was joking or not. "Okay, enough fooling around," he said. "I'll go, and you guys can monitor the ship's computer in case David gets captured by the police." He turned to Rauph and Bhakat, who had been listening intently to the Humans. "Sorry about this. Sometimes things need to be worked out amongst ourselves. Yvette, will you come with me to the airlock?" She nodded, and the two left the bridge.

Rauph nodded slowly as James and Yvette left the bridge and headed for the airlock. "An interesting discourse—" he began to say to Bhakat. His eyes suddenly grew wide and rolled back to whites as he fell to the floor.

"Master!" Bhakat cried. He bent over the unconscious Rajani, checking his pulse and breathing. "Janan, you have the bridge. I'll get him to the medical bay." He picked up Rauph and quickly left the room.

"I'll go with him," Kieren said. "In case he needs help."

"I'll come too," Gianni added.

"No," Kieren said. "I think you've done enough already." She turned and left.

Gianni stood near the door, watching Janan push buttons on the control panel in front of him. "So," he said after a moment, "need any help?"

Janan turned to look at him. His usual smile was gone. He turned back to the control panel without saying a word.

"Well, I'll be in my room, then," Gianni said softly. "In case anyone asks. Or anything." He was met with silence as he turned and walked out into the corridor.

◊

Bhakat walked as fast as he could, hoping that his initial

diagnosis was wrong. Rauphangelaa had been under a lot of stress since the Krahn had attacked. Bhakat could tell it had taken a toll on his Master. He prayed silently that it was a fainting spell brought on by all of the excitement, but feared it was more than that. He would know for sure once he had Rauphangelaa hooked up to the medibot. His arms were burning by the time he reached the medical facility. Rauphangelaa was not light. He would have to put him down on the floor to hit the button that opened the door.

He was getting ready to do so when the Human female named Kieren appeared behind him and pushed the button for him. He gave her a quick nod of thanks and hurried into the room, placing Rauphangelaa on the table nearest the door. He made sure his Master was positioned correctly for the medibot to scan him and placed an air mask over his nose and mouth. He walked quickly to the machine's control room across the corridor. The door to the medical bay closed after him.

Bhakat had received extensive training with the medical robot, and he quickly punched in the required information. He stood back and watched as the medi-bot began to work on the unconscious figure of Rauphangelaa. Its arms quickly cut off his robe and attached sensors to his chest and temples, all the while scanning his body for injury. Another arm gave Rauphangelaa a shot of a vaso-expander. From the initial readings, Bhakat could see that Rauphangelaa was breathing on his own, and his heart had not stopped beating. He let out a breath he hadn't realized he was holding. It wasn't the best outcome, but it could have been worse. Much worse. Rauphangelaa's vitals were stable. The question was if there was any permanent damage, and how much.

"How is he?" Kieren asked. Bhakat jumped, having forgotten that the Human female was still there.

"He should be fine," he said, hoping that it was the truth. "We'll know more after a full examination by the medical robot."

"Good," she answered. "I'll let the others know."

Bhakat nodded, though she had already left. He didn't notice that she had been speaking Talondarian Standard perfectly, or that she had understood everything he'd told her.

◊

James and Yvette reached the airlock, and he stopped and faced her. "I need you to keep things civil while I'm gone."

"I was kidding—" she started.

"I know you were, but I don't want things to get out of hand," James said. "I think it's best if everyone stays away from each other for a while to let the situation cool down."

"You're probably right," Yvette said, smiling. "Good luck finding David."

"Thanks," James said. It was hard to concentrate with her standing so close. He could smell her hair. He studied her face for a moment, noticing a small mole on her right cheek that he'd somehow missed before, along her jawline. He noticed that he'd been looking at her intently for a few seconds. "Uh, I'd better go," he said sheepishly.

Yvette smiled. "Yeah. Good luck." She stood on her tiptoes and gave him a kiss on the lips before turning quickly and walking down the corridor. He watched her walk away, pleasantly surprised by the kiss. He still wasn't used to having a woman in his life. That, as well as their present circumstances, made it difficult to think about romance.

He took his time once he left the ship. He had a better sense now of the port's layout, and he didn't want to miss David in the crowd. He felt like it was nighttime, or close to it, though he couldn't tell anything from the crowd waiting to enter the port. The length at the security checkpoint was the same as it had been on their earlier visit.

The fly-headed alien wasn't working anymore. A different shift must have started, and the alien working security appeared to have no eyes at all. It was tall, maybe seven feet, and very pale. It had a large, round, bald head. Twin nostrils flared below the place where eyes would be on a human being, but there was nothing above them. Its mouth was a long slash below them, filled with small, pointed teeth. Its ears were large and cup shaped, extending out four or five inches from the side of its head.

James, who had been invisible since leaving the ship, attempted to pass by as he had done before while coming aboard the port with Rauph. As he approached the front of the line, the alien's head perked up and followed his course.

"Sir, please wait your turn like the rest of the customers," the bald alien said, turning its head toward where James stood.

James remained there a moment, mouth open in surprise. He could understand enough of what the alien said to know he'd been caught, somehow. He also knew he'd be in real trouble if he was forced to speak Talondarian Standard in complete sentences. He could only think of a few words and phrases. He remembered taking Spanish in high school because it was a graduation requirement. He had been able to understand what was being said by his teacher a lot earlier than he could carry on a full conversation. The same thing was happening with the alien language that Rauph was teaching him and the others.

"Sir, the line ends back there," the bald alien said, now through the translator, motioning toward the end of the line of aliens. Some of them were looking around in confusion, wondering who the alien security guard was talking to.

James turned slowly and walked back to the end of the line. The line moved along gradually, while James's mind raced. The guard must have had some sort of extra perception ability. He watched as the guard interacted with customers, and it finally dawned on him. Sonar. It must have been using some sort of sonar, like a dolphin or bat, only the sound it made was either above or below human range. He couldn't hear anything that sounded like it could be coming from the alien. As James proceeded in line, he wondered if David had come through, and if so, how he'd been able to pass security. Finally, he made it to the head of the line.

"What is your reason for visiting the Mandakan Space Port today?" the alien asked disinterestedly. It either couldn't tell James was invisible or didn't care. To it, James was another solid body waiting in line.

"Refueling my ship," James answered in English, happy he had learned enough of the language to understand what was being asked of him. The translating device beeped once. "Language log verified," it said before translating what James had said.

The alien doorkeeper moved his head toward the device, as if curious why it had been forced to recognize a new language. "Ship's name?" the alien asked, its appendage poised over a control panel.

"The *Tukuli*," James answered, hoping he had not blown their cover.

The alien ran its appendage over the control panel. "Your ship's language has been logged with the second verification for future interaction. Have an enjoyable stay."

James realized that the first verifications must have been David when he'd come through the line earlier. He said nothing as he walked past the guard, incredulous that it had been so easy. Then he realized it would probably be more difficult to get back to the ship, due to the riot he had witnessed earlier. He'd deal with it when the time came. He needed to find David.

◊

David was amazed at all of the different forms of life he saw aboard the space port. He'd become so used to Bhakat, Rauph, and Janan aboard the *Tukuli*, he'd almost forgotten he was so far from home. That fact was brought back to him as he walked down the short corridor to the main concourse of the port.

The port was much larger than he thought it would be. He had no real plans beyond his initial defiance, so he was wandering through the concourse when he was approached by a small furry creature pushing a cart filled with what looked to be some sort of food. The creature spoke in a high-pitched, sing-song cadence as it proffered its wares. When it stopped speaking and looked at David expectantly, David shook his head and walked away. He couldn't understand the alien's language. It occurred to him he was out of his element, and he should head back to the ship now that he'd cooled down from the argument with Gianni.

But there were too many interesting things to experience, and he was taking them in like a wide-eyed tourist, which he supposed was exactly what he was. He stopped briefly to watch what he assumed were cops taking away a few aliens in restraints, wondering what they had done, before losing interest and walking toward another corridor away from the concourse.

David watched as aliens got off an elevator and others stepped on. He walked toward the doors and waited for his turn. He was startled when a large alien with long black hair and a horse-like face walked up and stood close to him. He saw it was wearing a large metal collar with what looked like a speaker built into the front of it. *Did someone's pet get loose?* he wondered.

When the door to the elevator opened, he waited for two aliens that looked like green fish with red crab legs for feet to exit before stepping through the door. He turned to see the hairy alien had joined him. He felt the first stab of fear as he saw none of the other aliens had moved to get on the elevator.

As the doors closed, the alien reached over and pushed a button on the elevator's control panel. The car began to move, and the alien reached up and took off the collar. It smiled as it turned to David and held the collar out to him.

"Uh, no, thank you," David said, holding his hands up, palms out.

The alien pushed a button on the collar and then held it up to its face. It spoke, and the collar spoke in what sounded like a much different language. David finally understood. It was a translating device, but much more advanced than the one on the *Tukuli*. The alien held it out to him again. He took it and looked at it, seeing the small buttons on one side. The inside of the collar was lined with a soft material, which David thought would make it more comfortable to wear. The alien reached over and pushed a button, then motioned with both hands at its throat, then at its mouth, then pointed at David.

"You want me to speak?" David asked. He really did feel like a tourist now.

The collar made a sound and then spoke in Talondarian Standard. "Analyzing language patterns." Then after a moment, it spoke again. "Analysis complete. Language log created." The alien reached over once more and detached what looked like an in-ear hearing aid from the collar and handed it to David. It pointed toward its own large ear, then at David. David put the aid in his ear. The alien finally spoke.

"I am Punjor. You have come from the *Tukuli*, Rauphangelaa's ship, correct?" As he spoke, the translator spoke through the device in David's ear.

"Yes," David answered. His words were translated and broadcast in Talondarian Standard by the collar. "My name is David."

"David," Punjor said, as if studying the word. "It brings joy to my employer's heart to see your kind once again, but I have been sent to caution you. The port is not safe for you at the moment. Rauphangelaa's visit has riled up the ASPs. It would be in your best interest to return to the *Tukuli* until the situation is not so ... complicated."

Even though the piece in his ear was speaking in ever-improving English as the conversation progressed, David was still confused at what Punjor was telling him. "Thank you," was all he said.

Just then, the elevator's doors opened. Punjor took a step as if to leave.

"Wait, your translator," David said, holding the collar out to the alien.

"It is a gift from Zazzil." Punjor said. "He only asks that you remember his kindness and return the favor in the future if you meet again on Mandakar."

"Oh. Well, thank you again," David said, now even more confused. Who the hell was Zazzil?

Punjor pushed a button on the elevator's control panel. "This should take you back to the main concourse. I trust you can find your way from there." He turned and left without another word. The doors to the elevator closed, and David thought about the strange encounter, still not understanding what had happened. In a few minutes, the doors opened once again, and he stepped out onto the concourse. He thought of putting the collar on, but it didn't seem right to him after seeing it on Punjor's neck. Could he catch something? Who knew what was hiding in the alien's long, black fur.

He walked faster than he had on his way to the elevators, the earpiece allowing him to pick up snippets of conversations as he walked. He realized that it was what he would expect to hear at many public places back on Earth. Some aliens were complaining about food quality or prices. Some were boasting about money won at the casino games, and some were yelling at their kids to behave and stay close in the crowded concourse. It reminded him of what a large airport back home would look like to someone from a foreign country. That is, if the airport also happened to have Vegas-sized casinos and hotels contained within it. At this thought, he began to relax.

David was feeling much more at ease in the situation when he was suddenly grabbed by the arm while trying to make his way through the traffic of alien life. He looked down on his arm, and there was nothing visible, though he could still feel something holding his arm below the wrist.

"Are you finished with your sightseeing?" a voice close to his ear asked in English.

"James?" David asked as a mixture of relief and trepidation rushed through him.

"You know anyone else here who can make themselves invisible?" James asked. "Head for the ship. I'll be right behind you."

"That's where I was going," David said.

"Sure," James said. Without seeing his face, David couldn't tell if James was being serious or not, but it sounded like he was smiling as he said it.

"I guess they told you what happened on the ship?" he asked as he walked.

"An abbreviated version, at least," James said. "I wish you had waited for Rauph and me to return, instead of leaving the ship without telling anyone."

It was unnerving to be talking to air. David felt like he was talking to a figment of his imagination. *I might be crazy,* he thought, *but I'm not that kind of crazy.* He smiled at his own little joke. "Well, no harm done."

Getting back through security was uneventful, though the large blind security agent did inform them all ships were commanded to stay docked until the investigation of the riot was completed, and he was sorry for any inconvenience it might cause.

◊

The next day, James pushed the button to announce his arrival at the medical bay. The doors opened, and he stepped through, wearing the collar translating device David had been given on the space port. He saw Rauph sitting up on the nearest bed. Bhakat was looking at a handheld tablet, which showed Rauph's vital statistics. He looked up at James.

"Only for a minute, then he needs to rest," Bhakat said and walked across the corridor to the control room. James had wanted to talk to Rauph the night before when he'd returned with David, but Bhakat had flatly refused, citing a need for the medi-bot to keep Rauph under close observation.

James nodded to Bhakat as he walked to the edge of the bed.

"A mild cardio fluctuation, and I'm now a slave to the medical robot," Rauph said, smiling. "I'm happy to see you, Officer Dempsey."

"Yeah, me too," James said. He meant it in both senses. He still wasn't comfortable turning invisible for long periods of time. It somehow made him feel ... insubstantial; like he wasn't really there at all anymore.

"I heard you found your missing team member," Rauph said, "and he procured a new translating device." He pointed toward the collar around James's neck.

"Yes," James replied, noting how tired Rauph looked. He would indeed have to make this a short visit. "David was angry because of his fight with Gianni. Don't the Rajani ever get in fights with one another?"

"I would be lying if I said no," Rauph said. "But we do try to not let them escalate into physical violence, if we can help it. The Kha teaches us to strive for understanding, not only a cessation of hostilities."

"Do you always achieve it?" James asked.

"No," Rauph said, smiling sadly. "Unfortunately, no. Much like your own civilization, from the information I gathered."

"How much information did you gather on our world?" James asked, now curious.

"Quite a bit, actually," Rauph replied. "I would have thought you had guessed by now. When we first arrived at your world, I tasked the three of us with finding out as much as we could about your species and your civilization. Janan was to research your culture and arts, through teleplays, books, music, and artwork. He discovered a wonderful resource called the congress library or some such. Bhakat was to search out your technology and medical capabilities. It was my task to search out you specifically, and those around you who might form your team."

"So you did your research, and still managed to get it wrong in the end," James said, smiling to soften the words.

"Somehow, I don't think I did," Rauph replied, smiling back at him.

"Well, I'm glad you're feeling better. I'll leave you to your rest."

Rauph nodded and closed his eyes, already almost asleep.

James walked across the corridor to where Bhakat still stood, looking over charts and vital statistics on his handheld tablet. "How bad was it, really?" he asked the large Rajani.

"Like Rauphangelaa said, it was minor," Bhakat replied. "He should be better with rest. There was a partial blockage in one of the minor arteries near his heart, but the medi-bot was able to clear it out."

"So I guess we'll be here at the space port for a while," James said.

"No, we're going back as planned," Bhakat said.

"What?" James asked loudly. They both winced, and James looked over at the resting form of Rauph. He was still asleep.

Bhakat nodded toward the doors, and they both walked out of the control room. Bhakat closed the doors to the medical bay.

"If Rauph is sick—" James began.

"Rauphangelaa's orders are to proceed as planned," Bhakat said, cutting James off. "There are still a few weeks of travel between here and Rajan. He will be better by then."

"You're the doctor," James said. "If you say he'll be fine ..."

"I said he'll be better," Bhakat said tersely. "I'm only his Pledge. If he says we go back, then that's what we'll do. There is nothing I can do to change it."

James nodded, looking Bhakat in the eye, sensing his frustration on the matter. "I understand."

"I don't need your understanding," Bhakat told him, "only your compliance."

"Fair enough," James said. He nodded to Bhakat and walked away down the main corridor.

Interlude

"Is this Dr. Phillips?" Dennis asked, holding up the piece of paper he had jotted her name on so that he wouldn't forget it. He'd never met Kieren's boss, but his sister had told him what a mean old bird the woman was, and how difficult she was to deal with.

"Yes?" came the matter-of-fact reply on the other end of the line. "How may I help you?"

"My name is Dennis Gray," he replied. "I'm Kieren Gray's brother."

"Oh, Mr. Gray," she said, all hints of toughness gone from her voice. "Have you heard anything new about Kieren?"

Dennis was taken aback by the abrupt change in the woman's tone. Maybe she wasn't as bad as Kieren had led him to believe. "No," he said. "That's actually why I'm calling. I've been calling around everywhere, asking if anyone has heard from her recently."

He didn't add he was doing it because the police still didn't know exactly how long she'd been missing. It had been a Friday when she'd last gone to work, and no one had known any different until she hadn't shown up for work on the next Monday. He was ashamed of the fact he didn't know. He should have known.

"No, I'm sorry," she said. "I haven't heard from her since the last time she was at work."

"Okay," Dennis said. "Thank you for your time."

"No problem, Mr. Gray," she told him. "Make sure you let us know if anything new turns up. We all miss her, especially her students."

"Thank you. I will," Dennis said, hitting the end call button on his phone. He put it down on his desk and leaned back in his chair. *So what now?* he thought, running a hand through his already disheveled hair. He'd called everyone he could think of, with nothing to show for it. He was beginning to lose hope.

Chapter 9

Commander Ries an na Van, Chief Protector of Sector Seven, Subsector Two, which included the Mandakan Solar System, could not have been stationed at a better port of call. Besides his impressive quarters aboard the Galactic Alliance Society for Peace ship *Interceptor,* he also had a richly appointed suite aboard the space port, as well as three vacation homes on Mandaka itself; one in the mountains, one on a private tropical island, and one in the global capital City of Pervan.

While his official capacity at the Mandakan Space Port was keeper of the peace and protector of the Kingdom of Mandaka, he had become as powerful as any figure in Mandakan society, excluding the king himself. Even the crown prince showed deference to him, for he was the key to Mandaka's success. He had the power to deny access to the space port for all ships in the name of security if he chose to. He had control of all commerce that passed through Mandaka; even the illegal trade was subject to his leniency in enforcing Galactic Alliance law. The kickbacks and bribes alone had made him rich. So it vexed him when events happened that were outside of his control.

His anger made his antennae throb and his fur stand up

on the back of his four arms. He clenched two of his fists, the three fingers on each hand making nail impressions on his white palms. There had been fights before on the port. There couldn't be gambling without someone eventually feeling cheated, especially when the port sold various mood-altering substances. It was expected. Bad seeds bore bad fruit, as his mother used to say. What had happened in the main marketplace was a first, though; officers of the Alliance Society for Peace were not attacked openly, with no fear of repercussions. It could not be tolerated. Order must be maintained.

Without order, there was only chaos. Chaos meant possible reassignment for him, and that would not happen if he could help it. Ries would kill—had killed—before he'd let anyone come between himself and his current assignment. He would restore order if it meant coming down on the inhabitants of the port with an iron fist. He'd been aboard the *Interceptor* at the time of the riot, but reports were, the fight started with a single attacker and had quickly escalated from there.

He had declared martial law at the first report, and his officers were systematically searching for the offender or offenders, who had managed to escape during the melee. He'd also declared a stop-leave, meaning no ships could leave the port or enter it until the investigation was complete. He would find those responsible, and they would be punished. Severely.

◊

James was in his room reading poetry on a handheld tablet. He'd never understood Yeats. Especially the poem entitled, 'The Second Coming.' It had always felt so ... pessimistic. He found himself at the local library one day a few years before performing research on the man and the poem, something that had surprised him. He hadn't been to the library since he was a kid, and even then it had been a Bookmobile, and not an actual building.

The anarchy James saw every day at his job was trivial to what Yeats had been writing about, he'd discovered. Most people couldn't imagine the horrors that came from living through, and fighting in, a war unless they actually experienced it themselves. Yeats had lived through World War I, and at the time he wrote the poem, was aware the world was on the brink of yet another war.

The five human beings brought aboard the alien spacecraft were now on the way to a war, as well, and he wasn't sure if they could handle the psychological ramifications of what they would experience if conditions on Rajan were as bad as he thought they would be.

If the others developed powers on par with what he had from the stone implanted in his head, then they would at least have a chance to survive physically. But the cost to their psyches, he wouldn't discover until later. He knew from his job experience what a difficult thing post-traumatic stress disorder could be to deal with. He'd had even veteran officers involved with shootings who could no longer perform the job afterward. He hoped that the Krahn would be gone when they arrived. He fervently wished he and his team would not have to experience the things soldiers had to deal with every day in a theater of war. The center wouldn't hold. It couldn't hold when anarchy reigned.

◊

Rauph had lain down in bed for the night. He had finally been moved back to his own room aboard the *Tukull*, despite Bhakat's protests. It felt good to be in his bed again instead of the one in the medical bay. As he was lying there, a thought brought his mind to a stop, and he sat up straight. He had been bothered by the mention of the Talondarians by Zazzil when he was aboard the Mandakan Space Port. He still had not known why the Cauterfan had mentioned the old Galactic Alliance species at all.

The Talondarians were one of the original founders of the Galactic Alliance. They were so influential at the prime of their civilization that their language and measurements for time and space were adopted by the Alliance as standards for a common system all members could relate to. All Rauph knew about them was the emperor and empress of the planet were killed while traveling from one of their colony planets back to Talondaria, and the emperor's brother had seized the throne, causing a civil war on the planet and Talondaria to be placed on suspension among the members of the Galactic Alliance. This had all happened shortly after he'd been named an Elder on Rajan, half a lifetime ago.

There had always been rumors the royal couple's young daughter had escaped the attack on their star cruiser and was in hiding, waiting to return and depose her uncle and reclaim the throne. The Talondarian civilization had been in a steady decline for hundreds of years, and their emperor had cut them off completely from the Alliance when he'd come into power.

Rauph sat a moment longer in his bed. Now wide awake, he thought about the sudden realization that had made him sit up so abruptly. It had come out of nowhere, but now he could think of nothing else. He slowly got out of bed and walked over to the desk and chair in his room. There was a tablet on the desk, opened to its largest dimension. He sat down and picked it up. Unlike all of the other tablets aboard the ship, he had left this one the capability of oral communication with the ship's computer. In case of emergency, he wanted to be able to swiftly tell the central computer what to do without having to manually input commands. It could be the difference between life and death.

"Computer," he said, debating with himself about whether he even wanted to know the truth.

"Acknowledged," the voice of the computer responded. The screen before Rauph lit up, waiting for his input.

"Computer, display all information regarding the Talondarians." He waited a moment, dreading the knowledge he might be right, but needing to know for his own peace of mind.

The tablet lit up with the official symbol of the Galactic Alliance briefly, then spoke once more. "There are 13,460,354 Galactic Alliance files detected on specified subject: Talondarians."

Rauph sighed. He should have known he was being too vague. For a race as old as the Talondarians, asking for everything was a mistake. He'd have to be more specific. "Refine search," he told the computer. "I want to see a picture of a Talondarian."

"Acknowledged," the computer replied.

Almost instantly, a picture appeared on the screen, and Rauph felt his heart sink, hating the fact he had been correct. He knew now why Zazzil had mentioned the Talondarians. Somehow, the Cauterfan had been able to see Officer Dempsey in his invisible mode. Maybe he could see in a higher or lower band of light than most beings, but Rauph had no doubt that Zazzil had seen the Human. He looked again at the image on the screen. He'd known virtually nothing about the Talondarians, other than a brief recent history of the race and their downfall. He knew they were bipedal creatures, and they were now on the fringes of Galactic Alliance society and government. What he hadn't known until that moment was they looked almost exactly like the Humans now aboard his ship.

◊

Gianni was alone in his room, thinking about home. He had lived in Detroit long enough to consider it his place of residence, but home would always be Dyker Heights in Brooklyn. He hadn't been back in a couple of years, though. If the kids he'd grown up with could see him now, he thought, smiling sadly. He'd left them all behind a long time ago.

Working for a man like his uncle tended to scare people off, unfortunately, so he hadn't been surprised when he'd eventually lost touch with the kids in his old neighborhood. The only one he'd kept in touch with was his cousin Tomas. Of course, Tomas was in the family business as well, and they still saw each other almost daily. Tomas must have been surprised when he'd disappeared. Gianni smiled, picturing his cousin's face when he'd come out of the bathroom. He wondered if he'd ever see his face again.

He also missed his cat, a large stray he had named Rat Pack. He'd had the cat now for a couple of years, even though the apartments had a strict no-pet policy. He thought it was funny that he'd been kidnapped by aliens and one of the few things he truly missed was his cat.

Seeing his pet and his cousin all depended on what happened on the planet they were traveling to, and his ability to stay alive. He sighed, knowing it would depend on the people he was with on this little vacation. People he had managed to piss off pretty badly in the last few weeks. He needed to stop being such a jerk, he knew, but the act was the only way he knew to keep them at a distance. He was torn, knowing he had to drop his guard and start trusting them, but not really knowing how to do it, or if he wanted to.

◊

Rauph woke up feeling better than he had in days. It was

strange, this sense of mortality, of an impending end. He didn't feel old, though he did realize it was inevitable he was getting older. Did it have to happen so soon? He began to braid his hair and pray. He prayed he would live long enough to at least free his world from the Krahn Horde. He prayed for his Pledge, who was having such trouble with the tenets of the Kha. He prayed the Humans would forgive him for all he had done to them, and what he might do in the future.

Janan's voice came over the ship's communication system. "Rauphangelaa, they're here for the lander."

He reached over and pushed a button on a small control panel near his bed. "Thank you, Janan." He had expected them to come this morning, and had told Janan to inform him when they arrived.

He stood slowly. He had been sleeping in his own bed for two days, no longer subject to the medi-bot and Bhakat's attentions. *No, that's not fair to him,* he thought. Bhakat meant well, and was a good and loyal Pledge. He just became tired of Bhakat's constant worrying at times. He walked out of his room and made his way to the main airlock. He opened it to find the Makerfy, Zazzil's bodyguard, along with three others. These others were an Esbian, a Cloyan, and a Kkathrewn. Each of them carried a large crate.

The Makerfy bowed to Rauph. "Zazzil apologizes for the delay, but we had to wait for the situation to quiet down before we could begin to work on your ship."

"When will you begin to work on the ship?" Rauph asked.

"Now, if you will allow us to come aboard," the Makerfy answered, smiling.

Rauph bowed slightly. "Follow me," he told them.

As they were walking down the corridor toward the cargo hold, the Makerfy moved up next to him. "They will need to take some measurements and stress tests of the cargo hold for the modifications you requested."

"Good," Rauph said. "I want to leave as soon as the stop-leave has been lifted."

"Zazzil understands this," the Makerfy said. "The modifications should only take a day or two at the most, depending on the complexity of the work to fit the room into the space provided."

At the door to the cargo hold, Rauph stopped for a moment, out of breath. He knew he would have to slow down. "Bhakat, my Pledge, will assist you from here. He's in the cargo hold prepping the lander for takeoff, and should be able to answer any questions you may have."

The Makerfy bowed, smiling, and led the others through the door. After the door closed, Rauph sat down on the floor, breathing heavily.

Suddenly, James appeared on the floor, kneeling next to him. "That wasn't very smart," he said. Rauph could see that he wore the collar translating device the Makerfy had given to David.

"Officer Dempsey, I didn't know you were here, but I'm glad you were," he said. "How long?"

"Since you left your room," Dempsey replied. "These guys are acting too ... I don't know, nice. Something doesn't feel right."

Rauph thought about telling the Human about the Talondarians and their apparent similarities, as well as Zazzil's ability to see Officer Dempsey, but then thought better of it. Why complicate the situation further? Besides, he was too out of breath to go into any long explanations, and he still wasn't sure of Zazzil's intentions concerning the Humans. If the Cauterfan really thought Dempsey and his fellow Humans were Talondarians, then Rauph didn't want to get caught up in any type of politics that might go along with it.

"Help me up," he said, instead. "Zazzil will be true to the agreement we struck. The Cauterfans are known for their inability to lie. He will honor his side of the bargain. That's all that matters."

"Do you need help back to your room?" Dempsey asked.

"I am not going back to my room," Rauph answered. "I've been in my room for long enough. If you would assist me to the bridge, I would appreciate it."

◊

Ries had been in the Alliance Society for Peace long enough to know that sometimes officers made enemies. He started his investigation of the riot by calling in all of the officers involved in the fight. They met in the ASP office aboard the port. Usually he would meet them in his private suite, invite them in and provide a little luxury to keep them loyal by showing them preferential treatment, but not this time. They all knew what meeting in the office meant by now. Someone was likely to get fired. Or worse.

The ASPs were not an organization they could easily walk away from. They knew what they were getting into when they signed up. It was usually worth it to them to gain special privileges throughout the Alliance. If they had to give up a little personal freedom, then so be it.

His first appointment of the day was with Shinto Gwe'll, the Asnurian who was first assaulted in the riot. Shinto had only been on the Mandakan Space Port for a short while. Ries had met him when he was first assigned and had not spoken to him since.

Ries's assistant, a small Esbian named Tmal, showed Shinto into his office and then closed the door behind her. He wished she hadn't. Shinto came from a species that believed bathing stole part of their life-force. His stench was barely tolerable in the larger open areas of the port, but it was almost overpowering in the closed confines of Ries's office.

Ries pushed a button on his desk that opened the large picture window behind him, which looked out over the main concourse from four stories up. Clean, purified air flowed into the room, and Ries breathed deeply, while also pouring himself a drink. One of the benefits of having four arms was having a dual set of brains, one to control each set. He finally turned his attention back to Shinto, who had been left standing in the middle of the office while he waited for Ries to take notice of him.

Ries could see the dark bruising on the Asnurian's face and his still-swollen lips from the fight. He slowly took a sip from his drink while still appraising the officer standing before him. *Make him sweat, and he's not likely to lie.*

"Sit down," he finally said, turning to look out of the open window at the lights and life scattered below.

"Commander, I—" Shinto began.

"Silence!" Ries did not even look at him. "Sit. Now."

Shinto did as he was told.

"Tell me exactly what happened, from the beginning," Ries said, turning back toward Shinto, who had the appropriate look of fear on his battered face.

"My partner, Vidro, and I had finished our patrol of the upper level," Shinto began.

His breath is worse than his body odor, Ries thought with an inward shudder.

Shinto plowed ahead. "We saw a group of fellow officers on the main concourse and decided to compare notes with them on the status of port security," he said, looking down at his feet.

"You decided to take a break and gossip on company time," Ries said matter-of-factly.

"No, sir," Shinto began, leaning closer to Ries's desk. The smell almost made him gag.

How can his partner and the others put up with this? Ries thought. Then he remembered that the officer named Vidro was a Nefarian, a species that could close their nostrils at will. Ries wished he could as well. He gave Shinto his coldest glare, and the other stopped and sat back, ending his protestations.

"Continue with your report," Ries said.

"We'd been there a few minutes when a Xerbian approached from one of the hydrolifts." ASPs were taught to recognize every known species in the universe, or at least the ones that were officially recognized by the Galactic Alliance. Because of this, Ries formed a mental picture of a large creature with a bad attitude.

"It walked over to our table," Shinto continued. "That's all I remember until I woke up in the infirmary. I'm told the Xerbian never spoke a word; he just started swinging. That's all I know, honestly."

"You had never seen the Xerbian before?" Ries asked him.

"No, sir," Shinto answered.

"You were approached by an unknown individual," Ries said, "and you took no precautions. You let him walk up and lay you out cold. That's great. The finest, most highly trained security force in the galaxy, and that's the best you could do."

Shinto stared at his paw-like hands and kept quiet. A wise move, as it turned out.

"Well," Ries said after a moment, "I suppose you've learned your lesson, at least. Get out of my sight."

Shinto stood up quickly, backing away toward the door to Ries's office. "Thank you, Commander. Thank you. I thought ... I mean ... I'll do better. I promise—"

"Get out," Ries said, knowing what the Asnurian thought.

Brian S. Converse

Shinto knew what happened to ASP personnel who failed under his command.

Ries stood and leaned out of the window, breathing deeply through his large nostrils.

Tmal entered his office holding a hand to her nose. "Sir?" she asked.

"Send in Vidro Glor," Ries said. "And a fan," he said after a moment, regretting his choice for the first interview. It was going to be a long day.

◊

James was beginning to get antsy. The *Tukuli* had been docked at the space port for a week, by his count, and no one had been allowed to leave the ship. Ever since the events had transpired that first day, Rauph had made it clear no one would leave the ship again while they were docked. Zazzil had been true to his word. Repairs to the *Tukuli* soon began, as well as the upgrades that Rauph had requested, as Janan and Bhakat supervised and scrutinized everything done aboard the ship.

James had been surprised to find out that Zazzil's workers brought three crates of clothing made for the Humans aboard the ship, though not exactly of a style or cut they were used to. He'd been informed by Bhakat they had left the crates in the cargo hold with express instructions from Zazzil's head of security that they were to be given to the guests.

James had distributed the clothing according to size, noting all five of the team members received at least a set of shirt and pants. They were comfortable enough, though simple and unadorned, and all the same khaki material. It occurred to James it wasn't coincidence there were clothes for all of them, not only the two who had left the *Tukuli,* but he could worry about the implications later.

Finally, the workers had pronounced the work finished,

and Rauph called all of the Humans together to let them know they would be leaving as soon as possible. James had then held his own meeting with the others and made a last-minute plea to them regarding the battle that lay ahead.

"If anyone has had any last-second thoughts about any of this," he told them, "now is the time to voice them. We can leave you here and pick you up on the way back to Earth."

James had felt a small amount of pride in the fact none of them had volunteered to stay. Now, a day later, he sat and waited for the ship to finally begin undocking from the space port. For all he knew, they could already be on their way to Rajan, and the Humans hadn't been told yet. It wasn't like there were windows in his room he could look out of and see their location. He eventually couldn't stand it anymore, and made his way to the bridge. He pushed the button next to the door to announce his arrival, and the door opened. He stepped through and saw by the viewscreen they were still docked. It occurred to him then he could have punched it up on his tablet, but by then he was already there.

"What's going on?" he asked. He felt somewhat stupid when the three looked over at him, and it occurred to him the translating device was not in the room. He couldn't understand them if he wanted to. Janan smiled and pointed to the viewscreen. James saw a large, intimidating ship floating a short distance off the space port's docking station. Its colored stripes made it look like some type of predatory fish.

"ASPs," Janan said.

James felt his heart sink. It looked like the police were still keeping all of the ships from leaving the station until they sorted through the events leading to the full-scale riot involving their officers. He didn't need a translator to guess that. It's what he would have done. The question now was how to leave without being stopped by either the police or the Mandakan Imperial Warship that was still patrolling the system somewhere. As he was thinking about their dilemma, there came another chime at the door to the bridge. The three aliens turned to look at James. He smiled and went to the door. Outside in the corridor were Gianni and Kieren.

"What's going on?" Gianni asked. "Weren't we supposed to leave by now?" He stood on his tiptoes to look over James's shoulder, trying to see onto the bridge.

"The cops are stopping everyone from leaving the station," James told them, pointing toward the viewscreen.

"No shit?" Gianni said, smiling. "Guess they're a pain in the ass way out here too."

"Gianni," Kieren said.

"What?" Gianni asked. "I was only kidding. Big J knows that."

"Big J?" James asked. He wasn't sure if he should be offended or complimented by the nickname.

"So why can't we tell them it wasn't us and ask to leave?" Kieren said. "I mean, we haven't done anything wrong, have we?"

"I've found speaking up only tends to lead to trouble," Gianni said. "Cops want to find things out on their own. You come to them, and all that happens is they get suspicious of you, and the next thing you know, you're in an interrogation room and they're playing good cop/bad cop while you wait for your lawyer to show up. It's not worth it."

"I wish I could go over the finer points of police procedure with you," James said. "Except in this instance, you're probably right. Best to keep our heads down and not draw attention to ourselves, if we can."

"What's going on?" asked a voice from the corridor. They all turned to see Yvette walking toward them.

"Looks like we're stuck here for a little while longer," Kieren said.

Rauph rose from his chair and wordlessly directed them all to follow him. The four Humans were led to a nearby room, and they saw the large translating device sitting on the table inside. Rauph turned the device on and then spoke. "I would ask you not congregate on the bridge at this time. We're doing our best to figure out how to expedite our departure."

"Hey," Gianni said. "We wanted to know what was happening. No reason to get all pissy with us."

"I am not being, as you say, pissy," Rauph replied, not really knowing what the expression meant, but knowing if it came from Moretti, it couldn't be good. "I only ask that you stay off the bridge until we are on our way." He nodded to James and then left the room.

"Well," Yvette said. "Diplomacy strikes again."

"All I'm saying," Gianni told her, "is we're not prisoners here. We have a right to know what's happening. Right?"

"I agree," James said. "But we're also guests aboard their ship. There's no reason to antagonize him in an already tense situation."

"If we're going to be stuck here a while," Yvette said, "why don't we at least try out the new training room?"

"An excellent idea," came a voice from the doorway to the room, via the translator. They all turned to see Bhakat and Janan. "It's getting late tonight," Bhakat continued. "But we could start your training in the morning, when my shift ends."

"We?" James asked, surprised the Rajani would ever attend the training session. He thought it was against the Rajani's religious beliefs.

"Bhakat is the only one trained in the use of the room's

controls," Janan said, smiling. "Rauph refused to learn anything about it, so I guess you're stuck with us."

"This should be fun," Gianni said, sarcasm dripping from every word.

"Fun is not the word I would use," James said. "We have a limited amount of time before we reach Rajan, and in that time, we need to learn the full extent of our new powers and how to use them as efficiently as possible. Our lives, as well as the lives of thousands of the inhabitants of Rajan, depend on us knowing what we're doing before we get there."

"Easy for you to say," Gianni said. "You're already showing your new powers. The rest of us still don't even know if we'll get any, let alone what they'll be. Except for Kieren, I guess."

"Patience," Bhakat said. "They will come. From what Rauph has told me, sometimes they need a little ... incentive to manifest themselves the first time."

"Then I guess I'll see everyone bright and early tomorrow morning," James said. "Has anyone seen David around? He should be told as well."

"I'll tell him," Janan said from the doorway. "His quarters are near mine."

"No," James said, thinking it over a moment. "I think I'd better be the one to talk with him about it. Thanks anyway."

◊

After his meeting with the others, James went looking for David. It had taken a little while to figure out where everyone's rooms were located on the ship—the Rajani had not set them up in a row of rooms, so it was a chore to seek each other out. James wasn't sure if this was by plan or because the Rajani themselves were solitary in nature and had assumed the Humans would enjoy their own space as well. It was the reason he and the others had agreed they should have a common meeting room where they could hang out together if they wanted.

When he finally arrived at David's room, he pushed the doorbell and waited. When there was no answer, he pushed it again. Finally, the door opened and David poked his head out. He was bleary-eyed and his hair was disheveled. He was in only a pair of boxers and a white T-shirt. Unlike Gianni, though, he had been brought aboard the ship wearing a suit and tie. James saw the suit was now in a heap in the corner of the room, next to a heap of the clothes provided by Zazzil.

"Sorry if I woke you," James said. "Isn't it a little late for a nap?"

"Oh, is it?" David asked, pulling his dark slacks on and tucking in his T-shirt. "My body clock is all screwed up out here." He motioned for James to enter and tried to rub the sleep from his eyes. James could see he'd been drooling on himself.

"I wanted to come by and let you know we're going to start our training tomorrow morning," James said. "We've had a little setback, and it looks like we might be stuck here another day or two."

"Repairs?" David asked as he took a drink of water from a glass that had been sitting on a small table near his bed.

"Cops," James replied.

David raised his eyebrows. "Did we get caught? The Rajani, I mean."

"No," James replied. "But I have a feeling if we are caught, we might get stuck in quarantine for a while until they make sure we're okay. Your guess is as good as mine."

"Damn," David said, closing his eyes and scratching his head. "So what type of training are we talking about for tomorrow?"

"I think we'll take things slow at first," James replied. "I want to make sure we're all physically fit enough for this. Powers are great, but I think we should all be able to withstand anything that may be thrown at us, and that means making sure we're all able to build up our physical and cardiovascular endurance. We don't know exactly what to expect once we get to Rajan. Hell, we might already be too late."

"What do you mean?" David asked with a look of uncertainty on his face.

"The Krahn may have come and gone," James said. "We might be stuck picking up the pieces after we arrive. I don't think that's how this will play out, though, to tell you the truth."

"Why not?" David asked.

"I don't think we'd be that lucky," James replied. "Besides, what fun would it be?"

"True," David said. "By the way, I've been meaning to ask you, what does it feel like to use your powers?"

"It really doesn't feel like anything," James told him. "It's not like you can feel the power around you. The energy field is there, but is almost like a part of you. You can do things naturally. It took me a little while to get used to turning invisible and staying that way, but after a while it was easy. I can still see myself, even though no one else can."

"Cool," David said, before looking contemplative. "I hope I'm not stuck with some lame power that's no use to us."

"I'm sure you'll be fine," James said. "The important thing is getting everyone to work as a team."

"Good luck with that," David said, rolling his eyes. "I'm glad I didn't get stuck as the leader of this ragtag group."

"I'm still counting on you to be an important part of it, though," James told him, placing a hand on his shoulder. "I'll see you tomorrow morning."

"I'll be ready to go," David replied. "I think."

"Good," James said, walking to the door. "It's going to be a long day of training." He smiled as the young man groaned. He was looking forward to seeing what his fellow team members could do. He was especially curious about the ones, like David, whose powers hadn't yet manifested.

Interlude

Tomas Giovanni was getting a visit from the one person he didn't want to see: his father. He watched as the man walked around the room, inspecting the Get Well Soon cards and gifts that had been accumulating there since Tomas was admitted. Finally, he sat down in a chair close to Tomas's bedside.

"So," his father said, frowning, "what kind of shit are you caught up in now?"

"Nice to see you too, Dad," Tomas said. "Thanks for coming all this way to interrogate me."

"Don't give me that bullshit," his father said tersely. "You know I hate flying. Who knows what that knucklehead Rizzo is doing while I'm gone?" Rizzo was his father's right-hand man, but even Tomas knew the man was lost without a little direction. Handling the business side of things wasn't his strong suit.

"Sorry," Tomas said. "Guess I'm tired of everybody asking me questions. You know I've been getting regular visits from every asshole with a badge in Detroit?"

"And you told them ...?" his father left the question hanging in the air.

"You think I'm an idiot?" Tomas asked. "Nothing. It's the truth, Dad. I don't know who it was that jumped me, and I don't know what happened to Gianni, neither."

"Good boy," his father said, leaning back in his chair. "Leave Gianni to me. We got some people out there looking. We'll find him."

"I'm sure that Aunt Christina is worried sick," Tomas said.

"Yeah," his father confirmed, looking out the window. "He'd better have a good answer to all of this, or she won't be worrying anymore. She'll be grieving."

Chapter 10

James opened his eyes to find he was in a small round room with walls that were pure white. *Oh no, not again,* he thought, confused as to how he had woken up in another strange place. When his eyes had become more accustomed to the light, he noticed the whiteness surrounding him was not completely opaque. It was wispy, as various gasses swirled around behind a clear surface. The temperature was cold enough that he could see his own breath.

Then he noticed he was wearing a translating collar much like the one David had been given aboard the space port. There was also an earpiece in his ear. Something was wrong with the whole situation. He instantly powered up, and just as quickly, the energy field disappeared as searing pain coursed through his head, making him curl into a ball on the floor. The pain stopped, but he felt its aftereffects throbbing in his temples and a nauseated feeling in his stomach.

"My apologies," a soft voice spoke through the earpiece in his ear. "But I couldn't risk you lashing out with your powers. My home is made of one of the strongest substances aboard this space port, but I still couldn't trust you wouldn't cause a breach in its integrity. That wouldn't do either of us any good."

"Zazzil?" James asked when he was finally sure he wasn't going to be physically ill.

"Yes," the voice responded. "I wish we could have met under more formal circumstances, but there was a certain need for secrecy, as I'm sure you know."

"Why am I here?" James asked, slowly sitting up. Then he remembered he had fallen asleep that night next to Yvette, although he was happy he'd chosen to wear some clothing to bed. "How did I get here? And what happened to Yvette?"

"My staff brought you here," the voice said. "Your mate is unharmed, I assure you. We did nothing to her except ensure she would not wake while my staff attended to you."

"Wait," James said, standing up. His head almost touched the rounded ceiling of the room, and James could see it was not the same meeting room they had brought Rauph to in their original visit. "How did your people get aboard the *Tukuli?*"

"The lander," Zazzil replied. "Each ship and its lander are given a security code when they're manufactured. In the case of the *Tukuli,* Rauphangelaa had not changed the code on the lander before we took it away. It was a simple thing to look up the code on the lander and use it to gain entrance to the Tukuli."

"You planned this all along," James said, the idea sending chills through his body in the already cold room. "The day Rauph came to see you for the first time. You purposely agreed to take the lander as payment."

"I had hoped Rauphangelaa had not changed the code, yes," Zazzil said. "When I saw you with him, I knew we would have to meet."

"When you saw ..." James began, dumbfounded.

"Yes," Zazzil said. "I guessed that since you had accompanied Rauphangelaa while displaying powers, you must have been implanted with a Johar Stone."

"How do you know about the stones?" James asked. "Rauph said they were a closely guarded secret of the Rajani."

"My species has been a member of the Galactic Alliance for thousands of years," Zazzil replied. "We have very long memories. We were an ancient species when the Rajani were discovered. Their story is known to us, and not only the fable of what they believe to be true."

"Fable?" James asked, confused as ever.

"Enough about the Rajani," Zazzil said abruptly. "They have no part in what we need to speak of now. If you are to return to the *Tukuli* by morning, then we cannot waste any more time talking about them. I must admit, though, I was surprised to see you had leaned on them for assistance, considering the history between your two species. Though receiving the Johar Stones does explain it, somewhat."

"I haven't leaned on anyone," James said. "Rauph asked for our help. Look, I'm still confused about all of this. What history are you talking about?"

There was silence for a few minutes as James stood and looked around him for any sign of an exit. There wasn't one.

"I don't know why you are playing coy with me," Zazzil finally said. "But I'm sure you have your reasons. The girl is safe; I can assure you of that. You can also rest assured that the Harodet Clan of Cauterfa has remained loyal to the rightful rulers of Talondaria. We only ask this is remembered once your empire is restored."

James stood there while the Cauterfan's words echoed in his mind. *Talondaria,* he thought. *The ones who created the language? Which girl is safe?* He was still uncertain as to what Zazzil meant, but was beginning to understand that he was caught up in a case of mistaken identity, if Zazzil really thought he was a Talondarian. What exactly would happen if the Cauterfan found out he wasn't one? James decided it best if Zazzil didn't find out, at least not while he was in such a vulnerable position.

"Why don't you let me out of this room," James said. "Or am I a prisoner?"

"Of course you're not a prisoner," Zazzil said. "I only wished for privacy. My workers are loyal, to the extent they are paid very well. But there are always those willing to pay more to test that loyalty. We each have our share of enemies within the Alliance."

James was about to ask again if he could go when Zazzil's voice came over the translator. "I apologize; I had hoped to speak more with you this morning, but I'm afraid something else has arisen which merits my attention. We will speak again soon, if we can."

Suddenly, the portion of the floor that James was standing on began to lower, and James saw he was being brought down to the level below the Cauterfan's tank, where some of Zazzil's workers were waiting for him. One, a purple Humanoid with three eye stalks and four fingers on each hand, bowed to him. It came closer and removed the collar from James's neck, then pointed to the side of his head. James understood, and removed the earpiece, handing it to the creature. He looked around at the extensive network of large and small pipes that led to and away from the Cauterfan's tank. It was an engineering feat beyond anything he could have imagined. He supposed the tank held a limited quantity of the gases the Cauterfan needed to live.

Another of Zazzil's workers, this one a short, three-legged creature with long red hair all over its body, motioned for James to follow it, and he stepped off the platform he'd been standing on. As he did so, the platform once again rose into position in the room above, pushed up by a thick piston.

The worker led him to a door and opened it, motioning for James to step through. He did, wondering where he was being led. He followed the alien through various corridors before finally coming to another nondescript door. His guide opened the door and again motioned for James to step through. As he did so, he saw the doorway led directly to the docking station of the space port. He nodded to the alien and headed toward the *Tukuli,* wondering if he would ever truly understand what Zazzil had told him.

◊

Ries had expanded his questioning to include some of the better known off-market merchants aboard the space port. Most of them he had forced to meet him in his office, but the Cauterfan named Zazzil posed a problem. He knew he would have to go to see Zazzil in his room, an inconvenience he'd put off while questioning the others on his list. The time had finally come for a visit.

He waited at the door, flanked by two of his officers. When the door opened, he was greeted by Punjor Sarn, Zazzil's security chief. The Makerfy had ascended quickly up the ranks of Zazzil's employees, and Ries would have loved to nail him with something on principle, but couldn't prove anything. The Makerfy made his antennae twitch. One didn't rise to prominence so quickly without leaving a few bodies in one's wake.

"Commander Ries, what an unexpected surprise," Punjor said, showing his long, sharp teeth. "I'm afraid that Zazzil's schedule is very busy this morning, but if you call later, we should be able to fit you in sometime this afternoon."

"Don't give me that, Punjor," Ries said, pushing past the Makerfy. "He'll see me now or he'll regret it." He walked past the other workers and over to the meeting room. "Zazzil, I need to talk to you," he said. He sat down in the chair, detesting the waves of cold air coming from the tank. His own world was hot, and he kept his quarters the same temperature.

"Ries, what can I do for you?" came Zazzil's voice over the translator.

"That's *Commander* Ries," he said, absentmindedly looking at the nails on one of his hands. "I need to ask you a few questions about the recent trouble aboard the port."

"At so early an hour?" Zazzil asked. "I didn't think you woke up this early, let alone worked."

Ries ignored the jab. He was used to getting them by now. It came with the job. "My time is important, Zazzil. I have to fill my days speaking with important people. That's why I'm speaking to you, someone who is not so important, at such an early hour." He smiled at his own wit.

"Then I won't waste your time," Zazzil said. "I know nothing about the trouble you're referring to. Nor do any of my workers. Now, if you'll forgive me, I do have business to conduct of my own, however unimportant it might be. Good day, Commander."

Ries stood up, knowing he would get nothing else from the Cauterfan, and it wouldn't be worth rounding up his workers. Their loyalty was almost legend aboard the space port. This wasn't over, he vowed to himself, not by half. Zazzil would feel the squeeze on his operations for his disrespectful attitude. Ries thought he might have to order a review of all of the Cauterfan's business dealings since the riots, to make sure everything checked out. He walked to the door and ignored the grinning Makerfy, feeling his antennae twitch as he did so.

◊

Yvette woke up with a splitting headache. She rolled over and reached for James before discovering he was gone. *Damn,* she thought. *He must be getting ready for training already.* The wall panels were beginning to grow lighter, telling her that it was still early in the morning. She'd never been much of a morning person, but the headache was something new, making it impossible for her to roll over and return to sleep. She rubbed her temples with both hands, wondering if she was getting sick from some alien virus. Then she saw the small dot on her arm. She brought her arm closer to her face, thinking maybe it was a natural skin blemish. No, she decided. It was definitely a needle mark.

She sat up, too quickly, and had to lie back down for a moment while her head stopped swimming. Finally, she sat up again, slowly this time, and pulled on the clothes she'd left next to the bed. She took a drink of water from the container on the table next to her side of the bed. Her head was clearing rapidly as she left James's room and headed for the common room.

As the fog in her head dissipated, her sense of panic rose as she began to wonder where James was. She stopped at the common room, but it was empty. She then went straight to the bridge. She pushed the button next to the door, hoping James would be there. He wasn't. Only Bhakat was on the bridge. He looked up at her, a quizzical expression on his face. She realized that she hadn't brought any translator with her, so she asked, "Have you seen James?"

"No," Bhakat answered.

At least I understood that, she thought, regretting not studying the language better. "I can't find him," she said as she left the bridge, heading for the only other place on the ship where he logically could be. When she arrived at the training room, she found it empty as well.

◊

James returned swiftly to the *Tukuli*, wondering if

anyone was even aware he was gone. As he neared the tube-shaped walkway connecting the ship's outer hatch to the port's airlock, he also wondered how he would be able to get back on the ship if no one knew to let him in. He hoped the door had been left unlocked by Zazzil's workers when they took him.

He needn't have worried, he saw, as he reached the door to the airlock and saw Yvette, Bhakat, and Gianni walking toward him from the ship. He smiled as Yvette reached him ahead of the others and wrapped her arms around his neck. He returned the hug. "Did you miss me?" he asked.

"Where the hell were you?" she asked, pulling back from him as the others caught up to them. She didn't look happy.

"I think we need to get back on the ship before I say anything," he told her. He wasn't sure if they were being watched. He was glad to see Yvette looked unharmed, as Zazzil had promised.

They made their way to the common room, where they found Kieren, David, and Janan waiting for them.

"James!" Kieren said, smiling. "You guys found him."

"More like he found us as we were leaving the ship," Gianni said, sitting down. "I still didn't get to see the damn space port."

"Poor baby," James said. "I suppose that was the only reason you volunteered to look for me? Wait, don't answer. I don't want to know."

"Ignorance is bliss," Gianni said, smiling.

James ignored him and turned to Yvette. "You're okay?"

"Yes," she replied. "I had a doozy of a headache when I woke up this morning, but it's gone now."

"Good," James said. "Zazzil said they made sure you wouldn't wake up while they were here last night."

"Zazzil?" Bhakat asked.

"Yes, Zazzil," James said. "His workers came aboard the ship last night and kidnapped me while everyone was sleeping. He claims it was to talk to me privately, and he did let me go free, but it's still not an experience I'd like to repeat. By the way, Bhakat, you should change the security code on the *Tukuli* immediately."

"So you've been kidnapped twice now by aliens," Gianni said. "Some people have all the luck."

"Like I said, it wasn't the best experience in the world," James said. "I need to talk to Rauph about this. Zazzil thinks we're Talondarians. That's why he's been so nice to us lately, giving us gifts like the translator and clothing."

"I know," Rauph said from the doorway. He was holding the collar translating device that had been hanging by the door. He attached it around his neck before speaking again. "I'm sorry I didn't tell you, but I didn't think anything would happen. He mentioned the Talondarians when I first spoke to him. I didn't know at the time what he meant, but later realized it was because he had seen Officer Dempsey, somehow."

"You knew and didn't tell anyone about it?" Yvette asked.

"I didn't think it important at the time," Rauph replied. "I thought we would get our repairs finished and leave before he was able to take any actions. I was wrong."

"We can't do anything about it now," James said. "But like I told Bhakat, you need to change the security code on the Tukuli immediately. They took the code from the lander."

"Bhakat, can you take care of that for us?" Rauph asked. Bhakat bowed slightly and left the common room.

"We were supposed to start our training this morning," James said, "but I don't think either Yvette or I are up to it right now. I guess we'll postpone until tomorrow morning, same time." He also wasn't sure what Zazzil had done to him to make it so difficult for him to use his powers. He hadn't tried to power up since his meeting, so he didn't know whether he was being blocked somehow or not. He didn't want to find out with the others watching.

"If you'll excuse me, my duties are about to begin on the bridge," Rauph said, taking off the collar and hanging it up before leaving.

"Well, if all of the excitement is over for the day," Gianni said, "I'd like to have breakfast now." He stood and walked over to the cabinets that held the supplies of protein bars and other supplements. James wasn't paying any attention to what he'd said. He was looking at the collar, still rocking back and forth on the hook near the door.

Interlude

Josiah Manidoo was sitting in his richly appointed living room, having poured himself three fingers of scotch. He looked around his house, wondering how things had changed so much since he was a freshman senator, fifteen years before. Back then, he'd had to practically live at the House, coming home every other day or so to visit his daughter and to make sure her nanny was keeping her out of trouble. A tough job, it turned out, with his daughter. He took a sip of the amber liquid, feeling it burn his throat as it went down. He wasn't a heavy drinker, but he needed something tonight to help deal with Yvette's disappearance.

There was a knock on his front door. He had dismissed his housekeeper for the night, expecting company as he was, so he walked to the heavy oak door and looked through the spy hole. It was Byrnes. He opened the door and stepped aside to let the man through before quickly closing it once more after a brief look outside. He half expected to see one of those ambush paparazzi photographers sitting on his front lawn and filming, but there was no one visible. He turned to Byrnes, who was quietly waiting in the foyer, both hands gripping the handle of his briefcase.

"Come into the living room," he told the man. He walked to his chair and sat back down. "I've poured myself a drink. Feel free to help yourself to the bar." He motioned toward the corner of the room with the hand holding his drink before taking another sip.

"No, thank you, sir," Byrnes said, his right hand pushing a pair of dark glasses up the bridge of his nose. "I don't drink."

"Neither do I, usually," he told the man. "But I'm making an exception. Please, sit."

Byrnes sat down on the edge of the leather couch

and began to open his briefcase. Josiah appraised the man while he waited for him to get his papers in order. He was a smallish man with a bald head, neutrally dressed and totally unassuming to the casual observer. Yet he'd come highly recommended from another senator who had experienced some legal problems of his own. Byrnes was known in Washington circles as a man who could solve problems.

"So, what did you come up with?" Josiah asked him, too impatient, after all, to let the man get settled fully.

"Your daughter didn't have any relationships with the men she worked with, or the men she had gone to school with," he began. Josiah had thought maybe she had eloped with a lover or went on a vacation without letting anyone know where she was going. No luck.

"I could find no records of her buying any travel tickets," Byrnes continued. "Her car is still parked on the street near her apartment. You may want to have it moved, by the way, before it gets impounded."

"Thank you," Josiah said. "I'll take care of it."

"The police still have no leads, nor do they have any in the other similar disappearances in her apartment complex. There are no signs of foul play in any of the cases," Byrnes said. He looked up from his notes and actually sighed in frustration. "I'm sorry, sir, but that's all I have. The trail has grown cold. I'm afraid unless your daughter wants to be found, she won't be."

Josiah sat for a moment, silently feeling his own frustration building up inside of him. He felt impotent knowing there was nothing more he could do. "Thank you for your help," he finally said. He stood up, waiting for the man to button up his briefcase. As he walked him to the door, he handed the man an envelope filled with cash, which quickly disappeared into the man's suit jacket.

"I'm sorry I couldn't do more," Byrnes said.

"Me too," Josiah said softly, and closed the door. He turned and leaned against the door while looking around his home. He knew he would trade it all to see his daughter's face once more.

Chapter 11

Rauph wasn't surprised when the call came on the *Tukuli's* communication system from Zazzil. He'd never imagined the Cauterfan would be capable of coming aboard his ship without permission, let alone actually taking someone from it.

"*Tukuli*, this is Zazzil," the voice said. "May I speak to Rauphangelaa?"

"This is Rauphangelaa," he replied, his anger making his voice sound clipped.

"I would like to apologize for my actions of last night," Zazzil said. "I didn't handle the situation correctly by boarding your ship without permission."

"If you wanted to talk to Officer Dempsey, you only had to ask," Rauph said. "Now all you've done is made it so he will be reluctant to speak to you again. He certainly doesn't want to leave the ship again." He wasn't really sure if Dempsey felt that way, but it sounded good. He was angry.

"Then allow me to come aboard your ship," Zazzil said after a beat of silence.

How ...? Rauph thought, confused. He wasn't sure how it could be accomplished. "I'd allow it, but it would be dependent on whether or not Officer Dempsey wishes to speak to you. I'll send you his answer as soon as I can."

"Thank you, Rauphangelaa," Zazzil said.

Rauph cut off the signal and sat thinking for a moment. He couldn't very well refuse Zazzil's request. The Cauterfan would never help him again. He would have to believe Officer Dempsey would make the correct choice. He had little say in the matter. He sighed before pushing the button for the ship's communication system. "Janan, please come to the bridge."

◊

James was sitting with Yvette and Kieren in the common room when Rauph walked in and took the translating collar from the hook on the wall.

"Officer Dempsey," Rauph said, "may we speak together privately?"

James looked over at Yvette, who shrugged. "Yes, I'm not busy," he said, placing the tablet he'd been reading down on the table next to him. He'd been trying to do some research on training tactics from Earth, but was not having much luck. Janan hadn't downloaded very much on the subject to the *Tukuli's* central computer. He'd meant to ask Bhakat or Janan how to program the central computer to translate files from Talondarian Standard to English so he could read them, but had forgotten. He stood and followed Rauph into a meeting room. "I thought you were on duty aboard the bridge," he said, sitting down at the table.

"Janan is taking my place while I speak with you," Rauph replied, sitting down across from him. "I received a call from Zazzil. He would like to speak with you again, if he could."

"What?" James asked. "After everything he did last night?" He didn't know if he wanted to go anywhere near Zazzil's room again.

"I told him it was entirely up to you," Rauph said, holding

up a hand to forestall any arguments from James. "He even acquiesced to meeting aboard the *Tukuli*."

"How exactly would he do that?" James asked.

"I have no idea," Rauph replied. "I should remind you, Zazzil could make it very difficult for us to leave the space port if he wanted to."

James thought it over for a second. "Fine," he finally said. "But only if a few conditions are met. First, I want all of my team present to hear what he has to say. Second, he is to come alone, or with as few of his workers as possible. Tell him if those conditions are met, I'll talk to him."

"I'll inform him of your decision right now," Rauph said. "I'll set up the meeting for tonight, if possible." He stood up and turned to leave.

"One more thing," James said, sitting back in his chair.

"Yes?" Rauph asked, stopping to look at him.

"This is at least the second time you've withheld information from us. Information that might have been very important to the outcome of this entire mission. I don't like the pattern. If we're to succeed, we're going to have to know more than what you're telling us."

Rauph sighed and sat back down in his chair. "I do apologize, James."

James was surprised at the use of his first name. It was the first time Rauph had used it, even though he was constantly telling him to. Rauph was becoming more comfortable talking to him.

"I've kept my own council now for a long time," Rauph continued. "It's been many years since my wife died, and she was the only one I ever really trusted. I'm not used to this type of situation. I wonder sometimes whether life as I knew it has changed irrevocably because of the Krahn invasion. Things will never be the same on our world, I fear."

"I lost my wife, too, at a young age," James said. "It took me a long time to get over it and come to grips with the fact she was no longer a part of my life. I had to see that things can change and still be good. Life is about change, and if there's no change at all, then you might as well be dead too."

"I suppose you're right," Rauph said, standing up once again.

"If there's even a slim chance we can save your world," James said, "then that's better than none at all. It won't be as you remember it, and for that I'm sorry. All we can do is the best we can and hope that it's good enough."

Rauph smiled and took off the collar, placing it on the table before James. He squeezed James's shoulder and left. James sat a moment, thinking about what he had told Rauph and wondering if he believed it.

◊

David didn't know what to expect that night. All he'd been told was this alien named Zazzil was coming aboard the ship to speak to them, and James wanted them to meet in the common room beforehand. He'd returned from taking a shower and had just pulled on his pants when his doorbell rang. He pulled on his shirt and hit the button next to the door. When the door opened, he saw Janan was waiting outside. The translating device he was holding was almost as tall as he was.

"Hey, Janan," he said. "I don't really have time to watch TV with you. I have to get ready for the meeting tonight."

"I know," Janan said, putting down the translating device and sitting in the chair. "I wish I could come too, but I'll be on duty on the bridge. Rauph asked me to give this to you to take to the meeting."

"Bummer," David said.

"Bum ...?" Janan asked, looking perplexed.

"It's an Earth expression," David said. "It means 'that's too bad,' or 'I'm sorry.'"

"Oh, I get it," Janan said, pointing toward his own head. "It doesn't translate well through my implant."

"So, do you actually hear both languages when someone speaks to you?" David asked.

"It's hard to explain," Janan said, thinking it over. "The implant is connected directly to the language center of the brain. The brain isn't hearing two languages, because it's almost instantly receiving translations from the implant."

"Must be a lot easier than lugging around a translating device all of the time."

"Yes," Janan agreed. "It does take a while to get used to. I've heard that sometimes the implant can interfere with normal language learning, and in extreme cases, can actually cause the brain's language center to stop working completely. Imagine not being able to understand what anyone is saying to you ever again."

"Hmm. Think I'll stick with the portable translators."

"Probably a wise course of action," Janan said. "Well, I have to report to the bridge." He stood up.

"I'll let you know if anything interesting happens."

"Don't worry." Janan smiled. "I'll be listening in." He turned and left with a wave back over his shoulder.

David thought about what Janan had said. James had mentioned to them the Rajani could probably listen in to everything said in any of the rooms aboard the ship, but they'd never had any proof they did, until now. David knew he had a tendency to talk to himself at times without realizing it, especially when he was alone. He'd have to be careful about what he said from now on, especially with his dreams getting worse.

◊

James walked into the common room and saw David and Gianni were already there. "Hey," he said. Neither of them answered, and James could tell they had probably been arguing. "Gianni, I asked that all of you be present to listen to what Zazzil has to say. If you start causing problems, you'll have to leave."

"Me?" Gianni asked. "C'mon, Big J."

"Yes, you," James said. "Zazzil has enough influence on the port to cause us a lot of trouble. Let's not give him a reason. I need you to listen. If you have any questions or comments, please keep them to yourself until *after* he's left. Can you do that?"

"Sure, whatever," Gianni said, scowling.

Yvette and Kieren walked into the room, talking about their hair and what a pain it was to do anything with it aboard the ship.

"Ladies," James said, smiling at them. Yvette smiled back. He winked at her. "If you'll all take a seat. Rauph and Bhakat should be coming as well. I don't know what you've heard, but Zazzil is the alien Rauph and I went to see when we first arrived at the space port. Even though I was invisible, he somehow saw me, and that's when all of the trouble started." He looked up as Rauph and Bhakat arrived. Rauph took a seat, while Bhakat stood next to the open door. "Anyway," he continued, "I asked Rauph to tell you about the Talondarians." He sat down next to Yvette at the table.

"Thank you, Officer Dempsey," Rauph said. "Basically, the Talondarians are one of the founding species of the Galactic Alliance. They were a powerful empire for a long, long time, until the emperor and empress's ship disappeared about twenty of your Earth years ago. The new emperor, who was the old emperor's brother, was suspected in the disappearance, but nothing was ever proven." He took a sip of water from a glass in front of him before continuing.

"There are rumors, from what I've read, that there is a pocket of resistance somewhere, including the rightful heir to the throne, a female who was still a young child when her parents disappeared. The Talondarians had many allies within the Alliance, and I suspect one of them were the Cauterfans, like Zazzil." He pointed to a handheld tablet sitting at the other end of the table. "David, could you pass that tablet down here?" David complied, and Rauph punched in the information manually that brought up a picture of a Talondarian. He turned it around to show them.

James could see the alien looked like a human being, but there were differences. Aside from the cosmetic differences, like his haircut and clothing, the Talondarian's eyes were farther apart from each other and larger, and his face was broader as a whole. His ears were smaller and closer to his head. His nose was broad and flat. The one pictured, at least, had a skin tone that was close to Yvette's, a soft brown. Though their appearance must vary, James reasoned, if Zazzil mistook both James and David for members of the species.

"Wow," David said. "No wonder."

"Yes," Rauph replied. "Zazzil mistook James, and later David, for Talondarians. He obviously mistakenly came to the conclusion they were members of the Talondarian underground, and we Rajani were assisting you by giving you Johar Stones."

"Which is the reason they took me from the ship last night," James said.

"And drugged me," Yvette added, scowling.

"Yes," James said. He still wasn't sure what Zazzil wanted to talk about in the upcoming meeting that hadn't already been said. James would have to try to convince the Cauterfan that he and his teammates weren't Talondarians.

Janan's voice came over the ship's communications system. "Zazzil is here, Rauphangelaa."

"Bhakat, will you go let them aboard?" Rauph asked.

Bhakat bowed and pushed a button next to the door and spoke. "Acknowledged, Janan."

"Wait," James said. "I'll go with you." He wanted to make sure Zazzil had honored their agreement. He grabbed the translating collar near the door and followed Bhakat to the main airlock. When Bhakat opened the outer hatch, James saw the Makerfy, as well as about ten other workers, were waiting outside. All of them were armed.

"I said he should come alone," James objected.

The Makerfy smiled. "It is my job to ensure Zazzil is safe. Do not worry, this is only for his trip to and from the ship. He is vulnerable outside of his home." He looked over his shoulder. "Bring him forward."

James watched as two of Zazzil's workers wheeled a large, square, see-through case toward the hatch. He could see Zazzil floating in the gases inside the case, his wings moving slowly up and down. On one side of the case was a small speaker, much like the one in the meeting room. On the other side were two large tanks attached to the case via large tubes.

"Leave your weapon outside of the ship," Bhakat told the Makerfy.

The Makerfy stopped smiling and looked toward Zazzil for confirmation.

"It's fine, Punjor," Zazzil said. The Makerfy handed his gun to the closest worker, who strapped it over its shoulder.

"Could you assist me in pushing him?" Punjor asked Bhakat. "The case is heavier than it looks." They both lined up behind the case and began to push it down the corridor.

James hit the button that closed the outer hatch, and then

the inner door of the airlock, once they had passed through. He followed them down the corridor to the meeting room.

"Rauphangelaa," Zazzil said when they had reached the room. "Thank you again for allowing me to come aboard your ship."

"Thank you for asking permission this time," Rauph replied. James could tell that he was still angry about the breach in protocol. He also saw the others were in various stages of surprise at Zazzil's appearance. He never thought to warn them about it.

"If everyone could take their seats, we'll begin," James said.

"Thank you, James," Zazzil said. "I am here ... to apologize, especially to James and his mate."

James looked over at Yvette. She had a blank look on her face, at first, but then smiled at him, blushing. He smiled back at her and shrugged.

"I know now this was a misunderstanding on my part," Zazzil continued, ignoring the exchange between James and Yvette. "You are not Talondarians, as I had hoped. The sample we took from James proved that, beyond a doubt."

"You took a tissue sample from me without asking?" James asked.

"Yes," Zazzil answered. "The collar you wore stored it for our use. We grew suspicious after Punjor found your shipmate did not speak Talondarian, and then further after our talk last night. I'm afraid I was a little too zealous in trying to assist the Talondarians, and was blinded by my eagerness. You must understand, it has been so long. I'm coming to the end of my life cycle. I fear I will not see the return of our allies, if it ever comes to pass."

"I can forgive you, as long as you destroy any sample of mine you may still have in your possession," James said. "And if you promise not to repeat your actions from last night. No more gifts, either."

"No harm done," Yvette said. "I guess."

"Thank you," Zazzil said. "I'll leave you now. I wish you a profitable journey, wherever it may lead."

"Thank you, Zazzil," Rauph said, appearing mollified by the apology. "Bhakat, can you escort them back to the airlock?" Bhakat bowed again and helped the Makerfy push the case out of the room.

After they had left, Rauph stood and closed the door. "Well," he said. "That was unexpected."

◊

David had been surprised when they'd wheeled the alien into the room. He'd expected another bipedal creature, and instead, Zazzil had turned out to look like some type of manta ray with a head at the front of its body. He recognized the hairy alien pushing the case as the same one he'd talked to aboard the space port. As they'd stopped pushing the case, the alien (Pujor? Poonjob?) had looked over at him and smiled, showing his long white teeth. David had smiled back, reluctantly. The alien kind of gave him the creeps. He studied both aliens as Zazzil talked, fascinated by their appearances. All too soon, the conversation came to an end, and the two aliens had left with Bhakat.

"Well, that was unexpected," Rauph said.

David had to agree, though he hadn't been sure what to expect in the first place. An apology was not what he thought would happen.

"So, we're all fine with this?" Gianni asked. "They come aboard our ship without permission, kidnap one of us, and take a sample from him, and it's 'no harm done' and apology accepted?"

David was surprised Gianni had held his tongue until the

aliens left. He didn't think he could, even after James had asked him to.

"Like I said before," James said, "it was all a misunderstanding. We couldn't afford to make a stink about it. We need to leave the space port as soon as we're able."

"So now what?" David asked.

"Now," James answered, "we proceed as planned. We'll begin training tomorrow morning, and hopefully, we'll be done with any other surprises until we leave Mandaka."

"Okay," David said, standing up. "Then I'll be in my room; you know, in case anyone needs to talk to me." As he walked out of the common room, he hoped Janan had still been listening and taken the hint to come meet him in his room. He wanted to talk about everything that had happened.

And he needed a drink.

Interlude

Steve Montgomery was in a deep funk. He sat at his desk, which had previously belonged to his partner, and stared at the computer screen, not paying attention to the information displayed. He'd put in for a promotion to fill the slot vacated by his missing partner, and instead had been supplanted by some young hotshot from Chicago. It wasn't his fault the Infinity killings were still unsolved. The trail of clues, and bodies, had dried up right around the time James had disappeared.

Hell, the FBI still had their suspicions that James was the killer, which Steve thought was utter bullshit. He'd worked too closely with the man to think he was some psycho killer in his off time. It didn't make any sense. Yet some idiot at the FBI had come to the conclusion it was too much of a coincidence the killings stopped when James disappeared.

James had the knowledge of police procedures and knew how to get around the usual evidence linking him to the crimes. Seven killings and no physical evidence, the FBI said. The cop is either incompetent or complicit. Steve knew James was neither and had told them so. And why would he pick white women to kill? James had never so much as uttered a racial epithet in all of the years they had worked together.

Steve thought his defense of James probably played into them passing him over for promotion as well. He'd been pissed off when he found out the FBI had received a search warrant and ransacked James's apartment looking for any clues linking him to the murders, and without consulting with him. They hadn't found anything, of course, but by then, the damage was done in the press. They were calling James the 'Killer Cop' in some tabloids.

It made Steve's stomach turn; bad enough his partner was missing and might be dead, but now a good man, a good cop, was being crucified for something and had no way of defending himself. The fact that four other people in his building were missing never made it to the national news highlights, only appearing toward the end of the local paper's article about James's disappearance, with a quote from the captain stating they had no connection to James.

The only real hue and cry had come from the senator whose daughter was missing, but because the police could find no link between James and the Manidoo woman, they were treating their disappearances, as of now, as isolated incidents. In fact, there seemed to be no connection between any of the missing people from the apartment complex. The senator was pressuring some other poor badge, so Steve didn't have to worry about that case, at least.

It was a damn peculiar situation all around. Even worse was the feeling he couldn't be one hundred percent sure about James. It would be horrible if it turned out to be true, that James was a killer, and all this time, he'd been smiling in Steve's face and laughing at him behind his back. All Steve could do was drown his sorrows in a bottle, which was what he planned to do, again, as soon as his shift ended.

Chapter 12

Ries was sitting in his office aboard the space port when his assistant walked in, holding a tablet in front of her as if it were a shield.

"Commander?" Tmal asked, clearing her throat gently. "There's a group of merchants waiting in the outer office."

"What do they want?" He rubbed his eyes with one hand while straightening up objects on his desk with the other three. The investigation was going poorly. He was out of leads, and they had no one in custody.

"They want to talk to you about the stop-leave," Tmal answered.

"Blast," Ries muttered. "Fine, send them in." He sat up straighter in his chair and folded his bottom appendages. Appearances were important in his job.

Tmal led a group of eight into his office. Ries knew them to be the leading merchants aboard the port. If they had come together, he knew he'd run out of time.

"Commander Van," the nearest said. He was a Mandakan; cousin to the king and therefore considered royalty. "How is your investigation progressing?"

"I'm afraid the investigation has come to an end," Ries answered. He would have to make the declaration before being forced to do it by these merchants. He couldn't be seen as being forced to do anything. The illusion of power was still power. "The stop-leave is to be lifted immediately."

"Wonderful," the Mandakan said. "Because we've been losing revenue for a week now, without new customers flowing into the casinos, as you are aware, I'm sure."

"What I am aware of," Ries replied, "is my officers have received almost no cooperation from any of you in regards to our investigation. It would have lasted only two days if we'd been able to wrap up this case quickly. So don't complain to me about lost revenue. The stop-leave has been lifted. The announcement will be made soon, followed by a ship-by-ship exit interview. If that is acceptable to you, then our meeting is over."

The Mandakan looked at the others a moment. "It is acceptable, of course."

"Good," Ries said, rising from his chair. "My assistant will show you out. Have a good day."

After they had left, Tmal came back into his office. "I didn't know you had finished the investigation."

"I have now," he answered tersely. "Draft up the announcement, and I'll have a look at it."

She turned to comply with his order, but he stopped her. "Wait. First, get me the *Interceptor* on the com. I'm leaving."

◊

Bhakat had made up his mind already, but he wanted to talk to Rauphangelaa. He calmed his nerves a moment, and then pushed the intercom button next to the door to Rauphangelaa's quarters.

"Yes?" came Rauphangelaa's voice a moment later.

"Master," Bhakat said, "may I speak to you a moment?"

The door to Rauphangelaa's chambers opened.

"Come in, Bhakat," Rauphangelaa said. It was relatively

early in the morning, and Rauphangelaa was dressed in his sleeping clothes. His long white hair was not yet placed in the Ralik, the symbol of a Rajani Elder and Priest of the Kha.

Bhakat had finished his shift aboard the bridge, and wanted to talk to Rauphangelaa in his room, where they could speak privately, instead of on the bridge when Rauphangelaa reported for his own shift.

"Everything is well?" Rauphangelaa asked.

"Yes," Bhakat said. "I pray your rest was peaceful."

"And yours," Rauphangelaa replied.

Bhakat had practiced what he was going to say, but now that he was there, he wasn't sure where to begin. He sat down as Rauphangelaa busied himself getting dressed and braiding his long hair.

"Master," Bhakat began, hesitantly. "I've decided when the Humans begin training this morning, I will train with them."

"What!" Rauphangelaa asked, his fingers stopping and his eyes trained on Bhakat. "But the Kha ..."

"The Kha will not help win this fight," Bhakat interrupted, standing up. "The only way we can save Rajan is if we fight. All of us."

Rauphangelaa sat down now on his bed, his hair forgotten. "There is a reason we brought the Humans along, Bhakat. It was so we wouldn't have to abandon our beliefs. Would you still do so now? Would you abandon your studies and become as we once were—as the Krahn are now?"

Bhakat walked to the door before stopping. "If it means saving our species, I would make any sacrifice. Even if it means forsaking the Kha forever, I will do what I can to fight the Krahn. We cannot hide while the Humans free us from those monsters. I see that now." He turned away from his Master. "I'm sorry," he said quietly and left without looking back.

◊

The five members of the team, along with Bhakat, were gathered in the brand new training room aboard the *Tukuli*. James and Bhakat had agreed that all of the members of the team, including James, would stay away from the cargo hold while Zazzil's workers constructed the training room. That way they wouldn't know what to expect on the first day, and so they were all seeing it for the first time. The room was a large squared-off area in the cargo hold. Zazzil's workers had built it with reinforced steel beams that went from floor to ceiling and held up the double-thick steel reinforced walls. The inside of the walls were deeply padded in the event of any collisions that might occur during the training exercises.

The floor of the training room was also reinforced and slightly padded, but not enough to throw off their footing. The ceiling was fifteen feet high and had numerous trap doors within it. After looking at the room more carefully, he could see there were panels in the walls and floor as well.

Bhakat was wearing the portable translator around his neck. "I've programmed the ship's computer to prepare a low-level training program," he began. "It's not set on lethal force, but if you make a mistake,"—he paused to smile at Gianni—"it will hurt." Bhakat looked back to the rest of them. "It's hoped in this way you'll be able to more thoroughly explore your powers. Know this also, Humans: what I do here goes against all I've learned since Pledging with Rauphangelaa. My actions are not violent in and of themselves, yet they may lead to violence against others."

Kieren held up her hand. "Wait for a moment, Bhakat."

"Yes?" he said, looking at her, a confused expression on his face.

Kieren pointed to the translator. "Could you shut off the translator collar?"

He reached up to his neck and clicked it off.

"Okay, now talk to me," Kieren told him.

"What would you have me say?" Bhakat said, looking at her quizzically.

"That's all I needed to hear," Kieren said in perfect Talondarian Standard, a wide smile on her face. Even her accent matched his slightly Rajani-accented Standard.

"How ... how can this be?" Bhakat asked her, dumbfounded.

Kieren laughed, throwing her hands up as her energy field formed around her. She began to slowly rise off of the floor. "Ha-ha! I can understand him! I can understand what he's saying!"

"That's great," Gianni said, with an edge of envy to his voice. "She's Wonder Woman."

"More like Supergirl," David told him, earnestly. "Wonder Woman can't fly. Can she?"

Yvette rolled her eyes, her arms crossed before her.

Kieren, still smiling, was floating with her arms out to her sides, four feet off the floor. She faced Bhakat, who had his arms crossed. "I kept hearing a weird echo when he talked. I couldn't put my finger on why."

"An interesting development," Bhakat said. "If you'll excuse me, I'll leave the room now as you train." He bowed slightly and left, closing the door behind him.

James smiled and motioned toward Gianni with a come-here signal. "That's great, Kieren," James told her. "That talent should come in handy. Why don't you step outside and tell Bhakat that we're ready for the initial training program."

After Kieren had left the room, James turned to Gianni. "Listen, man. Your shit is getting old real fast. That girl is going to need our support if she's going to survive this. You need to cut the tough-guy macho bullshit right now. Got it?"

Gianni pointed toward the closed door to the training

room. "That girl is tougher than she looks, and I'm sure these 'crayons' aren't going to be a support group for us, either."

"My point exactly," James replied, still staring into the other man's eyes, hoping there was some depth to them. The man's answer suggested there was, but he wasn't going to let James know it easily.

Gianni smiled again, his arms crossed over his chest. "Glad we see eye to eye, Big J."

James and Gianni were still eyeing each other when Kieren stepped back into the room. "Um, James? Bhakat said you were to give the signal when you're ready. Hold up your hand. He's watching from outside the room."

"Thanks, Kieren," he told her, and then spoke louder to everyone. "Okay, people, get ready." He held up his hand. "Now,"

As James spoke, panels opened in the walls, and large gun-like weapons pointed out of them and began firing laser beams. Panels opened in the ceiling, and small flying robots with lasers descended out of them. Panels opened in the floor, and small Humanoid robots come out firing lasers as well.

David was hit in the side of the head by a laser beam and fell to his knees. "Holy ... ung!" He was hit again in the back by a gun to his left.

Kieren rose into the air near the ceiling and was attacked by four of the flying robots. James powered up and quickly disappeared.

Yvette turned and gave one of the Humanoid robots a kick to the head, with no effect. Suddenly, she powered up. She was surrounded by an energy field, much like James's, except hers was the dull yellow color of sulfur. "Get away from me!" she yelled as she pulled back her fist, and it formed into a sharply pointed spear. She punched the robot through the head, and then looked at her arm, which was still in the shape of a spear. "Whoa!"

Gianni was hit in the shoulder by a laser beam. "Ouch! Damn, man." He powered up, his energy field a ruby crystal color, and a wall of red energy formed in front of him, deflecting any laser beams directed his way. The robot continued coming toward him as he stood behind the wall of energy. "Well, great, and me without a gun," he said aloud.

He pointed his finger jokingly at the robot. He was surprised when a bolt of the same ruby energy fired from his hand and passed through the force field, knocking the robot off its feet. He pulled his arm back and clenched his fist. "All right!" He didn't see the robot coming up behind him. The machine was within five feet of him when its head flew off, hitting the wall. Gianni turned to see James appear. They looked at each other and smiled.

"You owe me one, Slick," James told him.

A blue blur went past them. It was David, running. He too was encased in an energy field, though his was the color of sapphire. He ran back to stand beside them. "Can you believe this? I haven't been able to run since college."

They all heard Kieren yell for help. They turned to see she was surrounded by four of the flying robots. One shot her point-blank in the chest. The energy field around her disappeared, and she fell, screaming.

Gianni reached out toward where she was falling. "Kieren!" He shot with both of his hands, hitting and destroying two of the robots, his energy bolts now stronger. Yvette formed a spear with her arm and extended it through another robot. James ran and jumped, grabbing the last robot and crushing it with his hands.

David ran and caught Kieren before she hit the ground. "I got ya," he said, breathlessly.

Outside of the training room, Bhakat and Janan were standing in the cargo hold and watching the training on a handheld tablet. "This cannot be," Bhakat began. "From what Rauphangelaa has told me, the stones have never produced these types of powers in the Rajani."

"The stones have never been implanted in these Humans before," Janan replied. "They're truly a remarkable species."

"Yes," Bhakat agreed. "One the Kha would condemn outright, I'm afraid. I need to tell Rauphangelaa about this."

"Why, Bhakat?" Janan said, smiling. His smile quickly disappeared. "What choice do we have, now?" he said softly, turning his attention back to the training room. "Besides, it's not like we're going to take the stones back from them."

Inside the training room, Gianni was kneeling down next to Kieren, who was sitting on the floor. He was holding out his hand for her. "Are you all right?"

"If you laugh at me," she told him, "I'll deck you." She grabbed his hand and pulled herself up.

James crossed his hands before him, and let his energy field disappear. "That was certainly a disaster. We have a lot of work to do. Bhakat!" As he looked around, he saw all of the robots were wrecked, as were some of the guns coming out of the walls.

The door to the training area opened, and Bhakat and Janan entered, looking at the destruction around them. "Excellent first training session," Bhakat said. "I suggest a slower approach from now on."

Gianni looked at Kieren. "No, really?" She didn't smile.

So it went that day and the next, although they found that the robots were a lost cause—they were wrecked beyond repair. Each day was a challenge, but they were slowly getting used to their new abilities. The days were filled with honing their skills. James and Kieren quickly taught the other three how to make their heads visible so that everyone could see each other's faces. Their teamwork improved greatly once they could take visual cues from facial expressions. It seemed a simple fix, but none of them had realized how much they relied on it.

Bhakat surprised them by joining them on the second day. He began learning self-defense from Yvette, lifting weights with James, though on a much smaller scale, and even running with David. James found he could lift a great deal of weight without trying—in fact, they had run out of things for him to lift already. It scared the hell out of him. The others had augmented strength from the stones as well, but none of them near the level of his.

◊

Rauph knew it was only a matter of time. The ASPs would be contacting the *Tukuli* at any moment, and he had to decide what the best course of action would be when they did. He hoped all they would do was ask him some general questions and let them leave, but in the case they wanted to board the *Tukuli* and search it, he wasn't sure what to do. He'd imagined some crazy scenarios already: trying to outrun them, having the Humans destroy the ASP ship with their newfound powers, leaving the Humans to their own fate aboard the space port so they couldn't implicate the *Tukuli* and its crew. He knew none of them would work. So he sat on the bridge and waited as patiently as he could. After a few days, there finally came a hail from the ASP ship, as Rauph was about to leave the bridge and go to his quarters for his evening meal.

"This is the Galactic Alliance Society for Peace ship *Interceptor* to the crew of the Talondarian alpha class ship, nomenclature *Tukuli*. Please respond. Repeat, this is the *Interceptor*, please respond."

Janan turned to look at him from his seat before the viewscreen, lifting his brows in question as to what he should do.

Rauph sighed and pushed a button next to his captain's chair. "This is the *Tukuli,* responding as ordered," he said.

"To whom am I speaking?" came the voice from the ASP ship.

"This is Rauphangelaa, owner of the *Tukuli.* You should be able to verify. To whom am I speaking, please?" he asked.

"Verified ownership," the voice replied. "This is Commander Ries an na Van, Chief Protector of Sector Seven, Subsector Two. What is your business at the Mandakan Space Port?"

"Repairs to my ship and supplies," Rauph replied.

There was a long pause, and Rauph suspected the commander was pulling up the space port's records to see if there were any inconsistencies with the story Rauph had told him. He could feel sweat breaking out on his brow and under his arms, but he knew Zazzil had been in business a long time, and the only way they wouldn't check out okay would be if Zazzil didn't want them to. He also knew the ASPs had the sensor ability to perform a full scan of the *Tukuli;* but they could not, by law, unless they had a reason. None of his reasoning made him feel any better about the current situation.

"*Tukuli,* you are cleared to depart Mandakan Space Port," came the voice over the communication system. "Please proceed on your stated course."

Rauph and Janan both slumped in their chairs in relief.

"Acknowledged," Rauph said, and then motioned for Janan to turn off the subspace communicator. "Janan, we leave immediately. I want us in nullspace as soon as possible." He stood up, feeling wobbly from the stress. "I'll inform the others." He walked out of the room and down the corridor toward the crew quarters. All of the Humans were located in their common room.

They really are a more gregarious species than the Rajani, Rauph thought. *More like the Jirina.* The Rajani didn't tend to come together often in large groups. The Elders only met when a situation arose that needed input from all of them; they preferred to tend to their own affairs most of the time, without interference from their peers. They ran their households and didn't care about others unless a conflict arose. Rauph considered this may have been why he and Bhakat had been able to get away when the Krahn first attacked. If the Rajani had all been in one place, they may have all been captured or killed.

Rauph could overhear the loud Human named Moretti speaking.

"... can't tell me you think anyone is going to beat the Yankees this year," he was saying.

"Tigers might surprise this year, that's all I'm saying," came the voice of the one called Morris.

Rauph had no idea what they were talking about, but then, he still didn't understand a great deal about the Human culture. The conversation stopped when he stepped through the doorway of the room. He was happy to see the portable translator Morris had procured on the space port was hanging from a hook on the wall near the doorway. He had asked James to keep the device close to him, in case Rauph needed to talk to him. He was tired of lugging around the larger, outdated device. He hadn't thought about finding the collar in his haste to seek out the Humans and was glad he wouldn't have to. He slipped the translator around his neck and turned it on.

"I have good news," he said to Officer Dempsey, who had

been sitting on a chair opposite the Manidoo woman. "We've finally been cleared to leave by the ASPs."

"Great," Dempsey replied. "When do we leave?"

"Immediately," Rauph said. "I've already instructed Janan to undock and prepare for nullspace."

Janan's voice came on over the ship's communication system. "Rauph, we have a problem up here. I need you on the bridge."

In his haste to return to the bridge, Rauph didn't remove the portable translator from around his neck. He hurried down the corridor to the bridge, where he saw the *Tukuli* had left the docking station and was now being confronted by the large ASP ship. The commander's voice was coming over the speaker on the bridge.

"*Tukuli*, I repeat, this is Commander Ries an na Van of the Galactic Alliance ship Interceptor. You are in violation of Alliance Code T879."

Rauph knew the code. It stated all ships with Rajani crews or owners must declare themselves when confronted by GA ships. He heard the ASP commander continue.

"Failure to declare yourselves has caused an automatic full scan of your ship," the commander's voice said.

Rauph motioned to Janan to keep prepping the ship for nullspace travel. He needed to set in the coordinates for Rajan. Rauph pushed the communication button next to his chair. "*Interceptor,* this is the *Tukuli*. What is the meaning of this? You said we were cleared for departure. Haven't you kept us here long enough?"

"*Tukuli*," the commander's voice came back, "we ran your ship through the GA mainframe and discovered you're a Rajani vessel. This was not logged on your docking manifest. Neither were the seven unknown occupants aboard your ship in addition to your two registered crew members. Please power down your engines and prepare to be boarded."

Rauph jumped when Dempsey appeared at his side as he turned off the collar. "What are they saying?" the Human asked.

Rauph hoped Dempsey had not heard the commander's voice being translated through the portable translator around his neck. He had enough problems to deal with at the moment. "We failed to declare ourselves as Rajani when we docked," he told the Human.

"And that's a crime?" Dempsey asked.

"Yes, it is," Rauph said. "We told you, we're not a very well-liked species within the Alliance."

"Apparently not. So what do we do?"

"The *Tukuli* is not equipped with weapons. There's nothing we can do, except let them board or try to run." He watched as the Human thought for a moment, rubbing his hand along the growth of hair along his jaw.

"Maybe there is another alternative," Dempsey finally said. "Keep stalling them and preparing to leave," the Human told him. He turned and left the bridge.

◊

James knew what he was thinking sounded insane. Hell, he knew it was outright crazy, but it might be the only way they could avoid rotting in some intergalactic prison for the rest of their lives. He ran down the corridor to where the rest of his team was still waiting.

"Yvette, Gianni, come with me," he said when he got there. "Kieren and David stay here for now, please." He turned and ran for the main airlock. Once he arrived, he opened the inner door and stepped inside.

"What's happening?" Yvette asked as she and Gianni caught up to him.

"Step inside and I'll tell you," James replied. The two

others stepped through the doorway, and James pushed the button to close the inner door. "The ASPs are threatening to board the ship, and we can't afford to let that happen," he said. "I need you guys to help us get away." He looked at the controls to the outer hatch. He'd seen Rauph open the hatch once before, but couldn't remember at first which button he had pushed.

"You're turning into a regular criminal mastermind," Yvette said, smiling.

"Ha-ha." James rolled his eyes. He finally remembered the correct button. "All right, I want you guys to power up." All three of them powered up, and James continued. "When I open this door, Gianni, I want you to put up a force shield across the doorway. I'm going to hold on to the two of you, and then I want you to drop the shield."

"What?" Yvette asked.

"Listen," James said, "when he drops the shield, I want you to send the largest energy spike you can toward their ship. I think they should have their force field down because they're not expecting an attack from an unarmed ship. Now hopefully you can damage one of their engines or something, but even if you can't, the distraction should buy us enough time to get out of here."

He turned to Gianni. "In case they decide to fire back at us, I want you to put up a shield between us and them as soon as she pulls back. Do you both understand? We need to make this as quick as possible because I don't know how well our energy suits will protect us in space. I'm hoping they'll at least protect us from the cold." James strapped an arm through the cargo webbing hanging to one side of the outer hatch and grabbed both of the others around the waist. As he did so, each of their energy fields flared brightly as they touched one another.

"Guess that means I should push the button too," Gianni said.

"Uh, yeah," James said, looking up from where he was bent over, holding onto them. "Didn't think about that."

"Right," Gianni said. "Here we go." As he said this, a red force field appeared before the outer hatch. Gianni pushed the button, and the door slid aside. "Ready?" he asked, and a second later the force field disappeared, and the air was quickly sucked out of the small room.

James held on, feeling the pull from the vacuum of space, but not even close to straining to hold on to the others. He looked up to see Yvette's arms pointing out and lances of energy extending from them. He could see the brightly striped ASP ship was still a couple of hundred yards away. Its coloring made it seem like a poisonous fish, its stripes meant as a warning to others, which James supposed was close to the truth. Behind the ship, the planet Mandaka was lit up in orange and reds from the great yellow sun at the center of its system.

"I don't know if I can reach them," Yvette said, her voice echoing the strain she was under.

"Pull back," James said, seeing she wasn't going to come close. He watched as the lances retreated quickly back into her arms. "Okay, Plan B. Gianni, shoot the damn thing. But let me get out of the way first." James let go of the other two and stepped away from the door to give Gianni a clean shot.

"Okay, Big J," Gianni said, pointing both of his hands at the other ship and letting loose with a volley of energy shots. They all watched as the beams struck the ASP ship close to one of its engines. Small explosions erupted from the engine, though they could hear nothing. The fires were quickly extinguished by the vacuum of space, but they could also see the engine was no longer functioning.

"That did it, I think," James yelled, pointing at the controls. "Close the hatch, Yvette."

Yvette stood there a moment before finally nodding her head in understanding. She reached over and pushed the button, and the hatch slid closed.

James pushed the button to open the inner door. He dropped his energy field and turned to the others. "Good job, you two. Gianni, I need you to do one last thing."

"What now?" Gianni said, as both he and Yvette dropped their own energy fields.

"That ship is going to fire on us any second now," James said. "I need you to put up a shield between us, if you can, until we're far enough out of their range."

"If I can?" Gianni said, rolling his eyes.

"Just try, Hotshot," James replied, and smiled.

Gianni closed his eyes and stood still, his face scrunched up in concentration. James and Yvette turned and ran down the corridor.

"Is he doing it?" Yvette asked, following James down the corridor toward the bridge.

"We haven't been blown up yet, so that's a positive sign," James replied, smiling at her. He was happy they were finally seeing some action instead of waiting around on the ship.

When they reached the bridge, Rauph and Janan were still sitting in their chairs. Rauph stood up quickly and turned on the translation collar. "What did you do!" he demanded.

"Don't worry about it," James said. "We need to leave. Now."

Janan looked askance at Rauph, who stared at James a moment longer and then nodded. The Sekani quickly punched a variety of buttons and smiled at his monitor. "*Tukuli* has achieved full speed. We're in nullspace in five, four, three, two ... nullspace achieved." He sat back and sighed, smiling.

"We need to speak right now," Rauph said. "Alone." He looked at Yvette.

"It's okay," James said, looking at her. "Why don't you go tell Gianni to drop the force shield if he hasn't already."

"No problem." Yvette smiled at him and then walked down the corridor.

"Follow me," Rauph said, walking off the bridge without looking back to make sure James was following.

James looked over at Janan, and the little alien smiled and shrugged. James walked out into the corridor and saw that Rauph had entered the small meeting room they had been using since the trip began. He followed, and Rauph closed the door before turning to face him.

"What did you do?" Rauph asked again, vehemently.

"I bought us some time," James replied, sitting down on a chair. He was suddenly feeling tired and hungry—a side effect he'd noticed after each training session as well. "We partially disabled their ship so they couldn't follow us."

"Partially ...?" Rauph said, and stopped, a confused look on his face. "How?"

"Gianni shot out one of their engines," James answered, smiling sheepishly. He realized how it sounded.

Rauph sat down on the nearest chair and put a hand over his eyes. "Please tell me we did not fire on an ASP warship," he said softly.

"It was the only thing we could do," James said. "We had no alternative." He felt like adding 'they started it,' but thought better of it. Rauph probably wouldn't get the joke.

Rauph put his hand down. He looked miserable. "I suppose not. The ASPs have long memories, and I fear we haven't heard the last of this. We cannot worry about future repercussions now. The important thing is, we're finally on our way to Rajan."

"And we learned Gianni can be a team player," James said. "When he wants to be, at least. If not for him, we'd still be back at the space port with interstellar cops boarding your ship and placing all of us under arrest."

"Yes, of course," Rauph said, standing. "We shall meet in the morning, all of us, to speak more about this. But for now, I'm afraid I've had about as much excitement as I can take for the night."

"Good night," James said.

"And to you, Officer Dempsey," Rauph replied. He turned off the translator collar, placed it on the table, and left the room.

James smiled. It would be a while before he could go to sleep. He had too much adrenaline in his system at the moment. After grabbing the translator, he headed back to the common room to eat and talk to the others about what had happened. It was a good first start, but obviously, they needed to train better when it came to working together.

Interlude

Tomas had spent too much time in the hospital for his own liking, but now that it was actually time for him to leave, he was feeling apprehensive. His father's people still hadn't determined Gianni's whereabouts, even after more than two months had passed.

The strange thing was, there wasn't even a rumor on the streets as to what could have happened to his cousin. He had vanished without a trace. He was either facing some serious heat from the Feds and needed to take an extended leave of absence while things sorted themselves out, or he was dead – probably from the same people who jumped Tomas. He was itching to find out who they had been.

The Feds, however, acted like they didn't know what was going on. Tomas had learned his father's contacts within the agency didn't know about any secret deal Gianni had cut or a witness relocation program for his cousin, either.

Which meant the alternative; Gianni's body would be found in a landfill somewhere, or washed up on shore, or they wouldn't find it at all. Tomas planned to return to New York as soon as he could. He'd always liked his Aunt Christina. He thought he should be the one to break the bad news to her that Gianni might not be coming back.

Chapter 13

Bhakat was at the wheel of the transport vehicle as he and Rauphangelaa drove back from central Melaanse. Before that, they had visited Rauphangelaa's farm. It had been a productive day, as Rauphangelaa had talked to his farmhands, letting them know what the Elders had decided must be planted for that growing season.

Bhakat looked over at his Master, seeing that Rauphangelaa had fallen asleep in his seat. He'd walked over the entire breadth of the farm, determining what would be planted where, and inspecting the state of various fruit trees in the large orchard adjacent to it. Bhakat could tell it was something he loved to do, and looked forward to doing every year. Now it was growing late, and it would be dark before they arrived at Rauphangelaa's estate to the north of the city.

Suddenly, Bhakat saw a string of black dots descending from the darkening sky. He couldn't see them clearly, but he knew what they were: ships. Who would be coming to Rajan in such large numbers? He turned around in his seat and saw more dots appear in the sky above Melaanse. Then his heart sank as he saw the ships begin to fire at the ground below.

"Rauphangelaa!" he shouted. "Wake up! Rauphangelaa!"

His Master finally stirred, opening his eyes and sitting up

straight in his seat. "Bhakat, what is it?" he asked, still bleary-eyed from sleep.

"Melaanse is under attack. Look!" Bhakat said, pointing with one hand toward the windshield of the transport vehicle.

"What?" Rauphangelaa asked, wide awake now. He looked in the direction Bhakat was pointing. "Who are they? Can you tell?"

"No," Bhakat answered. He steadily began applying pressure to the accelerator of the vehicle, but it was a simple hydrogen-fueled transport, and its top speed wasn't fast, compared to some of the other Elders' vehicles. Rauphangelaa was not one for using the most modern technology.

"Head for the estate," Rauphangelaa said. "They must be warned."

Bhakat nodded, hoping they weren't already too late. They both watched as more ships appeared in the sky, firing at the city. They could see black smoke columns rising from various sections as it began to burn. They finally made it to the estate, but knew by then nothing could be done. Many of the buildings were in flames by that point. They could see some smoldering bodies lying on the ground around the engulfed structures.

"No," Rauphangelaa said softly. "No, no, NO!" he said, his voice growing louder every time he said it.

"Rauphangelaa, we must escape," Bhakat urged, dodging past the body of a Sekani with a large hole in his chest. Bhakat could see that it was Nebreni'kela, Rauphangelaa's chief estate gardener.

Rauphangelaa broke out of the state of shock he'd been in. "Yes," he said. "Head for the *Tukuli*. We have to escape. Find help, somewhere."

Bhakat saw a body lying in the path of the transport. It

was a Sekani male partially covered in rubble.

"Why are you stopping?" Rauphangelaa asked, wide-eyed, as Bhakat stopped the vehicle.

"It's Janan'kela," Bhakat replied, opening his door.

"Leave him; he's dead," Rauphangelaa said, grabbing his arm. "We must escape."

"I have to make sure," Bhakat insisted, looking down at Rauphangelaa's hand on his arm. His Master let go, reluctantly. Bhakat got out of the transport and ran the short distance to his friend's body. He could see the blood streaming down the Sekani's face from a head wound. As Bhakat knelt next to him, he could see his friend was breathing. Just unconscious, he thought. He hoisted the little Sekani in his arms and ran back to the transport. He laid Janan'kela gently down in the back of the vehicle and returned to the driver's seat. He pressed on the accelerator and turned in the direction of the *Tukuli,* praying they would find it in one piece. It was not easily seen from the air, or so he hoped.

"Bhakat, are you well?" Janan asked from the back seat.

Wait, Bhakat thought. *Janan was unconscious until after we flew through the blockade of Krahn ships above Rajan. He didn't wake up until the next day.*

"Bhakat?" Janan asked again.

Bhakat opened his eyes. He'd dozed off, lost in his memories of the day they'd been attacked. Janan was standing next to his chair, smiling at him. He'd entered Bhakat's room without Bhakat even knowing he was there.

Looking at his friend, he was suddenly happy he'd gone against his Master's orders and saved him. "Yes," he told the Sekani pilot. "Yes, I'm well."

"Good, because it's time for your shift," Janan said. "You'd better get to the bridge. Good night," he said as he left the room.

"Good night," Bhakat said, standing up and stretching. He smiled at his friend as the Sekani walked away, happy he was alive.

◊

The next morning, the team was training once again, as it had been every day since that first disastrous session almost three weeks before. Yvette, with a staff of yellow power, was trying to get past Gianni's force field; he was yawning, his hand to his mouth, feigning boredom. David was a blur, running around the perimeter of the group. James was lifting heavy machinery, and Kieren was flying through hoops in an obstacle course.

James found the hardest thing about having super strength was to *not* destroy the things he was lifting. Most of the training sessions he spent picking things up and putting them back down in an effort to not demolish them by grasping too hard or smashing them into the ground. It was harder than it looked. At this point in his training, he was afraid of what would happen if he ever had to catch a teammate or pick up an important piece of heavy technology without completely destroying it.

The most difficult part of their training, though, appeared to be concentration. It took a while to use their powers without concentrating on them. Kieren had the most difficult time; her energy field would disappear if she was too distracted. James had done his best to come up with drills to reinforce their abilities to keep their fields up without much thought. It was sort of like building muscle memory.

Bhakat and Janan were in the corner of the training room, watching. Bhakat had begun talking to James about fighting strategy and working out himself, but when the Humans were in full training, he tended to stay back so as not to be in their way.

"Impressive," Janan said, smiling.

"Most," Bhakat replied drily.

Gianni walked up to Bhakat and Janan, smiling. "Hey Chewy and Yoda, watch this next trick." He looked at the running blur of David, concentrating. A foot-high hurdle of red energy appeared in David's path. David tripped and flew toward the wall, screaming. His energy field disappeared.

Yvette quickly formed a slide with her arms that whisked him away from the wall. "I've got you." She'd learned from training that she could form all sorts of shapes with her powers, not only lances of energy. She'd been practicing with other parts of her body as well. She dropped David straight in front of Gianni, who was bent over laughing.

David pushed him. "You stupid jerk! I could've been killed!"

Gianni put up a shield between them. "But you weren't. C'mon, it was good for you. Good training."

"Put down your shield and we'll see how good my training has been," David said, pounding on the red energy shield between them.

Janan came between them. "Come, Da-v-vid," the small alien said. Do not let him ... get to you."

"You speak English?" David asked, incredulous. In all of the times they had spoken together in David's room at night, Janan had never even attempted to speak English to him.

"A small amount," Janan replied. "We had been in orbit a short while before you were ... contacted. I had a head start learning the language, but did not want to speak it until I was better. English is the language of the Central Authority on your planet, is it not?" Janan asked him.

Kieren was standing next to Bhakat. "Central Authority? Of what?"

"The U.S.," Yvette said, frowning. "He means the U.S."

Bhakat was nodding in agreement. "That's correct," he said in Talondarian Standard. He had been working out earlier, and wasn't wearing the portable translating device.

Gianni had his thumb cocked in Bhakat's direction. "What'd he say?"

"He said that James is right," Kieren told them.

"Couldn't he nod his ugly head or something?" Gianni said with a sneer.

"Why don't you lay off, Gianni?" David asked, wearily.

"He is only ... being a jerk," Janan said. "It is clear."

Gianni grabbed his crotch. He was leering at the alien. "What did you say to me? I got your 'jerk' right here."

James had his hand over his eyes; the hopelessness he felt about ever getting these people ready was beginning to grow. "I think that's enough training for today."

◊

Dinner that night was like something out of an old sci-fi movie. Except for the fact the alien was sitting down to dinner with them, instead of attempting to have them for dinner. The team and Janan were seated around a large, round table they had moved to the common room. Rauph was in his room for the night, and Bhakat was on duty aboard the bridge. There was food, though their supply from Earth had run out, so it was mostly from the supplies they'd acquired from Zazzil on the space port, along with bottles of water and a darker liquid.

Janan was smiling and talking to Yvette. She took a sip of the dark liquid from her glass, which Janan had poured for her. She made a face, as if it was the worst thing she'd ever tasted, which it might have been. "Oh, this stuff is awful!"

Janan and David laughed, remembering David's first impression of the strong, heady liquid called fernta.

Gianni and Kieren, who were sitting side by side, were

doing their best to ignore each other.

James stood and addressed the group.

"I know we've had our problems on this trip. Throwing together a group this diverse would pose problems for anyone, let alone people kidnapped by aliens. No offense, Janan. The hardest part of our journey is still in front of us. We've all made great strides in learning how to use our individual powers, and in integrating our talents into a team. I want to say that I'm proud of all of you-even Gianni." He waited as most of them at least acknowledged that he was joking before continuing.

"All kidding aside, though," he said, growing more serious, "when we get to Rajan, I want all of you to remember something: we're here to help them, but my first priority is your well-being. It's still not too late to change your minds. There are escape pods on this ship stocked with enough supplies to last several months. You could always be left on the nearest inhabitable planet, and we'll pick you up on the way home."

David waved away the suggestion. "Robinson Crusoe in space? No, thanks."

"I'm afraid it's the only option left to us at this point," James continued. "Any takers?" He paused a moment before he continued. "Didn't think there would be, but I had to ask one last time. I have faith in all of you and your ability to get the job done. We all know what needs to happen. Rauph tells me we have only a couple of days until we come out of ..."

"Nullspace," Kieren interjected.

"Nullspace," James said. "Thank you."

Kieren stuck her tongue out at Gianni.

"We're sitting ducks until we can get to the planet's surface," James continued, not noticing the interaction going on between the two. "Once we do, we contact any resistance and assess the situation from there. Any questions?”

“What if there isn’t any resistance?” Yvette asked.

“Why wouldn’t there be?” David asked back.

“That’s the reason we’re here, isn’t it?” Yvette answered. “This ‘Kha’ of theirs forbids them from fighting.”

“It is true,” Janan said. “Most Rajani males are devout in their faith.”

“Which means they won’t resist,” Kieren said. “Or at least won’t fight, right?”

“Wonderful,” Gianni said, rolling his eyes. “So what do we do, sit around and sing Kumbaya with the Krahn?”

James’s face was deadly serious. “No, I’m afraid not. Not this time. This is going to be war, people. From this point on, the gloves are off. That means no more showboating in training, Gianni.”

Gianni shrugged in reply. David face said he’d believe it when he saw it.

“With that, I wish you goodnight,” James said. “We all need our rest, so I suggest you do your best to get some.”

◊

On the bridge of the ship, Rauph was seated, with Bhakat in his customary spot, standing behind his Master. Rauph had found that he was unable to sleep, and he was also curious about what the Humans would talk about at their meal. He’d been invited, but had declined. They were both listening to a portable handheld tablet. James’s voice came from the tablet, which was tuned to the communication system for that particular room. “... the gloves are off.”

“Master,” Bhakat began, almost hesitantly, “They must be told.”

Rauph turned to Bhakat. “Must they?” he asked, rhetorically. “There will be much anger in them.” He turned off the tablet and set it down on the small table next to his chair. "They may wish to return to their home planet. Can we risk that, all for the lives of so few?"

Bhakat gently placed his hand on Rauph's shoulder. "There is only one way to tell. They must see it was necessary."

"Ah, my Pledge." Rauph smiled. "Always so sure. I'm afraid this time, I cannot share the sentiment. They place as much importance on a Human life as we do on our own." Rauph stood up. "But I believe you're right. They must be told, eventually. I'm afraid tonight, though, I am too tired to deal with it. Good night, Bhakat."

"Good night, Master," Bhakat said, sitting down in the seat his Master had relinquished.

◊

A few days later, James and Yvette returned to his room from another dinner with the others in the common room. It had become a routine in the weeks since they had left the space port. The group would work out separately in the morning; some of them running, others lifting weights or performing aerobics in the training room. After breakfast they would meet in the training room and talk about strategy and the best ways to use their powers. Mostly it was a brainstorming session. After that, they would practice with their powers until lunch. They would return from lunch and practice using their powers together. After a few hours, they would break for the night.

They had all started having dinner together early on in their trip, and had continued the tradition, even after spending so much time together for training during the day. After dinner, they would stay in the common room or return to their own quarters for the night. Sometimes Yvette or James would feel like being alone, and they'd say their good nights and go back to their own rooms. Most of the time, Yvette would come to James's room, and they would talk or make love or go to sleep in each other's arms, too exhausted to do more.

James wasn't sure if what he felt was love, but if it wasn't, it was damn close. Neither of them had mentioned the 'L' word, though. James was afraid of what complications might arise if they did. He'd told her about his parents and brother and about being a US Marine. She'd told him about growing up as a politician's daughter, about her mother's murder at the hands of a mugger, and about law school. It wasn't as if he was keeping a tally or keeping track of what each told the other, but he was mindful of not keeping secrets from her. It was still difficult to open up to someone after being alone for so long.

There was only one subject he hadn't talked about, and he still wasn't sure he wanted to. Yvette would ask him about her eventually, he knew.

"I could have used a beer or two with that dinner tonight," James said, sitting down on the chair in his room. "There's only so much of that fernta stuff I can handle." They had eaten some type of pre-made meat and vegetable dish that had come from the ship's new stock of supplies from the space port. He'd been afraid to ask what kind of meat it had been, but it had the texture of chicken and a very gamy flavor, like squirrel or opossum or something. The vegetables had been colorful, but almost tasteless in the overpowering sauce the contents were cooked in. The best part of the meal had been a dark bread that was heavy and moist and came in small, individually packaged loaves.

"I've never really cared for alcoholic drinks," Yvette said after she sat down next to him, leaning her frame into his. "But I do crave a pop every now and then. Probably better for my teeth, though, that I'm not drinking any."

James had never consumed a lot of pop, not even as a

child. Jenny had loved her Dr. Pepper. James couldn't stand it. He looked up, realizing he'd been lost in thought for a few minutes.

"You were gone again," Yvette said, smiling.

"Sorry," he answered. "Thinking about the past. Guess I'm tired tonight."

"James," Yvette began, "I know we've never really talked about her, but what was your wife like?"

James thought for a minute.

"You don't have to answer that," Yvette said. "I didn't mean to pry." She started to stand up.

"No, you're not prying," James said, grabbing her hand and gently pulling her back down to the chair. "I've spent so long avoiding thinking about her, I mean *really* thinking about her—not only the things we did together or what happened to her—that it takes a few minutes to remember. It's been a while." He thought for another moment before continuing. "She was quiet, thoughtful. Practical would be a good word too. She knew how to have fun. She was very pretty. What I can remember the most is how ... how young she was. All of my memories of her ... all the time I knew her was a brief period when we were in our early twenties." He stopped, knowing he was getting too emotional.

"James, I'm sorry," she said, looking down at her lap.

"Shhh," he murmured, pulling her into his arms. "It happened a long time ago. I guess it still hurts a little to think about." He held her for a moment. "I think I'm going to hit the hay," he said. "It really has been a long day."

"Okay," she said. "I'll see you in the morning."

"Yeah," he said, walking her to his door. He felt bad for her, but needed to be alone for a while to work through his emotions.

"Good night," she said.

He kissed her on the lips briefly. "Good night." The door closed, and he sighed before undressing and climbing into bed.

Interlude

Lisa was disgusted with the man who almost became her father-in-law. She'd learned Jeb had planned a memorial service for David without even waiting for the police to close their missing person investigation. She was surprised he hadn't had David declared dead, but learned he legally couldn't do it for a couple of years. *Thank God for that*, she thought.

Then he'd had the gall to act like the grieving father at the service, playing it up for all he was worth as anguished family members consoled him. All she could do the entire day of the service was cry, and David's father treated her like an outsider who was lucky to be invited at all.

Her only consolation, if you could call it that, was the fact she would never have to see or talk to the man ever again, if she had her way. David had told her what his father was like, but she still hadn't believed him until she was forced to get to know Jeb better after David disappeared.

She still woke up at times crying in her sleep because she might never know what happened to David, and the last time she had spoken to him had been when she'd refuse his proposal.

Chapter 14

David wasn't quite awake as he headed down to the main corridor of the ship. He still wasn't used to getting up early and running, a practice he'd kept from junior high school until his knee injury as a sophomore at Michigan State. After his surgery and rehabilitation, he'd felt there was no point in running again. He would never play football again, so why bother? The doctors had repaired his knee well enough for him to walk without a limp. At the time, it was the best they could do. Even if he had come back and was able to run, he'd lost his burst; what the NFL scouts he'd talked to had termed 'suddenness.' He wasn't big enough to out-jump the defensive players he played against in the game. His greatest asset had been his speed, and that had been taken away. His future in the NFL had been taken away by one hit to the side of his leg.

Somehow, his knee felt stable now, though. It no longer felt like it would buckle if he stepped wrong. He no longer felt a twinge of pain when he straightened it out all the way. He'd been thinking about it, and he didn't think it was fixed, exactly. More like the stone's power was helping to stabilize it better. He had no idea if that was the truth, but he didn't really care. He could run now, and fast. With his new powers, and especially when he was powered up, he could run faster and farther than he'd ever dreamed. It was an exhilarating feeling. He didn't know how fast he could run, as they hadn't found a way to time him yet, but he guessed he was probably the fastest human being. Ever. Perhaps even faster than any living thing on Earth. He didn't really care how fast he was, though. All that really mattered was that he could run again, which was what he had woken up so early to do. He was surprised to find he wasn't the only one with the idea.

"Hey, Kieren," he said to the figure he saw stretching in the corridor before him. He felt awkward, but he didn't want to startle her.

"Oh, hello, David," she replied, smiling, her head near her knees as she stretched.

He began to stretch his legs, not knowing what else to say. He and Kieren hadn't really spoken to each other much since coming aboard the ship. He hadn't really spoken to any of the others much, except for training and small talk at dinner. He spent most of his time alone in his room or with Janan.

"So," Kieren said, "am I going to be able to keep up with you if we run together?" He saw she was still smiling.

"Uh, yeah," he said, feeling stupid. "No powers, I promise." He smiled back at her. She had seemed like a nice person when they had first woken up, and he'd been around her enough to see it wasn't an act.

"I have to warn you, though," he said. "I haven't run for exercise in a couple of years. I don't know what shape I'm in or how long I'll hold up."

"Why is that?" she asked, a look of concern on her face.

"Blew out my knee playing football," he replied with a shrug.

"Oh no," she said. "Were you a professional?"

"No, college," he replied, stretching his arms over his head. "I never got a chance to go pro."

"Hey, is that a tattoo?" Kieren asked, seeing a small dark shape on his stomach, just above the waistline.

David pulled his shirt down, looking embarrassed. "Oh, yeah. When I was a freshman in college, me and some of the other new guys went and got our numbers tattooed on us. Stupid, huh? I was number eight."

"Not that stupid," Kieren said, showing him a small, brightly colored butterfly on her ankle.

"Ha," David said. "Don't tell anyone. Especially James. I don't want him to think I'm some dumb kid."

"No problem," she replied, smiling. They started jogging side by side down the corridor.

"Thanks," he said, returning her smile.

"So what do you do now for a living?" she asked.

"I work for a marketing firm," he said. Though he'd told them all what he did when they were first woken up, he didn't really expect Kieren to remember. It seemed like a long time had passed since then. "Or at least I used to. I doubt I'll have a job waiting for me when I get back. My boss is a real jerk."

"Oh, I'm sorry," she said.

"Yeah," he said. "It wouldn't be so bad if he weren't also my father."

She laughed. "Oh, I really am sorry."

"Probably better this way anyway," he said, chuckling. "Clean break and all that."

They jogged along for a moment in silence, each lost in their own thoughts.

"What about you?" he asked. "You said you're a teacher, right?"

"Yes," she replied. "I'd only been working in Detroit for a few months when ... well, you know the rest."

"How did you like it?" he asked.

"Well," she paused for a while, gathering her thoughts. "It was definitely ... different. And it was a huge challenge."

"You said you were from Colorado, right?"

"Uh-huh," she said. They were both running out of breath now. "Colorado Springs. I worked at a really nice school there."

"Then why did you move?" he asked. "Did you have family in Michigan?"

"Well," she said, "my older brother had been transferred to Detroit with his job. He asked if I would be up to moving out there to be closer to him. He said he could find me a great place to live; aka cheap; and the schools paid more there. That was before I knew what the economy was like and how underfunded the schools actually are in my district."

"Not quite what you pictured?" he asked.

"No, not quite," she answered.

By this time they had run from one end of the corridor and back four times, David was ready to stop. He would have stopped earlier, but had been engrossed in their conversation. Kieren was an interesting woman. He definitely found her attractive. He could see himself falling for her. He'd seen the way Gianni looked at her, so he'd probably have competition, but that could be solved easily enough.

"So," she interrupted his train of thought, "I think this is it for me."

"Oh yeah," he said. "Me too. I'm surprised I lasted this long."

"Same time tomorrow?" she asked, smiling.

"Sure," he answered, smiling back. "If I can get out of bed." Her smile was contagious. He watched her walk away and wondered what it would be like to kiss her.

◊

One inconvenience Kieren had found in being placed in the Sekani crew quarters was her room didn't contain a shower of its own. Another was the showerheads lining the wall of the shower room were all set too low. She practically had to bend over to wet her hair. When she entered the shower room, she noticed that Yvette was already there, and hesitated.

"You're welcome to join me," Yvette said, noticing the hesitancy that Kieren displayed. "The water is hot."

"Oh, I can wait," Kieren replied. She'd never been into cheerleading or any type of sport in school where she would have had to shower with other girls, so it felt weird to shower next to another naked woman.

"Don't worry," Yvette told her, laughing, "I'm not that type of girl. I thought you might want to save some time."

"Oh." Kieren blushed. She hadn't been thinking that at all. She decided it was okay to venture into the water. As she undressed, she noticed she was taller than Yvette, and probably skinnier. No, not skinnier, she decided, just not as sturdily built. Yvette looked like she could handle herself in a fight.

Kieren moved under the warm spray of water, feeling the sweat from her run rinse out of her hair. It was a good, satisfying feeling. One she hadn't felt for a while, having had no real time to exercise back home due to her school schedule. She was proud of her improvements with her own body as well as with her powers, though she was still frustrated at times by her inability to concentrate enough to keep her energy field up.

"So, how are you dealing with things?" Yvette asked her.

Kieren jumped. She'd almost forgotten the other woman was still there. She laughed. "Well, I'm still not used to all of this, really. There are some times when I think I must have been crazy to come along. Like I was too impulsive for my own good. You know what I mean?"

"Yeah, I do," Yvette answered. "I don't know why I decided so quickly. My dad would probably remind me I've been this way my entire life." She chuckled.

"Is your dad really Senator Manidoo?" Kieren asked her.

"The one and only. Who told you?"

"James. He sounded impressed," Kieren said.

"Oh, really? That's good," Yvette said, now drying herself off with an oversized towel. "Did you vote for my dad?"

"Um, no. I voted Democrat," Kieren said, looking away quickly.

"Don't worry, I won't tell him," Yvette replied, laughing again.

Kieren liked her laugh. It wasn't some little girl laugh, like many of her friends from college still affected. Yvette definitely wasn't a demure creature. "So what do you think of James?" she asked the other woman.

"I really like him," Yvette replied. "I mean, what's not to like? He's six-foot-four, two hundred and forty pounds. He's taken care of himself physically, which is good for his age, and he's not bad to look at. Not to mention the fact that he knows what he's doing."

"I didn't mean like that," Kieren replied, now toweling herself off. "I meant as the leader of the team."

"Oh." Now it was Yvette's turn to blush. "Well, like I said, he knows what he's doing."

"Not to mention he's single," Kieren teased.

"Yeah, there's that too," Yvette said, smiling. "And he's good in bed."

Kieren's eyes opened in surprise. "Really?" She burst out laughing, her face turning red.

Yvette laughed with her. "Oh, maybe I shouldn't have said that."

"Actually, I had wondered," Kieren told her. "I've seen the looks you two have been sharing. And that Zazzil guy referred to you as James's mate."

"Yes, that. Well, it's not like we were hiding the fact we've been seeing each other, but I guess I'd hoped it wasn't that obvious," Yvette replied.

"It isn't," Kieren told her. "But a woman knows, right?"

"Yeah, I guess so," Yvette told her. "Men can be so dense sometimes. Well, okay, most of the time."

"You're telling me," Kieren said, thinking of Gianni.

"How are things between you and Gianni?" Yvette asked, almost as if she were reading Kieren's mind.

"Oh, you know. Horrible," replied Kieren. "He makes me furious sometimes. It's like he enjoys seeing me angry."

"I figured you two were either going to fall in love or kill each other on this trip," Yvette said.

"Or both," Kieren said, as they both laughed.

◊

Yvette had never intended for things to become serious so quickly with James. Who knew she would have to be kidnapped by aliens to find someone? Of course, her father would throw a fit if he found out she was dating a man so much older than she was. That fact didn't seem as important, light years from Earth and months from home. At night, she sometimes wondered if her father missed her at all. Their relationship was complicated, to say the least. There were times in the past when she was sure she would never speak to him again. She'd wanted to live her life her own way, and he couldn't allow her to do that. Perhaps it was one of the reasons she'd agreed so quickly to come along on this trip.

Now, she had extraordinary powers that she'd never dreamed of, and she could hardly believe she wasn't dreaming now. She had to train herself how to use them properly, trying her best to remember everything she'd been taught in various martial arts classes. She was a brown belt in karate, but she had attempted to learn what she could from other disciplines as well. She'd never used weapons, other than a bo staff and nunchaku.

Since she was capable of creating any shape with her powers, a staff was easy. She tried other shapes, such as spears, swords, clubs, and even tried an old-fashioned mace like she'd seen in history books. The only limitation of her powers was that the shape had to stay in contact with her at all times. She couldn't throw her spears like Gianni shot his guns. But she could extend her arms from one end of the training room to the other, and wouldn't have known she had limits if not for the incident with the ASP ship. She was glad she had found out now instead of in a more dangerous situation.

◊

Now that the team's powers had manifested during their training, James had to figure out how to best use them once they arrived on Rajan. Although he had been in the Marines for a few years, he was not a trained military tactician by any means. His police training provided only a limited amount of strategy, and most of it was for searching a building or disarming a single person, not fighting in an all-out war. He needed to think on a grander scale.

On top of that, he was working with a team of people with no training at all, and one who could possibly be too dangerous, considering her martial arts background coupled with her powers. It wasn't that he didn't trust Yvette, but he would hate to see what could happen if she was ever really pissed off. Melding them all into a cohesive team would be the most difficult task of all.

◊

Kieren thought it was interesting that the stones had given them each powers that coincided with their individual personalities. James was a strong man, mentally and physically, but at times, she could tell all he wanted to do was disappear for a while and be left alone. David was a runner, pure and simple. From the little she knew about him, he had been running all of his life, whether in sports or away from his father. Yvette was as fast and sleek and tough as any woman Kieren had ever known. Gianni was an expert at putting up walls around himself and sniping from protective cover.

She was always trying to reach out to people, to make contact, whether it was the kids she taught or other people she communicated with on a daily basis. And the flying—well, she had always dreamed of flying, and not only to escape, like the others might have, but to simply soar above the Earth and feel the wind rushing past her face. It was the ultimate form of freedom. She couldn't wait until they were off the ship and she could really go all-out without worrying about bumping her head on the ceiling. They could, of course, be landing in the middle of a war zone, but she hoped the Krahn had left already.

At this point, she would be grateful if the fighting only lasted a short period of time and then they could all go home again. It was too late to change her mind about coming along on the trip.

◊

Bhakat was stunned at the powers shown by the five Humans. He'd grown up hearing stories about the Johar Stones and the power they gave to those implanted, but by now those stories were as much myth as anything in Rajani society. As far as he knew, the last time a Rajani had been implanted with a stone had been more than two thousand years earlier. It was difficult to know for sure, because records from the time were either lost or classified by the Galactic Alliance. Not much was really known about the life of Ruvedalin, besides what was passed down in his teachings, which, collectively, were called the Kha. The end of his life, which was chronicled by the Elders, was part of the information not classified by the Alliance.

Bhakat was still torn by his decision to go against those teachings and help the Humans train aboard the ship, but it still felt right, at least most of the time. He felt better knowing he was doing something instead of sitting, useless while the Humans prepared to save his planet.

◊

Gianni was in the training room shooting small moving targets, or at least attempting to, while thinking about Kieren. That explained why he was missing half of what he aimed at. Finally, he gave up in frustration. He typed a command into a handheld tablet telling the computer to halt, and turned off his field of power, defeated. He'd spent a lot of time recently experimenting with his powers. He had found he could generate walls of energy now without keeping them in his line of sight or concentrating on them too much. He could still feel them in his mind as existing without having to visually verify it, as he had been doing in most of his training. It was getting easier to use his powers.

He sat down on the floor of the training area. His body clock was telling him it was late and he needed some sleep. But his mind wouldn't rest, which was why he'd found himself in the training room in the first place. The trip so far had passed too quickly for him to sit and take stock of how he really felt about what he had stumbled into, and what still lay in store when they arrived at their final destination. Then there was Kieren, which complicated matters even more.

He'd set out determined not to get to know her; not to get to know any of the others, really, but especially her because he knew the dangers of becoming emotionally attached to anyone. He sighed and then swore, knowing he needed to talk to her, but unsure what he would say.

◊

Kieren was sitting on her bed, which was made up properly. She was a neat person as a rule, and being in space hadn't changed that aspect of her personality. She was flipping through a magazine on her handheld electronic tablet. The doorbell sounded as she skimmed an article entitled, "Attract Mr. Right!"

She went to the door, already knowing who was on the other side. Just as she expected, Gianni stood in the hallway. "Hi," he said. "Can I come in?"

"That depends," she answered, trying to sound annoyed. "Are you going to apologize?"

Gianni's expression was incredulous. "For what?"

"For yelling at me the other day," she said, wondering if she was taking the act too far.

He turned and walked away, throwing a hand up. "Fine. Forget it."

Kieren stood in the doorway and watched him leave, knowing she had pushed him too far yet again. "Fine," she muttered, and closed the door. She felt like throwing the tablet at the wall but restrained herself. It wouldn't do any good to destroy her only source of entertainment. She sighed and wondered what David was doing.

◊

David was falling. No, that wasn't right. David was in some type of vehicle that was falling; spinning around so that the G-forces pinned him effectively against the side where he sat. He turned his head with difficulty and saw with amazement that Janan was sitting near him, the alien's eyes closed so that David couldn't tell if he was awake or not—or if he was alive or dead.

The scene shifted violently and he was walking through a desert, with dunes all around him and a merciless sun shining overhead. Again, a shift, and he was running swiftly through an unknown city in the dark. Large stones blocked his path in places so that he had to carefully weave among them.

He stopped suddenly, and his eyes filled with tears as he looked over the edge of a cliff and saw alien bodies strewn below. He turned, and the scene changed again. He was standing beside what looked like a grave next to a group of alien trees. There were others standing near him, but he couldn't make out who they were, so he had no idea who was buried there.

David woke with a scream held behind his teeth. He could feel sweat beading down his back. Another bad dream. He'd been sleeping a lot lately, and not just because of the rigorous training schedule. He'd been able to keep his depression in check for most of the trip, but he had entered another of his black moods, where all he wanted to do was lie in bed. And now, it seemed he couldn't even do that because of the persistent nightmares.

He reached over and took a sip from the glass of water sitting on the table next to his bed, and then ran a hand over his face. That dream had been the worst of all because it was clearer than any of the others. Before he had only had feelings of dread and fear. Now the vision was beginning to reveal itself.

He stopped for a moment, a thought beginning to form in the back of his mind. What they really were visions? What if the stone in his head was giving him some sort of extra-sensory power, so that he could see what was going to happen? He thought about it a moment. Thought about when he'd started running during training. It had almost seemed as though he could anticipate what was going to happen a split second before it did. It hadn't helped him when that asshole Gianni had tripped him, but that had happened so fast. Maybe to coincide with his speed, the stone had given him the ability to glimpse the future.

If that was the case, then he needed to pay attention to his dreams from now on. They might help him to avoid what he'd just seen.

Interlude

Dennis Gray was going to confession for the first time in twenty years. He didn't know what else to do. As he sat in the confessional booth, he heard the priest sit down on the other side of the screen. "Forgive me, Father, for I have sinned. It's been ... twenty years since my last confession," he said. That was all he could remember from the ceremony.

"And what are your sins?" the priest asked quietly.

"My sister went missing, and I think it was my fault," Dennis said.

"How so?" the priest asked with alarm in his voice.

"I'm the one who invited her to Detroit," Dennis replied. "If I hadn't done that, she'd still be okay. I'm the one who brought her to this shithole. Sorry, Father," he said, feeling bad about his language. He was silent for a moment as tears came to his eyes. "I've ... always been ... selfish. Even when we were kids, I would always want things to go my way or I'd throw a tantrum. When I was older, I would storm out of the house. Even ... even after our parents died. I was supposed to be the one taking care of her. And instead, I left her alone to fend for herself, until I got lonely, and I forced her to come here. Now she's gone. She's been missing so long the police have stopped looking for her." He began to cry silently, too ashamed to make a sound. Why should he receive any sympathy, when it was his sister who was missing, not him?

"My son," the priest began, "you've said it's been a while since you've confessed your sins, so I'll overlook the fact we're not exactly following the script here, and that's fine. While God can forgive your sins, only you can forgive yourself. You didn't know what would happen to your sister; you couldn't have known."

"I should've known!" Dennis said, too loud for the

confessional booth. "I'm sorry, I shouldn't have yelled. I'm not doing this very well."

"I sense you love your sister very much," the priest said. "You wanted her to come to Detroit because of that. But this was also a form of coveting, and that is a sin. If you are truly not responsible for your sister's disappearance, that is your only sin, as I see it."

The priest paused a moment to let his words sink in. "Your act of repentance is to first talk to someone who can help you work through your feelings of guilt. Now, normally, I would also ask you to say some Hail Marys and an Our Father, but I get the feeling that you've been praying enough without my guidance. Do you understand what I'm telling you?"

"Yes," Dennis replied.

"Good," the priest said. "Secondly, I don't want you to lose faith in God. Everything happens according to His plan. There is a reason your sister is missing; we don't know what it is at the moment. You must trust in God."

"I'll ... I'll try," Dennis said, wiping his nose with the back of his sleeve like a six-year-old.

"Now," the priest said. "Join me in saying the Act of Contrition."

"Um, I've forgotten it," Dennis said, a hitch in his voice still from crying. All he heard from the other side of the screen was a sigh.

Chapter 15

Kieren was jogging down a dark corridor near the engines early the next morning. To conserve the ship's energy, the Rajani kept the lights at half power at night, and the central computer hadn't yet turned them up to full power. She'd waited for David to show up, but after about ten minutes, had decided he probably wasn't coming. *Probably stayed up too late with Janan,* she thought, knowing the two could usually be found together drinking after dinner on most nights. She thought David might have a little bit of a drinking problem.

She stopped when she saw her shoelace was untied, and bent over to tie the shoe. As she did so, she bumped her behind on a button on the wall. A section of the wall slid open, startling her. She powered up instinctively. "Whoa. How did I do that?" The door had been hidden, with no signs to show it was there while closed.

She walked into the room, looking around. She turned a corner into another section of the room, and her eyes went wide. "Oh. Oh my God!"

She turned and quickly ran out.

Half a dozen large metal capsules occupied the room. Each capsule was approximately six feet long and two feet wide, with six-inch square windows on one end. They were laid out side by side in the room, each connected with the wall via large tubes with valves along their lengths. There were humans in two of them, and they could be seen through the frosted glass windows. One of the bodies was an older black man, and the other was a young white woman, from what Kieren could tell. Both of them looked peaceful, in repose, but they clearly weren't sleeping.

◊

The common room was filled with the sound of angry voices as the Humans and two Rajani shouted to be heard. Kieren had come to James and Yvette and told them of her discovery. James had rounded up Gianni and David and asked them all to wait in the common room while he went to wake Rauph. Rauph had then asked Janan to take his shift on the bridge while he and Bhakat spoke to the Humans. The room now rang out with accusations and questions and the mechanical sound of the large translating device as it attempted to sort out the individual conversations.

"Everyone settle down," James finally said, holding up his hands. "Please."

"Whatever you say," Gianni said, angrily. "Did you know about this too?"

James stepped up to him and looked him in the eye. "Let's you and me get this straight, once and for all. I'm a patient man. I don't like to jump to conclusions, on anything. You are very close to pissing me off, so calm down and back the hell off before you step over the line."

"Well said, Officer Dempsey," Rauph began.

James turned to him, cutting him off. "Save it. What in God's name are other Humans doing on board? Are they dead?"

Bhakat answered, his teeth bared in a snarl. "We don't need to explain anything to you."

"It's all right, Bhakat," Rauph said, holding a hand on his Pledge's arm. "We knew this might occur before I had a chance to tell them." He turned back to face the Humans. "When we first came to your planet, all we had to study were television and radio transmissions. We couldn't be sure if you were biologically compatible with the Johar Stones."

"Until you had test subjects," Yvette said.

"Yes," Rauph answered, looking down at the ground.

James took a step closer to Rauph. "Are they dead?" he asked again.

"Yes," Rauph answered, after a beat.

"Son of a bitch!" Gianni raged, looking like he was ready to hit someone. James was afraid the situation still had the threat of escalating if he wasn't careful. He needed to know the truth before anything could be decided. The last thing he needed was Gianni going off and complicating the situation even more.

◊

Rauph was looking down at his feet, trying to think of the best way to calm everyone down. He knew the fate of his home world rested on what he said in the next few moments. *Is it really coming down to this?* he thought. "Unfortunately, we needed to perform a complete physical examination, as well as a complete post-mortem examination."

Kieren's hand went to her mouth. "My God. They were alive when you brought them aboard?"

Rauph now had his arms spread as if to entreat them all with his words. "We needed living specimens. If it's any consolation, these Humans were going to die soon."

"What the hell is that supposed to mean?" David asked.

"Please," Rauph said. "Listen." Rauph looked at a handheld tablet that Bhakat handed to him. "First subject was an unknown female Human. Age was approximately thirty-two Earth years. She ... fell from the top of her apartment building, and her injuries were fatal. Second subject was a male Human, approximately seventy-three Earth years. He was living in the alley behind your dwellings. Upon examination, Bhakat found that his lungs were full of tumors."

Gianni was incredulous. "A homeless guy? You expect us to believe this shit?"

"Mr. Moretti," Rauph answered, "Humans die on your planet every day."

"So you 'borrowed' them before sending them on their way," James said, feeling like someone had kicked him in the stomach.

"We had to be sure," Rauph continued. "I can assure you that these Humans did not suffer. They were never conscious aboard our ship."

Kieren had tears streaming down her cheeks. "You killed them!" She turned to Gianni, who was next to her, and started crying. He held her, surprised at first she would seek him out for consolation.

"We understand your feelings—" Rauph began.

"You understand nothing," James cut him off. "My God, do you know how disgusting we find you right now?"

Bhakat pointed at James. "Human, if you don't stop your tongue—"

Yvette powered up. "I suggest you stop yours."

David and Gianni followed her example and powered up as well. Kieren backed away from Gianni, looking from him back to James.

Rauph had a sinking feeling in his stomach, knowing the situation was quickly getting away from him. It had gone from tense to dangerous.

"No. No, we will not do this." James turned to his

teammates. "Power down."

"But, James ..." Gianni started.

"Power down," James said again. "Please. If we treat them the same way they have our people, where does it get us? And where does it stop? We have to draw the line. I draw it here. Now."

He turned back to Rauph. "We'll help your planet, but on one condition."

"And what is that?" Rauph answered, warily.

"Don't ever come to Earth again," James said.

"That is ... more than fair," Rauph said, eyes downcast now.

The Rajani turned and left, with Bhakat giving James one last defiant glance. In the room, Gianni, David, and Yvette stayed powered up for a moment.

◊

James wondered how the situation had become so complicated so quickly. Things had been going so well since they'd left the space port. They had escaped the ASPs, begun their training with the powers the stones had imparted to them, and started coming together as a team. Then Kieren's discovery had changed everything. Janan told him it would still be a week before they reached Rajan. Instead of concentrating on the Krahn and their plan for freeing the Rajani on the planet, James had to worry about a full-blown mutiny aboard the *Tukuli*.

He'd stopped the situation from getting out of control right after the initial confrontation but was afraid things might get out of hand quickly if there were more angry words between them and the Rajani. Not that he could blame any of his team for being angry. Hell, he was angry himself. But he was also practical about their situation. What was he supposed to do, take over the ship and turn it around?

Head back to Earth and leave an entire species, actually three species, to suffer at the hands of their conquerors? He couldn't do that—couldn't punish an entire planet for the actions of two of their members; actions that, at the time, they'd felt were necessary. Of course, that didn't mean he could look at himself in the mirror anytime soon. He made a promise to himself, though, no matter what happened on Rajan, those two people would be taken back and given a proper burial on Earth. No matter how long it took.

◊

David sat on his bed and felt like crying. He'd thought everything was working out so well. Now, he didn't know. He had found it difficult to make friends while growing up. It didn't help his father usually disapproved of them for one reason or another. He rarely, if ever, asked anyone to sleep over or come to a birthday party. As a consequence, he was also never asked over to other people's homes.

Even when he became the star receiver on the high school football team, he didn't have any real friends; only people who wanted to be around him because of his popularity. Yes, he was popular, but it didn't translate to friendship. The girls who wanted to go out with him were all clueless bitches looking to glom onto his fleeting popularity in the hopes of elevating their own social standings. His father had warned him women were more trouble than they were worth, but he didn't start to believe him until high school.

It had taken a while to warm up to everyone on the ship, especially Gianni, but he'd thought he'd made a real friend in Janan. Then came the discovery on the *Tukuli*, and he'd found out Janan was like all of the rest of those people who had tried to use him for their own purposes. He should have known better. He wouldn't make that mistake again.

◊

James knew what needed to be done, and also that it was going to be difficult. He had to calm everyone down. First, he went to the common room, but found it empty. Not surprising, considering the shock from the day before. Then he went to the training room in the cargo hold. Empty. He sighed, knowing it was going to be more difficult to get everyone to leave their rooms and talk. He went to Yvette's room in hopes of gaining an ally to help coax everyone else back to the common room for a meeting. By the look on her face when she answered the door, he could see it wasn't going to be easy.

"Come in, if you want," she said, turning away and walking toward her bed. She was wearing her workout outfit, which had come as part of the supplies they had received on the space port. He must have missed her in the training room.

"I want to talk to you," he said. "Well, to all of you, actually."

"Let me guess," she said, sitting on her bed and glaring at him.

She really is naturally beautiful, he thought. *Even when she's angry.* He knew her well enough to tell she was furious.

"You're going to try to talk us into still helping them," she continued, running a hand through her hair in a way he had come to recognize. He noticed her hair was growing quite long.

"Maybe I came here to tell you how beautiful you look this morning," he said, smiling. He was no good at giving compliments. He was out of practice. She stood and faced away from him, her arms wrapped around herself.

"Oh, is that how it's going to be?" she asked. As her shoulders began to shake, he could tell she was crying. He slowly walked over to her and put his hands lightly on her arms. She turned and buried her face in his chest, and he let her cry as he held her close. Finally, she pulled away, wiping her eyes with her hands.

"Thanks, I think I needed that," she said, looking up at him.

"No problem," he answered. "You still look beautiful, by the way."

Her face broke into a wide smile as she wiped away another stray tear. "Shit. How am I supposed to stay mad at you?"

"You're not," he said, serious now. "I promise you, I knew nothing about this."

"I know," she said. "I wish we didn't know about them at all."

"But we do," he said. "Now we have to learn how to deal with that knowledge without anyone else getting hurt in the process."

She looked up at him and smiled. "Later," she said, gently pulling his face down to hers.

◊

"How long before we reach Rajan?" Rauph asked. He was seated in his regular chair aboard the bridge.

"Two days," Janan answered quietly. None of the Humans had talked to him in days. Not even David.

"Notify me if anything happens before tomorrow," Rauph said. "I need to get some rest." He rose slowly and walked to the door of the bridge before turning. "Janan, I wanted to ... apologize to you. For not telling you about—"

"You don't have to—" Janan began.

"Yes, I do," Rauph insisted. "We should have told you. You're my pilot and a member of my House. After everything we've all been through, you should have been told. I wanted you to know I'm sorry."

"Thank you," Janan said as Rauph turned and left. He only hoped David would eventually understand. He had come to consider the Human his friend. Yet he also considered Bhakat his friend, and the Rajani had not told him about the first Humans taken aboard the ship. It was all so complicated. How could he hope to be forgiven by David if he could not bring himself to forgive Bhakat? And yet he felt so betrayed by his Rajani friend. Was this what David was feeling as well, this sense of disloyalty? Janan had learned in his time with the Humans they felt many of the same emotions. Their physiology might be different on the surface, but under it all, they were more alike than not.

He made up his mind he would to speak to both Bhakat and David after his shift was over. He was also worried about what would happen once they arrived back home. With everything that had happened since they had left Rajan, it was strange to realize they were almost back. He was scared about what they might face once they reached the planet, and what he would have to face when he returned to what was once his home.

◊

Bhakat was late for his shift on the bridge. His last shift aboard the *Tukuli,* most likely. Even if they were able to free their planet and repel the Krahn Horde, he thought his relationship with Rauph wouldn't allow him to stay his Pledge. He didn't think he could be a Priest of the Kha, or a Rajani Elder, for that matter. He wasn't meant to sit around studying history and the teachings of Ruvedalin and ruminating on their meanings; he could see that now. Perhaps he would go back into practicing medicine, as he had before becoming Rauph's Pledge. He felt almost free from the weight of expectations. He wasn't sure what would happen once they reached Rajan, but he did know his life had changed forever the night the Krahn attacked. He arrived at the bridge and pushed the button to open the door.

"Good night, Janan'kela," he said as he walked onto the bridge.

Janan only looked up at him from where he was seated in the pilot's seat. "We need to talk about what happened," the Sekani said. "Please sit down."

"Janan—" Bhakat began.

"Sit. Please, Bhakat," Janan said, motioning toward the empty captain's chair.

Bhakat sat down. "I knew you would be angry," he said quietly, looking at the control panel instead of his friend.

"Angry is not a strong enough word for what I felt when I heard what had happened," Janan said. "You knew about the other Humans, yet you didn't tell me?"

"Rauph—" Bhakat began.

"I don't want to hear about Rauphangelaa!" Janan almost screamed. "I want to know why you wouldn't tell me. Are we friends or not? Am I not trustworthy enough? What's the reason for not telling me?"

Bhakat sighed. "Yes, I knew about the Humans. I performed the physical examinations on them. We needed to know, before we wasted any more time and energy researching them." The big Rajani stood up and began pacing. "I knew you would be angry, but I also knew it wouldn't matter, in the end. All that matters is we're almost home. We—no, *I* did what I thought needed to be done to get us here. I don't feel right about it, but it was my choice. I was trying to spare you from this rotten, guilty feeling I've had inside of me since then, but I made things worse, and for that, I'm sorry."

Janan stood and walked up to his friend. "I know you are, now. I'd hoped that you were, anyway. I hope we can still be friends when we get back home."

"Yes, we're still friends," Bhakat said, placing his hand on the diminutive Sekani's shoulder. "If you'll have me."

"Good," Janan said. "Now that we have that out of the way, I need to get some sleep." He turned and headed for the door.

"Good night, my friend," Bhakat said, his mind already preoccupied by the thoughts of what lay ahead.

◊

Janan headed toward David's room, wondering along the way what he could say to the Human that could let him know he wasn't some kind of monster from space. He was disappointed to find David wasn't in his room. He thought about turning and going to his own room, but he needed to settle things between himself and the Human, or he wouldn't be able to fall asleep. He'd left the bridge feeling much better about his relationship with Bhakat. Now he wanted to fix things with David as well, if he could.

It occurred to him David might be in the common room the Humans had set up, so he walked in that direction. When he finally arrived, he pushed the button that opened the door. He was surprised to see all five of the Humans were there, and they weren't happy. He could sense the tension in the air, but all of the conversation stopped abruptly when the door opened to reveal him standing there.

"I am ... sorry," he said in English. "I was looking for David."

James stood and walked toward him. Janan looked up at the large Human, wondering if he should be afraid. What were they doing here at this time of night?

"Janan," James said, "we're kind of busy right now. David will come see you when we're finished, okay?"

Janan nodded as the door closed in front of him,

wondering if the Human actually would come to see him that night. He'd caught a glimpse of David's face when the door opened, and could see how upset he was. He walked to his room, the ebullient feeling from his earlier conversation with Bhakat now forgotten.

Interlude

Senator Manidoo was the Chairman of the Senate Committee on Appropriations. With a vote scheduled on the passage of the Democratic president's new appropriations bill coming soon, it was his job to come out against it as forcefully as possible, both in the press and on the floor of the Senate. His mind wasn't on his speech or the partisan wrangling that would come with it as he made his way toward the podium to stand before the gathered reporters. It was on the realization he'd had that morning. His daughter was gone. His baby. His only family outside of a creepy uncle who lived somewhere in the Upper Peninsula and thought he was a scout for Lewis and Clark.

He'd done everything within his considerable powers to find her, whether she was alive or dead, but it was as if she had vanished. The FBI and Secret Service had told him he should be prepared for ransom demands, but nothing had ever come. He'd waited as long as possible before accepting the inevitable. She was gone. It hit him almost as hard as his wife's death all those years ago. Not knowing for sure was like a knife twisting in his chest.

On top of that, some sleaze from a popular paparazzi website had the nerve to stand up at a news conference and ask him about his wife's murder, an event that had happened when Yvette was fourteen. As if it had anything to do with the present situation at all. He'd become so angry, he almost attacked the man physically. He'd heard the whole incident was a popular video on the Internet, but he didn't care. He hoped no one asked about Yvette today. His broken heart couldn't take it.

Chapter 16

It was early in the morning when James arrived at Rauph's room. He was still tired from the night before. They'd all stayed up late, each arguing for and against abandoning the Rajani to their fate, whatever it might be. In the end, cooler heads had prevailed, and they'd decided to finish the job they'd traveled all that way for instead of demanding to be taken back to Earth. Now he needed to speak to Rauph about the plan for arrival at Rajan. He had the collar translating device affixed around his neck, with the earpiece in his right ear. When the door opened, James noticed how much healthier Rauph appeared. He was out of danger, at least for now. "Good morning," he said in Talondarian Standard. "I pray your rest was peaceful."

"Much better pronunciation, Officer Dempsey," Rauph said. He returned to sit on his bed and continued braiding his hair. "I must say, when I heard the knock on the door, I was worried it was going to be all of you, informing me you were taking control of my ship." He smiled before becoming serious again. "You're not here to tell me that, are you?"

"No, I'm not," James said, remaining serious. "I need to know what is going to happen today so I can get my team ready for action. What's the plan?"

"The plan is to hide behind one of Rajan's two moons until we can determine the location of the Krahn Horde's colony ship. Hopefully, the colony ship and most of the other ships will be bunched together and we'll be able to get past them to the planet's surface."

"That's your plan?" James asked, surprised. "Try to outrun them?

"You must understand," Rauph said. "The Krahn Horde's fleet is made up of ships that are either stolen or created from scrap parts. The *Tukuli* should easily be able to outdistance them. The colony ship, however, is a different thing altogether. We must use the element of surprise if we hope to achieve our goal. It's our only choice, I'm afraid."

"That's not very encouraging," James said, thinking over the implications of what Rauph had told him. He forgot sometimes he was basically dealing with interstellar monks. He couldn't count on them to know anything about fighting—or in this case, avoiding a fight.

"Once we land on Rajan," Rauph continued, "we must make contact with the other Elders, if they're still alive."

"And if they're not?" James asked.

Rauph was silent a moment, thinking. "I don't know. What would you suggest we do?"

"We'll have to see if there are any pockets of resistance," James said. "If there aren't any, we'll have to create them ourselves. There's also the question of medicine, sanitation, food, and clean water. If things are as bad as you've said, we could find they are lacking in all of these."

Bhakat's voice came over the ship's communication system. "Rauphangelaa and Janan, report to the bridge immediately."

"Oh no, now what?" Rauph said, finishing his braiding and standing up. "Walk with me to the bridge, if you would, Officer Dempsey."

"Sure," James replied.

"I have thought quite a bit about what we may find when—"

The *Tukuli* shuddered wildly, almost throwing both of them to the floor of the corridor.

"Rauphangelaa!" Bhakat screamed over the ship's communication system.

James's power field appeared instinctively as he ran. It felt like the ship had been hit by something. When he reached the bridge, he saw Bhakat frantically pushing buttons and pulling desperately on the steering yoke.

Bhakat glanced over at James, a look of panic on his face. "Where is Rauphangelaa?" he yelled.

"I passed him in the corridor," James said. "What happened?"

"We've been fired upon," Bhakat replied.

"Krahn?" Rauph said, breathlessly, appearing at the doorway to the bridge.

"No," Bhakat said. "I came out of nullspace on the outskirts of the Rajani system, as planned. I was met by an ASP patrol ship."

"What?" James asked.

"Where's Janan'kela?" Bhakat asked, ignoring James's question. "I'm doing my best to outmaneuver them, but he's much better at this."

"I'm here," Janan said as he ran into the room and sat down in the seat vacated by Bhakat.

"How could they have arrived here before us?" James asked Rauph as the Elder entered the bridge.

"They didn't," Rauph said, out of breath. "The ASPs regularly patrol the outskirts of our system. They must have called ahead and told them we were coming."

"Is that even possible?" James asked. "I thought you said

you couldn't communicate over long distances in space."

"I said we couldn't," Rauph said. "The Galactic Alliance has the capability. It has something to do with cosmic ray technology, from what I understand. Up until this point, the Rajani have had no need for it." *Nor would they give it to us, even if we asked for it,* he thought.

"This is all very interesting," Janan interrupted, "but what am I supposed to do now? Our heading is taking us away from the Rajani system, and the ASP ship is still in pursuit."

There was another shudder, milder this time, as the *Tukuli* was hit again.

"Hull integrity at sixty percent on the rear panel," Janan said. "They're aiming for our engines." There was a loud beep as the communication system light lit up on his panel. "Rauphangelaa, they're calling us."

"Put them on," Rauph said. Janan pushed the button.

"*Tukuli*, this is Commander Thydosh Complin of the Alliance Society for Peace ship *Waverider*," the voice said. "You are in violation of Alliance law. Shut down your engines and prepare to be boarded."

"I have to find Gianni," James said. He ran from the bridge and headed for Gianni's room. He met Gianni, Yvette, and Kieren heading toward the bridge. All three looked disheveled and in various stages of dress, having been abruptly awakened from sleep.

"What's going on?" Yvette asked.

James dropped his energy field. "We're under attack by an ASP ship," he replied. "Gianni, I need a force shield put up behind the *Tukuli*."

Gianni closed his eyes. After a moment, he opened them again. "Done."

"Something tells me they didn't appreciate our escape from the space port," James said.

"Imagine that," Kieren said.

"Kieren, I want you to go tell Rauph to stop the ship," James said. "Gianni, concentrate on your shield. Yvette, come with me."

"Not again," Gianni said.

"Trust me," James yelled over his shoulder as he ran down the corridor toward the airlock, with Yvette following close behind.

Gianni looked at Kieren. She shrugged and headed for the bridge.

◊

Yvette wondered what James was thinking as they arrived at the cargo hold. Gianni was right; they'd already tried having her pierce the other ship with her powers. She didn't know how he thought this time would be different, especially if the other ship had a force field around it. They went through the doors of the cargo hold and closed them, then walked over to the airlock.

James pushed the intercom button next to the airlock door. "Let me know when we've stopped," he said. He turned to Yvette. "Believe it or not, I do learn from my mistakes," he said, smiling at her. He took off the collar translating device and removed the earpiece as well. He looked around at the cargo hold before walking over to a small tool locker and placing them inside. "Thing isn't very comfortable," he said and walked back over to her, rubbing his throat.

"We're stopped," Kieren said over the intercom.

In the background, Yvette could hear Gianni talking. "I hope he knows what he's doing," he said. Yvette quietly agreed with him.

"Acknowledged," James said, pushing the button once again. "This is going to be a little dangerous," he said to her.

"What is?" she asked.

"Power up," he said, doing so himself. She followed his example. "I need you to grab onto the *Tukuli* with one hand. When I open the door, I want you to extend us both out into space and then extend me over to the ASP ship."

"You think that will work?" she asked, uncertain.

"I guess we'll see," he answered.

She looked at him a moment in doubt before searching the cargo hold for something strong enough to hold them. Finally, she settled on one of the support pillars for the training area. She wrapped a beam of energy from her arm around the pillar, and then wrapped her other arm around James.

As the energy from their two fields came together, there was the same flash of light that had occurred the first time in the airlock. She nodded to James. "Got you."

James opened the outer hatch. There was a loud, extended *whoosh* as all of the air was sucked out of the cargo hold. Suddenly, the locker he had placed the translating collar in opened. The collar and earpiece flew out of the locker and through the open airlock door.

"Um ... oops," James said when he saw them fly out into the darkness of space. Like the last time they'd opened the outer hatch, the energy fields that surrounded them had trapped enough air for them to breathe. That also meant there was a finite amount of time before the air ran out, Yvette knew. They looked out and saw the ASP ship, this one smaller than the one that had pursued them from the space port. It was also farther away than the other had been from the *Tukuli*. They could see Gianni's force shield between them and the ASP ship. Suddenly, it disappeared.

That's interesting, Yvette thought, not knowing if it was a good or a bad development.

"Okay, extend us out," James said.

After the sound the air had made leaving the cargo hold, Yvette was startled at how loud his voice sounded in the vacuum of space. They left the airlock slowly, and then sped up as Yvette became more confident. She could hardly believe what she was doing. *This trip is definitely one for firsts.*

She came to a stop, knowing she had extended the arm as far as it would go. "Now what?" she asked.

"Extend me to the ship's hull."

She began to extend him toward the other ship with her other hand, then stopped. "James, are you sure about this?"

"What other option do we have?" he answered. His face was unreadable behind his energy field, he hadn't thought to make invisible around his head.

"Be careful," she said.

"Don't worry, I will."

She extended him over to the other ship, feeling her powers stretched to their limits, and hoping they weren't making a dangerous mistake.

◊

As James moved closer to the ship and farther away from Yvette, he thought about the first time he, Yvette, and Gianni had been in the airlock trying to disable the other ASP ship. He'd assumed when they spoke to each other, the reason they could hear one another was because they were close. Now he wasn't so sure. He knew enough about space to know you couldn't hear anything in a vacuum. It had always bugged him when watching a science fiction film when a starship would scream across the screen when there shouldn't have been any sound at all. It was impressive, and gave the sound effects people something to do, he supposed, but it wasn't accurate.

So this must have been something else. Maybe when the energy fields came into contact with each other, something happened. He looked back and saw he was fifty feet away from Yvette. It should have been physically impossible for her to hear him. "Yvette, can you hear me?" he asked softly.

"Yes," she immediately responded, sounding like she was standing next to him.

Amazing, James thought. He smiled widely, like a little kid who had discovered that Santa had been there the night before. Rauph had never told them their powers might work together when their fields touched. *Maybe he didn't know.* "I want you to get me to the ship's hull, and then let me go once I have a hold of it," he told her.

"What?" she asked.

"I want you to let me go," James said, then thought better of his wording. "But be ready to grab me again," he said, laughing. "Don't go anywhere." He was rapidly approaching the other ship now. "Okay, slow me down." He slowed as he came within a few feet of the hull. He saw a ladder running along the top of the small wing structure, where it met the body of the ship. He grabbed the closest rung.

"All right, let me go," he said. He immediately felt his body drifting up as he began to float. "Yvette?" he asked. "Can you hear me?" There was no answer. His guess about the energy fields was confirmed. He grabbed the next rung on the ladder and continued along the wing toward the engines. He knew he had to disable them somehow.

He also knew he couldn't punch a hole in the engines, or he'd likely be sent flying out into space. He remembered enough of science class to know about actions and reactions, which meant he'd have to tear the engines apart, if he could. He could see a slight distortion around the entire ship from its force field. He had figured Gianni may not have had the same success against a ship with a force field, which is why he didn't ask him to shoot out its engine again.

He reached the end of the ladder and saw he was still about twenty to thirty feet from the engines, with no handholds in sight. He'd have to make his own. He held on tightly to the last rung with his left hand and drove his right hand through the hull, about two feet closer to the engines. The force field sparked as his hand passed through it, but he felt no resistance as his hand pierced the ship. *Well, they probably know I'm here now,* he thought, hoping that they didn't take off away from the *Tukuli*.

He thought he'd have at least a few moments while they attempted to assess what had breached their hull. He quickly made his way along the side of the ship, holding on tightly to the previous hole with his left hand and punching through with his right.

He finally reached a seam in the ship where the engine parts were fitted to the main body. The two sections folded into each other. *Must be bolted together inside the ship.* He felt a tight thrum in the ship and realized he was running out of time. The engines were starting up. By the quality of his breathing, he also realized his air was getting thin. His exertions had depleted the oxygen too quickly.

He made up his mind about what he needed to do and punched through the hull next to the seam, on the main body side. In his years on the force, he'd come to learn when someone's door had multiple locks on one side, you took out the hinges on the other side to get in. Most of the people didn't augment the cheap hinges installed by most housing contractors. They relied on a few screws to keep out a police battering ram. He split the hull of the ship and kept pushing with both hands, opening it like a Ziploc bag. When the hole he created was large enough, he climbed into it and started spreading it wider and wider with his hands, the metal buckling under the pressure of his grip.

When his arms were extended as far as they would go, he moved along the tear and extended them again, making it larger as he went. After a few minutes, his breath ragged in his ears, he looked back and saw he'd made a split in the hull that spanned the entire width of the ship on one side. If they tried to accelerate, it would probably tear the engines right off. He made his way back toward the side of the ship closest to the *Tukuli*. He was starting to feel light-headed when he finally reached the ladder over the wing. He moved slowly along the wing, beginning to see dark spots in front of his eyes. He was almost out of time.

He looked to the *Tukuli* to see where Yvette was, hanging in space from the outer hatch. At first he thought his eyes were playing tricks on him from the lack of oxygen. But then he blinked rapidly a few times and nothing changed. Yvette was glowing. It definitely wasn't a light from either ship. She was creating her own light from her suit. And she seemed to be getting brighter. He smiled fondly. She had another power. He continued along the ladder slowly. Halfway along, his vision went dark, and he knew no more.

◊

Bhakat was standing on the bridge with Janan, Rauph, Kieren, and Gianni. Rauph had been doing his best to stall the ASP ship, whose commander had demanded they drop the force shield Gianni erected in return for their vow not to fire on the *Tukuli* again. They were going to board her and place them all under arrest. Gianni had complied on Rauph's orders. Rauph had been negotiating their surrender for the last twenty minutes, taking issue with anything he could to buy the two Humans more time. Communications from the ship had cut off abruptly ten minutes earlier.

Yvette's voice came over the intercom. "Help! We need help down here," she screamed frantically. "James is hurt."

"Bhakat—" Rauph began.

"I'm going," Bhakat said, already leaving the bridge. He ran down the corridor toward the cargo hold and the airlock and briefly looked behind him to see both Kieren and Gianni following. When he arrived at the cargo hold, he could see the door standing open. He went in to see Yvette kneeling next to James, who was lying on his back on the floor. Yvette looked up and saw him and the others enter.

"He lost consciousness out there, and his energy field disappeared," she said. Bhakat could see she was crying.

"Oh my God," Kieren said.

"How long was his exposure?" Bhakat asked, kneeling down next to James.

"What?" Yvette asked.

"He wants to know how long James was exposed," Kieren translated.

"I don't know," Yvette said. "Maybe ten or fifteen seconds, at the most. When I saw his field disappear, I surrounded him with my own and pulled us both into the cargo hold as fast as I could."

"You were both out there?" Gianni asked. "What the hell were you doing?"

"Disabling their ship," Yvette said, her expression blank.

Bhakat bent over the Human and listened for his breathing. Nothing. He gave the Human a breath and then checked his pulse. Weak and thready, but at least he had one. He gave James another breath, and then another. The Human vomited as Bhakat was leaning down to give him another breath. Bhakat turned the coughing, retching Human onto his side so he didn't aspirate his own stomach contents.

"We must get him to the medical bay for tests, but I think he'll be fine," he told Kieren.

"He says James should be okay, but we have to get him to

the medical bay," Kieren repeated. Bhakat could see she was crying as well.

"But he was out in space, unprotected," Yvette said, her hands wrapped around her arms as if she was cold.

Bhakat could see Yvette was going into shock. She'd need observation as well. He turned to Kieren. "I need you to escort her to the medical bay with me." She nodded. He placed his hands under James and lifted him, then slowly progressed from the cargo hold to the medical bay. When they finally arrived, Bhakat gently laid James down on a bed, his back creaking from the strain of carrying the heavy Human.

He turned once again to Kieren. "Tell her to lie down. Cover her with a blanket from the wall panel over there." He pointed at the wall near another of the beds. He began to hook James up to some monitors, after checking to make sure the Human was still breathing.

He looked up to see that while Yvette was now lying down on the bed, shivering, Kieren was staring intently at the wall. He'd forgotten the panel was difficult to distinguish from the surrounding wall. He walked over and pushed the panel, which slid easily out from the wall, revealing a compartment filled with blankets and towels of various sizes.

"Oh, thanks," Kieren said. She grabbed a blanket and covered Yvette, who appeared more aware of her surroundings now. She smiled gratefully as Kieren hugged her to help warm her up.

Bhakat grabbed another blanket and walked over to James. As he was tucking the blanket in around the Human, James stirred, opening his eyes slightly. "Don't talk; just rest," Bhakat said softly, knowing the Human probably couldn't understand him. James closed his eyes and soon was breathing regularly. Bhakat saw his vital readings had stabilized.

"So, you never answered Yvette's question," Gianni said. "How can James be all right if he was out there in a vacuum? Wouldn't his lungs explode or his blood boil or something?"

"Gianni!" Kieren said, shocked.

"What?" Gianni asked, and then saw the expression on Yvette's face. "Oh, sorry."

Bhakat looked over to see Gianni and Kieren standing next to Yvette's bed. Yvette was now sitting up, wrapped in her blanket. "Kieren, if you could translate," he said.

"Yes," she said, looking away from Gianni.

"It was a short exposure, from what Yvette said," he began, with a pause every now and then for Kieren to speak. "He was actually lucky he was unconscious, because he would have damaged his lungs, and possibly his eardrums, if he'd tried to hold his breath. At this point, he'll probably have some minor skin and tissue irritation and swelling, and maybe a minor sunburn on his exposed skin, if we were close enough to a sun for exposure to ultraviolet radiation, but physically, he should be fine in a day or two. I'll give him a shot for pain and to help him sleep."

"What about the cop ship?" Gianni asked.

"I think James succeeded," Yvette said. "He was heading back toward me when his field disappeared."

Bhakat walked over and pushed a button on the wall. "Rauphangelaa, the ASP ship is disabled," he said.

"We know," came Janan'kela's reply. "They've been spewing curses at us for the last five minutes. We're leaving now."

David appeared at the door of the medical bay. "Hey, guys, I was sleeping. What'd I miss?"

They all looked at him in disbelief.

◊

James woke up feeling like he'd been run over by a Mack

truck, and that the truck had backed up and hit him again for good measure. He looked around and noticed he was in the medical bay. "Damn, I hate waking up in here," he said quietly, his voice cracking.

"So do I," Yvette said.

James raised his head and looked over at the bed next to him. He saw that Yvette was lying down, covered in a blanket. "You all right?" he asked.

"Yeah," she answered, smiling and stretching her arms outward over her head. "Waiting for you to rejoin the party."

James put his head back down and closed his eyes. "I take it we got away?"

"Left the ASP ship floating out there somewhere," Yvette answered, pointing up. "We've been in a wide orbit around the Rajani system for two days now."

"Two days?" James asked. He slowly sat up. "No wonder I have to pee so badly."

Yvette was still laughing when he returned from the bathroom.

"C'mon," he said. "I'm starving. Let's go get something to eat." He jumped down off of the bed and almost fell to the floor. He stood, bent over for a moment while his body told him unsympathetically how much it didn't appreciate him moving quickly. "Ouch," he said quietly.

"Bhakat wanted to know as soon as you woke up," she said. "And I can see why."

"Well, we'll tell him as soon as we're finished," he replied, slowly standing up straight. He felt like he hadn't eaten in days. It occurred to him he felt this type of hunger after he'd used his powers for an extended period of time, like they somehow leached away his body's energy. He'd have to talk to the others about it when he had the chance. He was too focused on finding some food to do it right now.

"How 'bout this," Yvette said, placing a hand on his arm. "I'll go get you some food if you promise to go straight to your room and lie down."

"I can get—" he started to say.

"You can do what I tell you, or I can kick your ass," Yvette said sternly. "Do you know how badly you scared me?"

He smiled at her. "Okay, okay. I'm sorry if I scared you. I promise I won't do it again. I'll see you back in my quarters and apologize some more."

"Well, I guess you must be feeling better, at least," she said, standing on her tiptoes and kissing him lightly on the lips. "I'll see you in a few minutes. After I get you some food and tell Bhakat you're awake."

Chapter 17

David had spent the days since James was injured in his room alone. He was beginning to feel depression creeping in on him once again. He wanted to feel like part of the team, but it felt like they didn't need him. It didn't help that his super speed was absolutely useless on a space craft. They hadn't even woken him up for the last incident with the ASPs.

It was just like back home. No one wanted him around unless he was able to do something for them. It was the same with his college coach, with his so-called friends, with his girlfriend, Lisa, and with his father. He hoped things would change once they reached Rajan. He was looking forward to seeing what he could do once he was able to cut loose completely. Perhaps he could outdistance his own problems as well.

◊

The *Tukuli* had been in orbit around the Rajani solar system for five days, beyond the tenth planet's path. Rauph strode down the corridor toward Officer Dempsey's quarters. He still had a few Standard minutes before his shift began on the bridge, and he wanted to check on the Human's status. He placed the translating device on the floor and stood outside of Dempsey's room as he waited for the Human to answer his chime. He'd been disappointed to learn the collar device had been lost during the ASP ship attack. It had been much more convenient to carry around. He wished the translating device wasn't necessary anymore, but the Humans were having a more difficult time learning Talondarian Standard than he'd anticipated. Of course, the same could be said for him learning the Humans' language. After weeks together on the ship, the only ones who could speak the others' language without the assistance of the translating device were Kieren and Janan.

As the door opened, he started to speak before realizing it wasn't Dempsey who had answered the door. "Good morning to you, Ms. Manidoo," he said to the Human female standing in the doorway. "May I speak with Officer Dempsey for a moment? In private?"

"Sure," Yvette answered. She looked as if she was still angry at him, and perhaps she was. He couldn't very well blame her. "I was just leaving."

He smiled at her the best he could as she walked past, but realized how uncomfortable the Human female made him. There was something ... dangerous about her. He wasn't afraid to admit she would have scared him even without her stone-imbued powers. All his life had been spent in the search for peace and quiet contemplation. In many ways, she exemplified the opposite of everything he believed in. Even her calm moments felt charged with the potential for violence.

He found Dempsey still getting dressed slowly in the clothes he'd worn when he'd been brought aboard the ship. Rauph still didn't know what a wheel with a wing attached to it meant. "Are you well today, Officer Dempsey?" he asked, noting the Human was still sore. He'd given Dempsey the benefit of the doubt. The Human had been through a trying ordeal in his bid to disable the ASP starship. He could see the yellow-tinged bruises on Dempsey's torso.

"I feel much better, yes," Dempsey replied, slipping on his shirt.

"I hate to be blunt," Rauph said, setting the translating device on the floor, "but we're reaching a point, both with our supplies and in our patience, where we must either go forward to Rajan or go back to Mandaka. I don't wish to go back, if at all possible. I fear the ASPs would be waiting for us."

"I know," Dempsey said. "I suspected our food stores wouldn't last much longer, and I appreciate you allowing me to heal these last few days."

"I also fear our conflict with the ASP ship has taken away any element of surprise we may have once had," Rauph said. "The Krahn surely detected the presence of two large ships this close to Rajan."

"Damned if we do, or damned if we don't," Dempsey said. Although Rauph didn't know what the expression meant, he could guess well enough. They were left with no easy alternatives. "I'm ready," James continued. "We can proceed as planned, I think. Enough time has been wasted on my account."

"Good," Rauph said, picking up the translating device. "Then we'll return to Rajan today." He left the room with mixed feelings of excitement and apprehension.

◊

David, Yvette, Kieren, and Gianni were already in the common room eating breakfast when James arrived. It was the first time he'd left his room since waking up in the medical bay after his adventurous spacewalk.

"Hey, there he is," Gianni said, smiling.

"James, how are you feeling?" Kieren asked, standing up.

"Sore, but much better," James replied, sitting down gingerly. "I hear Yvette took over your training while I was laid up." She'd taught them all some basic moves during their time training together aboard the ship, but he had asked her to teach them as much hand-to-hand fighting as she could in the few days they had left before they arrived at Rajan.

"Yeah," David said. "She's like a drill sergeant and Mr. Miyagi combined."

James laughed. "I bet she is."

"Oh, quiet," Yvette said, hitting him lightly on the arm before handing him a protein bar.

"Well," James said, speaking around a mouthful of the bar, "you won't have to worry about it anymore. Rauph and I spoke, and we're going to Rajan right now. We should arrive within a few hours."

"Finally," Gianni said.

"Remember," James said, "we don't know what we'll find when we get there. The Krahn could already be gone, or they could be waiting for us. No matter what, we need to stick to the plan we've all agreed on. If the Krahn are still there, we make contact with the resistance, or if there isn't one, we create our own. If they're not there, then this turns into a humanitarian mission and we help the Rajani rebuild the best we can. We need to work together as a team, so remember your training and we should all be fine. Stay powered up once we set down on the planet's surface. I want everyone to get home safe."

◊

James had called off training for the day, so most of the team had spent their time alone in their quarters, waiting for the notification from the bridge telling them they'd arrived. When Bhakat's voice came over the ship's communication system, they all made their way to the bridge.

No one was surprised to see that Rauph, Bhakat, and Janan were already there; there would be no more down time for anyone aboard the ship. They saw the planet on the viewscreen, with numerous Krahn ships in orbit near the equator, where Rauph had said the city of Melaanse was located. The Krahn colony ship dwarfed them all. If James had to guess, he thought it looked to be maybe four hundred yards long and twice as wide. He'd never imagined it would be so big.

He felt a lump in his throat as he watched the smaller ships swarm around it, some leaving it and moving toward the planet's surface, and others returning from the planet and docking with it. Many of them stayed close to the ship in a protective formation.

The *Tukuli* was slowly moving toward them. After months of training and preparation, everything would depend on their ability to get past the blockade of Krahn ships.

Yvette moved up next to Bhakat, who was standing next to Rauph's chair. "My God," she said quietly, her eyes fixed on the screen.

"Far from it," Bhakat said, turning his head to look down at her before his eyes moved back to the mesmerizing spectacle before them.

"They can detect our presence by now, I'm sure," Rauph said, his back rigidly straight in his chair. "We have to get to the surface as quickly as possible. Janan, no matter what happens, do *not* stop the ship."

Janan turned and nodded wordlessly, his ability to speak having left him. He turned back toward the screen.

"What?" Gianni asked. "Are you crazy? We can't get through that."

Bhakat turned toward him. "We will get through it. It's the only choice we have left. Either we reach the planet's surface, or we die in the attempt."

"Fine," James said, his arms crossed before him. "All right, team, go to your rooms and strap yourselves into the emergency landing seats. There's nothing else we can do at this point, and it's not safe to stand around if we're going to be in a firefight."

"But, James—" Kieren began.

"I said, there's nothing we can do," James repeated. "Strap in, but be prepared to evacuate to the escape pods if this thing goes south. You may want to stay powered up as well. Let's go."

They all left the bridge and headed toward their individual rooms. James pulled Gianni to the side. "Hey, do you think you can throw up a force shield like you did back at the space port?"

Gianni thought for a moment. He'd been trying to create a curved force shield for a while, but had been unsuccessful up to that point. It still only appeared as a straight wall of energy. "I can, but I don't think I can protect more than one side of the ship at a time."

"It'll have to do for now," James told him. "Put a shield in front of the ship. It should protect us from a frontal assault. It's better than nothing, I guess."

"Thanks for the vote of confidence, Big J," Gianni said, smirking.

"You know what I meant," James said. "Do the best you can. And Gianni?"

"What?" Gianni asked.

"Don't call me Big J," James said.

They smiled at one another, and Gianni extended his hand.

James hid his surprise and shook it. It was an unexpected, though welcome, gesture. "Good luck."

◊

After all of the Humans had left the bridge, Bhakat moved to the second chair and sat down, knowing it would be a bumpy ride to Rajan's surface. "They're not happy with us," he said, thinking of the expressions of anger he was still receiving from most of the Humans.

"Did we expect them to be?" Rauph said curtly. His attention now was on the monsters between his ship and his home planet. "Janan'kela, take us in. Quickest route to Melaanse, please." He turned his attention back to his Pledge. "Bhakat, will you pray with me?"

Bhakat nodded, and they bowed their heads, just as a force shield appeared in front of the *Tukuli*. The ship streaked toward the surface of the planet. The Krahn ships quickly came into range and began firing at them. Most of the fire hit the energy field, and some continued off into space. The *Tukuli* continued on as more fire came, some of it hitting the sides of the ship as their firing angles improved.

"Hull integrity is down to seventy-five percent on the port side panel," Janan told the others. "Touchdown in five minutes."

"Try to rotate away from their fire," Bhakat said.

"I'm trying," Janan responded. "They're on all sides now!"

A flurry of energy beams and projectile fire struck the Tukuli from the Krahn ships that had moved in from behind. Silent explosions erupted from the hull of the *Tukuli* into space. Red lights popped up all over Janan's control panel. "Multiple hull breaches," he screamed as the ship began to shudder around him and alarm klaxons began to sound. "Our main booster is offline."

"What does that mean?" Rauph yelled, trying to be heard over the din.

"It means I don't think I'll be able to control the ship's descent," Janan replied. "We're going to crash."

Rauph was silent a moment as the Sekani pilot's words echoed in his mind. "Abandon ship," he said, and then said again louder as he realized he couldn't be heard the first time. "We must abandon ship," he yelled. "Get to the escape pods." He hit a button on his control panel. As he did so, a computer voice came on over the ship's communication system.

"Abandon ship—seek escape pods immediately—abandon ship." The voice repeated the message, alternating between Talondarian Standard and English.

"You two had better head for the pods," Janan yelled, not taking his eyes off his controls. "I'll keep the ship as stable as possible for as long as I can." He was doing his best to dodge the incoming fire as the *Tukuli* passed into Rajan's upper atmosphere.

Rauph was sitting with his head bowed. "No, Janan," he said, looking up. "Turn on the auto-lander. You and Bhakat go to the escape pods. I'll be along shortly."

"I'll stay with you—" Bhakat began.

"No, make sure Janan gets to a pod," Rauph yelled. "May the Kha grant you wisdom."

"And you as well, Master," Bhakat said, bowing stiffly before turning toward the door.

Rauph waited until his Pledge and the pilot had left before rising and sitting at the piloting controls. He switched off the auto-lander—he had to make sure the ship wouldn't crash into the city, and he wouldn't sacrifice the others to do so. He knew he probably wouldn't survive the crash, and he would have to make peace with that in the few minutes he had left.

◊

Bhakat and Janan ran down the corridor toward the

escape pods. Bhakat stopped as it occurred to him his Master might be attempting something both selfless and stupid. Janan stopped farther down the corridor when he noticed Bhakat wasn't pounding along beside him.

"You go on," Bhakat said. "Look after the Humans; make sure they all get aboard an escape pod."

"What about you?" Janan said, walking back toward him. "Aren't you coming with me?"

"Don't you understand?" Bhakat said, looking back toward the bridge. "He's not coming with us!"

"I don't care!" Janan replied. "He may be your Master, but I don't care if he makes it off this ship. You're my friend, Bhakat. I want you to be safe."

"And you're mine," Bhakat said, placing his massive hand on Janan's shoulder. "But I can't abandon him. You know that."

"Yes, I know," Janan said, wiping a stray tear from his cheek.

"Go now," Bhakat said, bending down to look at the Sekani face-to-face. "I'll see you on the surface. I promise."

"Goodbye, my friend," Janan said, hugging Bhakat's neck tightly.

"Goodbye," Bhakat replied sadly.

Janan turned and ran down the corridor toward the escape pods located near his room. Bhakat watched him a moment before turning and running back toward the bridge. He hoped he wouldn't be too late.

◊

When Janan arrived at the escape pods over the left wing, he noticed all of them were still present, though one of the pods' active lights was blinking, meaning someone had entered it recently. He opened the hatch to see David sitting inside.

David smiled when he saw who it was. "I ... um ... couldn't figure out the controls," he said.

"Thank you for waiting for me," Janan said, sitting down and strapping into the shoulder harness.

"No problem," David said. "Besides, I didn't want to go alone. Who would I have to talk to on the way down?"

Janan smiled and hit the eject button. The pod ejected from the ship, falling for a moment or two before the parachutes opened. The pod slowed as it headed toward the great Desert of Ambraa, west of the city of Melaanse. Its occupants were both unconscious as it floated down.

◊

James had gathered up the others who had rooms near his on the right side of the Tukuli. He herded Kieren, Gianni, and Yvette toward the escape pods, hoping David had found his own way to one. The corridor was beginning to fill with acrid smoke as they arrived at the pods. "Okay, one person per pod is supposed to be safest," he said. He opened the hatch of the first pod they came to and turned toward Yvette. "Be careful," he said, wrapping her in his arms. "I'll see you on the surface," he whispered in her ear.

She kissed him, and he returned it fervently, hoping they weren't saying goodbye forever. He pulled back to see she was crying silently. "Soon," she said, climbing into the pod.

He hit the button to close the hatch before turning to the others. "Who's next?" he asked.

"We're going together," Kieren said, reaching for Gianni's hand. Gianni looked down at her hand in surprise before looking back at her face.

"But ..." James began before seeing the determined look on her face.

"I don't want to go alone," she said. "Please, James, don't make me."

James knew there wasn't time for a prolonged argument. "Okay, it should be fine, I guess," he said. "Gianni, take care of her."

"Of course," Gianni said, without a hint of his usual smirk as he stepped through the hatchway of the pod.

Kieren gave James a quick hug. "Thank you," she said, and then stepped into the pod.

James pushed the button that closed the hatch. He walked down to the next pod and entered it, wishing he'd thought of going with Yvette before sending her alone.

Gianni and Kieren had powered up after strapping into the shoulder harnesses inside the pod. "It'll be fine," he said, though he sounded less reassuring than he wanted to be. He reached over toward her. She grasped his hand in her own, seeing the familiar flash as their power fields came into contact.

Gianni hit the eject button, and the pod shot off toward the planet's surface, almost immediately deploying its parachutes and slowing its descent. Inside, both Gianni and Kieren's power fields disappeared as they lost consciousness, though they were still holding hands.

◊

James's pod ejected and immediately deployed its parachutes, though it was already below the safe altitude point mandated by the pod's sensors. He was powered up and strapped in, feeling the familiar rush of adrenaline throughout his system, though he surprisingly hadn't felt it since coming on the trip, even when he'd gone out to disable the ASP ship.

All we've been through, he thought, all of the training, all of the planning. All of it for nothing.

All of their strategies were torn down like a straw house in a hurricane. James thought of the others, hoping they'd all land safely on the planet's surface. His final thoughts before he lost consciousness were of the Yeats poem he'd been reading on the trip about things falling apart.

◊

The *Tukuli,* now almost entirely a ball of fire and with Rauph and Bhakat still aboard, fell into the ocean off the coast of Melaanse, having missed the city. It skipped along the surface of the water like a flat stone before its momentum was slowed. The ship sank quickly into the dark water, disappearing from view.

The End - Stone Soldiers

Look for

The Rajani Chronicles II: Resistance
by Brian S. Converse

Coming in early 2018!

Updates on

www.BrianSConverse.com